Second Chance Grill

Christine Nolfi

Author website: www.christinenolfi.com

ISBN 978-1478342229

For Barry,
and a world's worth of second chances.

Chapter 1

Dr. Mary Chance feared she'd poison half of Liberty on reopening day.

Not that she'd personally put the town at risk. Ethel Lynn Percible's cuisine was to blame. Her slippery hold on culinary skills had Mary wishing she'd dumped antacids instead of mints in the crystal bowl beside the cash register. True, the elderly cook hadn't exactly poisoned anyone. But the historic recipes Mary hoped to serve were soggy, lumpy, undercooked or scorched to a fine black sheen.

A trim woman in a severe grey suit rose from a table. "I hope you were a better doctor than you are a business woman," she snapped. Storming past, she gave Mary a dismissive glance. "You should've opened an emergency room instead of a restaurant. Or better yet, both. *Then* you'd have a thriving business."

For a shattering moment, Mary connected with her frigid gaze. The woman had ordered the lunch special, Martha Washington's beef stew. She'd received a concoction that resembled glue and smelled worse.

In the center of the dining room, the young waitress Mary had rehired fended off a barrage of insults. Delia Molek's voice rose like a violin's plucked string. Cornered beneath antique pewter sconces, she ditched patience and favored the disenchanted patron with steely regard. The gum wadded between her molars snapped angrily with her retorts.

In contrast, the less confident Ethel Lynn remained hidden in the kitchen. She'd suffered a host of culinary calamities since the first customer appeared this morning. Perhaps she was infected with opening day jitters. Perhaps she *would* serve up savory meals once she got into the swing of things. In the fervor of new and disbelieving ownership, Mary had overhauled the menu, bringing back a delectable array of historic recipes. Many of the offerings graced the finest Colonial tables long ago, like succulent beef dotted with cloves and cakes sweetened with Rum. The new menu also featured a Civil War recipe of chicken seared with cherries. The dessert menu included rich puddings and a Spice Cake from the Roaring Twenties so beloved by Calvin Coolidge, he'd made the confection a White House staple.

No wonder Ethel Lynn's skills needed polish. The historic recipes were to blame for her bad start. With enough practice, she'd learn to make each dish with finesse. Customers would no longer risk upset stomachs, and the restaurant would thrive. Glancing heavenward, Mary prayed she'd hit on the problem.

The portly man fled toward the street. Delia marched up.

She said, "He didn't leave a tip."

Mary arched a brow. "Would you?"

"With Ethel Lynn running the kitchen? No."

Given Ethel Lynn's many years with the restaurant, the remark was unkind. Letting it go, Mary said, "Count your blessings. At least your customer didn't demand a refund."

"Point taken." The waitress popped a fresh stick of gum into her mouth and chewed thoughtfully. "So. Your first day as the owner of Liberty's one and only restaurant is a train wreck. Here's a fun thought. We still have the dinner rush tonight."

Mary surveyed the patriotic decorations she'd festooned throughout the dining room, a treasure trove of Americana harking back to the restaurant's founding in the 1800s. So many beautiful things, but they'd gone unappreciated. Diners noticed little but the glop on their plates.

Her heart sank. "There won't be a dinner rush. After the meals Ethel Lynn made for the breakfast and lunch crowds, we won't see a soul."

Delia wandered to the picture window. "I hope the town council doesn't burn up the phone lines scaring off our customers." She squinted at the courthouse anchoring the north end of Liberty Square. "Then again, they have a soft spot for Miss Meg. It might stop them from passing legislation condemning this place."

"Think I should ask my aunt to fire off an email?" Desperation made a grab for Mary's nerves, but she convinced herself long-distance lobbying could work.

"Don't intrude on Meg's retirement. She's half a world away, and no longer running the place. This is your problem, sister." The mirth on Delia's face died as she added, "We were sorry to see her go."

And sorry to see me take her place? Mary resisted the unwarranted thought. Since her arrival, the town had welcomed her with subdued kindness if not open arms. Sure, the townspeople gossiped whenever they thought she was out of earshot. She'd come around a corner in Liberty Square only to find chattering women huddled on the cobblestone walk. One glimpse of her and they'd burst apart like so much confetti showering down on Times Square. The men were no better. When she strolled the center green before the courthouse, they regarded her with ill-concealed curiosity. The way they acted, it was plausible she was the town's first new resident in decades.

Dismissing the thought, she said, "I know everyone misses Aunt Meg. She ran this place for so many years." Mary ignored the curiosity glittering in Delia's blue eyes. "She called an hour ago."

"From Tibet?"

"She wanted to know how we were faring on reopening day." Naturally Mary had glossed over the problems they'd encountered. "We didn't talk long. Said she had to get back to the monks."

Delia grinned. "She sure is eccentric."

Incorrigible was more like it. "She's practicing yoga with the monks then having a drink once they retire for the night. How she smuggled booze into a monastery is anyone's guess."

"Makes her own rules, that's how." Delia tipped her head to the side. "She's also an open book. You aren't. You never talk about yourself."

Mary crossed her arms. "I will when I have something useful

to share."

The young waitress wasn't buying. "Everyone has stuff to talk about," she pointed out. "Like, why did you take over? Everyone thought Meg would shut the restaurant when she retired. And did you like being a doctor? Do you miss it?"

"Not at the moment." Worry over bankruptcy occupied most of her thoughts. "Well, I miss my patients. If you don't mind, I'd rather not go into details."

Mostly because her emotions were sorely in need of CPR. And her bank account languished on death's door after generous Aunt Meg handed over the restaurant and waltzed into retirement.

In fairness, her aunt's largesse was perfectly timed. Though Mary was loath to explain, she'd eagerly left Cincinnati for a sabbatical from medicine. Slogging through her residency and working long hours in the ER had left her exhausted. Then the unthinkable happened. In a fog of grief, she handed in her resignation at the hospital and packed her belongings. Sorrow over the sudden death of her closest friend wouldn't end any time soon. The passionately driven and fiercely intelligent Dr. Sadie Goldstein was gone. Mary needed time to heal.

None of which was suitable conversation with the gum-popping Delia. Excusing herself, she returned to the kitchen.

The acrid scent of burnt vegetables spiked the air. Before the stove Ethel Lynn fluttered like a bird abandoned in the carnage of heaped pots and pans, and food-spattered counters. Her oversized apron swung in loose folds. She padded her fingers across the collar of her bluebell-patterned dress, a retro number that seemed better suited for the Eisenhower era, much like Ethel Lynn herself.

"Is the lunch rush over, dear?" she asked. "I'm ready if you need anything."

Mary hesitated. "Why don't I take over for a few hours? Walk home, and rest. You look frazzled."

Ethel Lynn threw back her shoulders. "I'm fit as a fiddle!"

Right. The woman possessed the metabolism of a sparrow on amphetamines. She'd worried her way through the renovations after the restaurant changed hands. Ethel Lynn had perspired in her delicate way, lace handkerchief at the ready, as the dining room took on a new coat of creamy paint and patriotic bunting was hung on the picture window. Now they'd reopened to disastrous results. Predictably, she seemed ready to fret into a full-blown state of distress.

Which was never good for a woman on the far side of sixty.

Gently, Mary patted her on the back. "About your cooking . . . there've been a few complaints. Do you need another pair of hands in the kitchen?"

Ethel Lynn turned her palms skyward. "What's wrong with this set?"

"I mean, well—it is a lot of work. Too much work for one woman."

"Nonsense. This establishment has always managed fine with one cook. You're willing to pitch in, and Meg did the same before she got it in her head to leave." Ethel Lynn puffed out her sparrow's chest. "You rehired the staff, didn't you?"

"I rehired Delia," Mary corrected.

"Only Delia?"

"I called the other waitress. She refused my offer."

"She's not coming back?"

The mysterious Finney Smith had blistered Mary with a few choice words before slamming down the phone. Shocking, sure, but who cared if they were short one waitress? "We'll find a replacement for Finney. Honestly, I can't imagine a woman like that waiting tables." Not unless the tables were in Sing Sing.

A squeak popped from Ethel Lynn's throat. "About Finney," she whispered, and something in her voice sent goose bumps down Mary's spine. "She wasn't a waitress, dear. Her job was— heavens to Betsy—a tad more important."

Mary's pulse scuttled. "What do you mean?"

Blossom's dad thought a lot about dying.

She supposed it was natural given all the pain, blood tests, and hospital visits they'd endured. Going through it, years of it, had changed him. It put lines on his forehead and doubt in his eyes. She'd watched the changes color him, as if he'd been a pencil sketch before the ordeal and was now bolded in by the blues and grays of his experience with cancer.

She wanted to tear up that picture, throw it into a garbage can of unwanted memories. She'd heard plain and clear the word Dr. Lash used. *Remission.*

The ordeal was over. Finished. They'd received the wonderful verdict—*remission*. The word always made her happy. Then she'd think about her dad, stuck on his thoughts of death.

Which made her sad.

The drone of bees hummed across the spring flowers set out in planters on the cobblestone walk. Skirting a group of women shoppers, Blossom darted into the shadows thrown by the row of brick buildings. Gathering up her courage, she tugged the book bag's straps across her shoulders and stuffed the paper bag beneath her armpit. Feeling self-conscious, she hesitated beside the restaurant's picture window. The curtain, patterned like the American flag, partially obscured the scene inside.

Hooking a curl behind her ear, she peered down the street like a spy afraid of being caught. Which was stupid. She was a sixth grader at Liberty Middle School and knew everyone in town.

Before she might chicken out, she peeked in the window.

No one in sight. The tables were neatly set, the chairs empty. Blossom toed the ground with the tip of her bright red tennis shoe. On a silent prayer she swung her gaze to the long counter in back, which was hemmed in by bar stools. Her mood soared. Mary was stacking napkins with the enthusiasm of a kid dreading a social studies test.

Ducking out of sight, Blossom leaned against the wall's rough bricks. Fizzy elation ran down to her toes.

Then she dashed across the street.

She ran diagonally through the park-like center green of Liberty Square. Maple trees wagged leaves in the breeze. The scent of freshly mown grass mingled with the sweet aroma of lavender spilling in waves across the sidewalk.

Moving faster, she narrowed her concentration with an adolescent blend of purpose and amusement. Sure, her dad worried about death. Grown-ups did all sorts of stupid things. He acted as if death lurked outside the door, a silly idea. Death wasn't cloaked in black, waiting to snatch you away. No matter how many times she reassured her father, he saw death as the enemy. He believed in it.

Yet Blossom knew that good doctors and positive thoughts outsmarted death. Wishing helped, too.

Buoyed by the warm May air and her foolproof plan, she ambled across the hot pavement of the Gas & Go. Inside the garage her father clattered around the pit, working beneath a late model Toyota.

"Hey, there." She spotted the vintage oak office chair, her favorite, and dropped onto it. "How ya doin'?"

"Hi, kiddo," he called from inside the pit. "How was school?"

"Just counting the days until my prison break." She yawned theatrically. "Guess what? The restaurant opened back up this morning. Been there yet?"

A rattling erupted beneath the car. "Too busy." Several bolts clanked into a tray.

"Go over and meet the new owner. She's nicer than prissy Meade Williams."

"Don't start. All right?"

Blossom ignored the request. To her way of thinking, Meade Williams posed the biggest threat to her emotional wellbeing since she and her dad high-tailed it out of the hospital last year. Rich and as genuine as a platinum-haired Barbie doll, Meade was now upping the ante. Lately the cosmetics entrepreneur had begun filling her Mercedes at the Gas & Go on a daily basis. She was probably siphoning off gas in a cornfield to keep her fuel gauge on empty.

Blossom said, "If you aren't careful, Meade will have you doing the goosestep to the altar. You don't know women like I do. I *am* a woman."

"We aren't having this conversation."

"Face it, Dad. If I don't give you advice, who will?" She wheeled the chair to the garage door. Sunshine dappled the quaint shops and the restaurant on the other side of Liberty Square. "The lady at the restaurant is pretty. You've got to meet her."

Beneath the Toyota, a tool clanked. "Meet who?"

She brought the chair closer, delighted to have nabbed his attention. "The lady who took over the restaurant. I heard she's Miss Meg's niece. She's real pretty."

"If you say so."

"Don't you want to give her a look-see? Make your heart pitter-patter?"

A grease-stained hand popped out from beneath the car and grabbed the air ratchet's snaking black hose. The hand disappeared underneath. An ear-splitting, motorized whirring roared through the garage.

When the tool fell silent, Blossom continued. "She has brownish-red hair down to her shoulders and green eyes. She's shy, like she's scared or something. Have you seen the new decorations? She dragged all sorts of cool stuff from Miss Meg's storage room to spruce up the place. She even changed the boring old menu. I'll bet the stuff she's making is better than your cooking."

"Hard to believe anyone cooks better than me."

"A lady that pretty is a great cook. One of the rules of the cosmos, like star-crossed lovers and Math teachers with yellow teeth."

"Whatever."

Frustrated by his lack of interest, she kicked away the bolts he'd tossed from the pit. "She changed the restaurant's name. It's now The Second Chance Grill. Cute, huh? Her name is Mary Chance, by the way."

"Great."

"She's younger than you. Twenty-eight or -nine. Nowhere near the old fart stage." *Like Meade.* "C'mon Dad, take me over for a sundae." Her father muttered a curse before climbing out of the pit. Plastering on a smile, she added, "This is an opportunity you can't miss."

When he paused before her, she wrinkled her nose. He was grease monkey all the way. Droplets of motor oil dotted his curly brown hair. Oil glazed the side of his large nose. Beneath deep brown eyes, smudges of black covered his cheeks. To top it off, he stank of eau de gasoline and perspiration.

"You're a mess." She pushed the office chair toward the garage door and the reprieve of springtime air. "And you're ruining your clothes. Geez, we'll never get the gunk out of your jeans. Not even with ten boxes of detergent."

Looking mildly offended, he ran his palms down his filthy

tee shirt. "Why are you always bugging me?"

"You're a good looking guy, that's all. Clean up once in awhile. Strut your stuff."

He sent the quizzical look that meant she'd crossed the line of father-daughter relationships—a line she didn't think existed. "Keep nagging, and I'll need therapy," he quipped. "A year of the talking cure to regain my confidence."

She rolled her eyes. "I hate to point out the obvious but you need a date. Meade's stalking doesn't count." She picked at the ragged nail on her thumb. "Here's an idea. Let's call the cops, put out a retraining order."

"Restraining order," he corrected, "and I don't need one. Meade's harmless."

"C'mon, Dad. How long's it been? Can you remember the last time you had a date?"

"Not really."

"That's *why* she's got you in her sights. It's about damn time you found a nice woman."

He threw a sharp glance. "You shouldn't swear."

"You shouldn't make me."

She pulled her attention from the ceiling and leveled on his sweet, teddy bear gaze. It never failed to warm her when he looked at her that way. It also made her sad, the worry lurking in his eyes, the concern he tried to hide.

He'd had that look her whole life.

Crouching, he clasped the chair's armrests. "Blossom, the last couple of years nearly did us in. A miracle we survived. And here you are, cooking up schemes. I can't imagine thinking about a woman or dating or—"

"You don't have to worry," she cut in. She patted his greasy cheek. "We're fine. Better than fine. We're great."

The concern in his eyes deepened. "I know."

"Try believing it."

A weary smile lifted the corners of his mouth. "I'm trying."

He let the chair go, and she snatched the paper bag at her feet. Following him across the garage, she announced, "I brought clothes. You can wash up and change."

From over his shoulder, he tossed a look of impatience. "You what?"

"Clean clothes. For you." She lifted the bag. "Let's go to The Second Chance for a sugar buzz."

"Shouldn't you go home, do homework or something?"

"All done, in study hall." She pulled out a pair of jeans and batted her lashes. "Can we go to Miss Mary's restaurant? Please?"

Her father leaned against the doorjamb, shaking his head. "Shit, you never give up."

She tipped up her chin. "You shouldn't swear."

He offered a lopsided grin. "You shouldn't make me."

The troubling revelation shared by Ethel Lynn was difficult for Mary to absorb: Finney Smith was the restaurant's missing cook.

How to convince the short-tempered Finney to return to work?

Mary was still pondering the dilemma when the now-familiar girl with the corkscrew curls and red tennis shoes entered from the street. There wasn't much to the girl in way of body mass, but her toffee-colored eyes, large and thickly lashed, glinted with high intelligence and an engaging hint of deviltry. She'd been peering in the window for days, an amusing state of affairs that provided a welcome respite from the hours of worry over the restaurant's prospects and the grief running through Mary like a low-grade fever. A tall man in jeans followed, and she nodded in greeting. Hopefully they'd arrived for an afternoon snack that wouldn't put Ethel Lynn anywhere near the stove.

To her relief, the girl asked, "Do you have sundaes?"

"With twenty flavors of ice cream." She reached for the order pad as they slid onto barstools. "Would you like menus? We have sundaes, malts and shakes."

The girl smiled broadly, revealing pearly teeth. "Don't need 'em. I'll take chocolate ice cream with chocolate sauce. And sprinkles, if you've got 'em." Light sparkled in her eyes. "I'm Blossom Perini. You're Mary, right?"

"I am. Nice to meet you."

Quietly the man studied her. Pangs of discomfort cramped her stomach. His eyes were remarkably expressive, twin mirrors reflecting emotions he seemed incapable of voicing. Like

Blossom, his hair was a rich brown, and curly. An older brother? Or Blossom's father? He possessed the well-toned build of a man who worked out, lending him a youthful appearance.

Blossom cleared up the mystery. "This is my dad, Anthony."

Mary extended her hand. "Hello."

"A pleasure." He surged to his feet to give a handshake formal enough for colleagues meeting at a medical convention.

He didn't release her after the obligatory three seconds. With a start, she wondered if an odd bit of food was stuck on her face. Flecks of ash from the sausage Ethel Lynn had burned? With her free hand she made a self-conscious swipe at her cheek.

Sensing her discomfort, he let her go and stepped back. He stood behind the barstool in what she decided was a state of utter confusion. She didn't know how to proceed, not with him gaping at her. Blossom watched the interchange with ill-concealed mirth.

The girl yanked on his sleeve. "Do you want coffee?" she prodded, and he dropped onto his barstool.

He nodded in the affirmative, and Mary searched for the coffee pot and her composure. She stole a glance at the mirror behind the bar—no smudges, no food anywhere on her face. What had startled him? Surely she appeared presentable, if exhausted. Given the apologies she'd doled out all day long, who wouldn't look haggard?

Shrugging off the bizarre exchange, she scooped ice cream then fetched the coffee pot. She'd just finished serving them when Anthony said, "So you're Meg's niece. How is she?"

"Traveling the world." His remarks were light, and much friendlier than his strange, first reaction and she added, "Meg's decision to turn over the restaurant came as a shock. I'd never visited. I should've found the time."

"I would've remembered seeing you."

He seared her with a smoldering look. Was he flirting? The possibility boosted her sagging spirits.

Steering the conversation to safe ground, she said, "I've had a crazy week. I'm still sorting through the antiques in the storage room and cleaning things up."

"This is the oldest landmark in town but Meg wasn't turning much of a profit." Anthony took a sip of his coffee. "I'm sure you'll have better luck."

"I hope so."

An attractive grin edged onto his mouth. "I hear Ethel Lynn is still around." He nodded toward the kitchen. "Keep her on a short leash. She's . . . high strung."

Mary chuckled. "And as eccentric as my aunt."

"You haven't seen anything yet. Wait until you get a load of Theodora Hendricks." He warmed to his story. "Closing in on eighty years old. She thinks yellow lights mean 'hurry' and red means 'floor it.' She's crabby and about four feet tall—drives a sky blue Cadillac. If you see her barreling down the road, get out of the way."

His eyes danced, drawing a laugh from Mary. "Thanks for the tip. I'll watch out for her."

The kitchen door swung open and Ethel Lynn fluttered out. "Now, Anthony, you know better than to frighten Mary with tales of Theodora's driving."

"She's had six fender-benders in the last year," he replied. "Trust me with the numbers. I'm stuck working on her car every time."

"You do bodywork?" Mary asked. *His* body didn't need work. He was a glorious study of lean muscle and commanding height. She wasn't in the market for a date, but he'd tempt most women. Squashing the notion, she added, "I mean, if you work on cars . . ."

"I'm a mechanic. The bodywork is a side business. Theodora is my best customer."

He shrugged and Mary decided she liked Blossom's father. He was attractive and sweet, and extremely protective of his daughter. Since they'd arrived, he'd reached behind his daughter's back repeatedly to pat her or rub her shoulders. In a world rife with broken homes and absentee fathers, his devotion to his child was heartwarming.

To Ethel Lynn, Anthony said, "Does the change of ownership mean you're retiring, too?"

"I promised Meg I'd stay until Mary settles in."

Mary savored the thought of ridding herself of the fretful woman. "Meaning you'd *like* to retire?" Guilt washed through her. Ethel Lynn was a lifelong friend of Aunt Meg.

Blossom, finishing her sundae, scanned the newly painted

dining room. "The restaurant looks cool with all the old stuff brought out of storage. Mary is doing great by herself."

Anthony nudged her shoulder. "She's Miss Chance to you." He gave an assessing glance. "Or is it Mrs?"

"Dad, I told you—she isn't married. Why can't you keep up? If you spent less time praying at church and more time eavesdropping, you'd hear all the gossip." The girl offered Mary an impish smile. "Well, *Miss* Chance, I like everything you've done to the place. Especially the new name."

Mary smiled. "I'm glad you like it."

"The Second Chance Grill. Really nice." The girl tugged on her father's sleeve. "Everyone deserves a second chance. Right, Dad?"

Blossom's inoffensive comment drove sorrow into her father's eyes. Mary's breath caught. The girl and Ethel Lynn missed the expression, vanquished quickly from his face. But Mary recognized the emotion, a demonstration of intense pain deftly hidden behind dulling eyes. It was an emotion she knew too well.

Like Anthony, she'd learned to hide the pain that leaked from her heart at unpredictable intervals. The sudden death of her closest friend, the loss of Sadie's calm presence and unwavering confidence—all the dreams they'd shared about building a medical practice together were vanquished in an instant.

She dispelled the memory gripping her. There was time enough to finish grieving. Once she had, she'd return to Cincinnati. She'd make The Second Chance Grill profitable and find a manager for the small enterprise. She'd create jobs in the town her aunt loved then get on with her life.

Drawing from the reverie, she blinked. Then she flinched with embarrassment. She was still staring at Anthony, a blunder that bleached the color from his face.

She pulled her attention to her shoes. But not before his eyes clouded. He understood: she'd glimpsed his pain. His emotions were laid bare before a perfect stranger.

Her mouth went dry as his expression closed. Fumbling for normalcy, she snatched a rag from beneath the counter and began polishing the gleaming surface. He rose and paid the check. Murmuring a farewell, he led Blossom out.

They skirted across Liberty Square.

After they'd disappeared into the Gas & Go, she whispered, "What . . . was that?"

Ethel Lynn looked up, confused. "What, dear?"

"Anthony was upset when Blossom said everyone deserves a second chance." Why had the comment rattled him? Searching for a plausible explanation, she asked, "What's the story between him and Blossom's mother?"

Ethel Lynn waved the question away. "Hells bells. Anthony dated Cheryl when they were teenagers. She got pregnant and he did the honorable thing by marrying her. Two years after Blossom came along, Cheryl fell for a guitarist and skedaddled off to Florida."

The explanation was depressing and common. "Does Cheryl visit Blossom?" Mary asked.

Ethel Lynn snorted. "Good grief, we haven't seen her in years. I doubt Blossom remembers her. Good riddance, I say."

"No wonder the comment upset him. With a wife like that, who'd believe in second chances?"

A chilling quiet descended. Ethel Lynn was lost at sea, the lines framing her mouth deepening. Foreboding stole through Mary.

Slowly Ethel Lynn withdrew a lace handkerchief from the pocket of her dress. "You don't understand," she said, dabbing at her eyes. "Blossom has leukemia. Last year she was so ill, we thought we'd lose her. The cancer is in remission, thank God."

The news struck Mary hard. "And Anthony?" she finally asked. "How's he managing?"

Sorrow bent Ethel Lynn's spine. "He's afraid to believe in second chances. He's learned to live each day as if it's Blossom's last."

Chapter 2

Learning of Blossom's leukemia added considerably to Mary's anxiety the following morning as she drove out of Liberty in search of Finney Smith's house.

She rechecked the address Ethel Lynn had jotted down before returning her attention to the road. Swatches of pink light brushed the newly plowed fields. Clouds sped across the sky, set loose upon a carpet of deep blue. Up ahead a farmer on a tractor tilled the brown earth, kicking up dust in his wake. Mary drove past with her thoughts wending back to the girl with the corkscrew curls.

Given her background in medicine, she couldn't help wondering about the prognosis. Leukemia was the number one cancer in children. Was Blossom's remission stable, or was she still undergoing treatment? And how did her single father manage the good months and the bad, and the dread every parent with a dangerously ill child was forced to confront? Like any doctor, Mary understood the stress of caring for such a child. Anthony's health may have been affected. Did he suffer bouts of insomnia? Have an ulcer?

Considering his wellbeing was the easier choice. She'd trained for a career as a general practitioner. Pediatrics had been the area of expertise of her closest friend, Dr. Sadie Goldstein. Before Sadie's death, during those nights when they'd stayed up late discussing the practice they'd soon share, she'd talked with excitement about serving Cincinnati's poorest children. Nothing about childhood illness frightened Sadie. During their residencies at Cinci General, she gladly did the rounds of common ailments like an ear infection or a broken femur. But she'd never feared working with the life-threatening cases, like cancer.

Mary had always known she didn't possess Sadie's fortitude. During a rotation in oncology she'd worked with a man losing his battle with prostate cancer. His smile said 'Surfer Dude' even though he was well past sixty. Throughout an increasingly unsuccessful course of treatment, he talked of taking one last trip to Hawaii with his wife. Too weak to surf the Pacific's whitecaps, he'd appeared eager, even serene, about one last stroll on the beach.

Many of the adults she'd one day serve would confront disease, even death. Maturity would see them through life's most difficult passage. Steering a vulnerable child through the frightening journey to death, as Sadie would've done with cool-headed compassion, was beyond Mary's emotional skills. Every doctor was required to understand her limits, and the cases she wasn't emotionally equipped to handle. Pity filled her as she imagined the impact of Blossom's ordeal on her devoted father.

Mary scanned the countryside for signs of life. This morning didn't afford the luxury of considering a father's struggles or his daughter's prognosis—or how, during her brief stay in their town, she might offer assistance. The restaurant demanded all her energies. If Finney Smith didn't resume her position as cook, The Second Chance Grill would shutter its doors within the month.

Mary cut a sharp right onto Elmwood, a woodsy stretch of road void of houses. On the side of the road a ravine swept down at a steep pitch. The soothing melody of the green, gurgling waters drifted through the air. A thick line of evergreen trees blotted out the morning light, throwing shadows across the road.

Where was the house? She slowed to a crawl to consider her options. Give up looking and return to Liberty? It wasn't as if she'd worked out a plan for convincing Finney to resume her job at the restaurant. Last night at closing, a nervous Ethel Lynn admitted she'd fired the cook. Why, Mary hadn't found the gumption to ask. Odds were, Finney was already working a new job. Convincing her to return might prove impossible.

Gravel crunched beneath the car's wheels. Beyond a stand of maple trees, a white house stood in a patch of yellowing grass. Music blared across the lonely expanse. Did Finney have a teenager? Or was the cook a fan of screaming guitars?

On a wave of anxiety, Mary parked and got out. She climbed the steps.

And might've knocked. The door was flung open.

"What do you want?" Without awaiting a reply, the woman jerked her chin toward the house's interior. "Dang it all, Randy! Turn the music down!"

Mary floundered as the house fell into silence. She was taller than the heavy-set woman before her. Finney's shirt was wrinkled but her brassy blond hair was neatly brushed. She was curvaceous, with a round, full mouth and wide-set eyes. Despite her rampant femininity, a decidedly masculine aura surrounded her.

Squaring her shoulders, Mary asked, "You're Finney Smith, aren't you?"

"Of course I am. Are you stupid?"

She attempted a smile, and failed. "Finney," she said, her lips frozen in a grimace. "An unusual name. Irish?"

The cook folded her arms across her ample bosom. "My formal name is Filomena and I don't know what it is."

"Filomena. Why, that's beautiful. Why don't you use it?"

"Too big a mouthful."

"Filly?"

Finney's nostrils flared. "Do I look like a horse?"

Mary stalled, her mind going blank. In point of fact, the cook was as voluptuous as a Rubens despite her Farmer Joe jeans and plaid shirt. The tight-fitting shirt was at risk of releasing her generous breasts from their unfashionable prison.

Starting over seemed wise. "I apologize for stopping by without an invitation," Mary began. "I'm the new owner of the—"

"I know who you are. Get in here."

Finney grabbed her by the wrist and Mary stumbled into the foyer. Down the hallway, a lanky teenage boy sauntered past. No time to offer a greeting—a push on the back sent her lurching into the family room with its beat-up green couch.

A teenage girl's voice rang out. Then the boy joined in and a squabble erupted. Meaning Finney had two kids. Mary recalled Ethel Lynn mentioning a deceased husband. A police officer, he'd died in an accident on I-90 years ago. The cook supported two teenagers on her own. And barely, from the looks of the place.

"Sit there," Finney said, breaking into her thoughts. Mary sank down onto the couch and the cook added, "Did the nibby old bat tell you *why* she fired me?"

"Ethel Lynn? No." Mary pressed her knees together, conscious she'd assumed the posture of a disobedient child. "Would you care to explain?"

"Hell, no." Finney paced before the couch. "Meade Williams has no right throwing her weight around when she's inside *my* restaurant. Complaining because I put sour cream in the low-fat ranch dressing! I don't use much, just a few tablespoons. So I threw her out."

"Who's Meade?" she asked, trying to keep up.

The cook snorted. "You haven't met Liberty's belle of fashion? She's chasing our town's favorite son. He owns the Gas & Go across the Square from the restaurant. Anthony Perini? He's Mr. Fix-it."

"We've met," Mary offered. "He's nice."

"God bless him, he's always fixing something at the restaurant. But he has a problem he can't fix. Meade's got him in her sights. He'll be hog-tied and hauled into marriage before the year's out."

The possibility sent relief through her. Ridiculously, she'd experienced the stirring of attraction when Anthony stopped by The Second Chance with his daughter. A true inconvenience since she had more pressing concerns than a romantic fling—like how to get Finney back to work, preferably today.

Defying logic, she heard herself say, "They're engaged?"

"More like Meade's on the hunt and Anthony is running for cover. Why do you ask? Do you have the hots for him? Half the women in town do."

Mary's brows hit her hairline. "I don't have the hots for him, no."

"Well, you *are* stupid. He's the only eligible bachelor in town. You put men off? You seem the type."

The rude comment stiffened her spine. "You don't know the

first thing about me."

"I put men off, too," Finney said, missing the heated denial. "I'm not strung tight, like you. Mine's a different problem. I come too strong."

"Like a bull?" The woman needed a seminar on polishing her people skills. An entire semester of *White Gloves and Party Manners.*

The insult stamped pleasure on the cook's face. "Men don't take well to strong women. The sissies." She changed track. "Your Aunt Meg is a good woman. Never so much as mentioned having a niece. Generous of her to leave you the restaurant."

"I thought she was joking when she called."

"Who jokes about real estate? I hope you thanked her."

"Of course."

Despite Finney's brusque nature, Mary found herself softening. The cook lived a hardscrabble life that seemed a place of meager hope and limited possibilities. A basket of laundry sat on the rug, the tee shirts and blue jeans folded with military precision. The jar on the windowsill brimmed with daffodils. Clearly she took pride in the smallest things.

"Meg knew I needed a change." Glad for an opening, she donned a look of sincerity. "Listen, Ethel Lynn never should've fired you. If I'd been in town, I would've stopped her."

Finney shrugged off the apology. "Why did you need a change?" she asked.

The question hung in the air. From the kitchen, the girl shouted and the boy let loose a string of profanity. The back door slammed shut.

She smiled gamely. "A friend died." Sadie had been so much more. Her touchstone. Her sister in every way except blood. "I needed a break from medicine and my aunt wanted to retire. When she suggested I come to Liberty, I jumped at the chance."

The explanation satisfied the cook. "We all need a change now and then." Her expression warmed to one shade less than sympathy. "What happened to your friend?"

Grief settled in Mary's chest. "A drunk driver hit her."

"Good Lord."

"Sadie was killed instantly," she said, wondering why sharing a ghastly memory gave a brief respite from the pain. "It happened so quickly ... they say she didn't feel anything. I'm grateful for that. I'll always be grateful."

"I'm sorry for your loss."

Murmuring her thanks, Mary returned to the task at hand. "Will you come back? The restaurant will go under without you."

"Now there's a news flash. Can't run the restaurant without me."

"Finney, *please*."

From the coffee table, the cook snatched up a notepad and a pen. She scribbled furiously then handed the pad over. "This here's my hourly amount. I'll work fifty hours a week . . . and this here's my weekly pay. I gave myself a raise for general irritation. You're letting that old bat, Ethel Lynn stick around. Makes you crazier than a loon but we all have our faults." She set her jaw. "You'll pay me on Fridays."

"I will?"

"Miss a Friday and I'll make your life hell." She tapped the edge of the notepad. "This is my final offer."

So begging wasn't required. Finney wanted to return. The pay she requested was more than reasonable. Mary was about to wholeheartedly agree when the cook spoke again.

"Now I have a few questions for you." She lowered her generous body onto the couch. "I like a good understanding of my employer. Ethel Lynn, well, she's as buggy as a flea-infested mattress. How 'bout you?"

"I don't conjure imaginary friends," she offered dryly. She might have laughed if the cook wasn't serious. "Finney, we'll get along fine."

"How many restaurants have you owned?"

"Before this one?" The nerves she'd put at bay wicked the moisture from her mouth.

"Were you the cook in a fancy place? If Meg left you the restaurant you must have culinary experience."

Wasn't it enough that she'd survived med school and a grueling residency? "I don't have experience in the restaurant trade. So what? How hard can it be to run The Second Chance?"

"You think running Liberty's only restaurant is a walk in the park? Are you crazy?"

"We aren't talking brain surgery. It's a *restaurant.*"

"What exactly *are* your qualifications?" The look Finney gave left the uncomfortable sensation that Mary was wearing a dunce cap.

"I'm a doctor," Mary snapped.

Finney sucked in a breath. "Run that by me again."

Stifling a yawn, Anthony dragged himself into a sitting position. On the railing of the small, second story porch outside his bedroom, three finches hopped to and fro on a flurry of chirps, greeting the new day. Swinging his legs to the floor, he cast his groggy stare toward the hallway with confusion. Once again a *thump, thump,* bounded through the house.

The noise grew louder as he shuffled from the bedroom. At the end of the hallway, and against his better judgment, he peered inside the bathroom. Before the mirror, Blossom gyrated wildly. A portion of her back popped into view as she struggled mightily with a stretch of slingshot-like material. Wrenching the strap up past her elbow, she growled with fury. The fabric snapped back and she veered into the wall with a *thump!* The commotion sent Anthony scuttling down the stairwell.

With horror, he resisted the notion sinking into his skull. The truth hammered his grey matter, forever ending the relative bliss of parenting.

Blossom had purchased a bra.

At age *eleven?*

Sure, female gadgetry loomed in her future. But she didn't need the contraption. Not yet, not if her petite and scrawny build was any indication. He tiptoed back to the landing and stared dejectedly up the stairwell. Thank God nothing was visible except the shuffle of her feet as she battled the elastic menace.

The fact he had no idea his daughter required feminine niceties sent him into a gloom that competed with his need for a morning caffeine fix. He fled toward the kitchen, away from the muttering irritation of his adolescent daughter, who might well strangle herself before she figured out the damn lingerie.

And therein lay the problem. Who would help Blossom negotiate the dangerous terrain of womanhood?

Single-handedly he'd steered his kid through early childhood. He'd attended school plays and picked out her clothing while Blossom sat in the shopping cart or leaned against his hip.

In retrospect, those days were idyllic. They'd melted beneath the volcanic eruptions that were now commonplace, her sudden squabbles with friends, the stalking through the house with her mood as black as her jeans. Blossom had acne now, a sprinkling of hormonal rage scattered across her forehead. When she appeared for dinner, Anthony was confronted with cheekbones gaining definition and a mouth veering toward sensuality.

Wasn't it bad enough she no longer considered Good Old Dad buddy material? If he dared to offer pithy advice or cracked a joke, she rolled her eyes with embarrassment.

Were they becoming strangers? Worried, he trudged into the kitchen. He yanked the coffee machine open and dumped grounds inside. The machine started brewing. Above his head, thumps bounded across the ceiling like balls set loose in hell's bowling alley. What was she doing now? He flinched as she stomped to her bedroom with the grace of a gorilla. Downhearted, he took down a mug.

By the time he'd poured a second cup, Blossom was talking loudly on her cell, something about Tyler's cute butt. He glared at the ceiling. Listening to the rest of the conversation wasn't an early morning elixir, and he retraced his steps to the front of the house and the sanctuary of his large front porch. On this bright Saturday morning a group of kids across the street, all fresh-faced and unencumbered by raging hormones, played hide-and-seek. The sky was a faultless blue, unmarred by clouds.

He'd barely settled into a wicker chair when he caught sight of Meade Williams sashaying down the street with her white poodle straining to escape its faux diamond leash. The miniscule Melbourne was spraying everything from Mrs. Osborne's petunias to the crabgrass beneath Anthony's mailbox. What the beast lacked in size he made up for in sheer male aggression.

"Anthony!"

Before he might duck back inside, she tugged her pint-sized companion due east. Melbourne gave out a yip, bells jangling as she dragged him forward. Midway up the stone path, she paused to admire the pink turrets and gingerbread latticework adorning his large Victorian house. Longing bloomed on her face.

Like her irritating dog, she knew how to mark her territory. Why she'd staked a claim for Anthony—and his beaut of a house—was too frightening to consider.

Even if her conquest *was* his fault, the energetic pursuit didn't make sense. Single, successful and too highbrow for his tastes, Meade was capable of winning any man she desired. The attractive cosmetics maven had seven years on him and more assets than his extended family.

Now she was determined to add matrimony to her list of achievements. And if he were honest with himself, he *had* begun worrying about how his single status affected Blossom. No doubt Meade had caught the scent of his desperation. What man in his right mind wanted to fly through his daughter's teenage years without a co-pilot? Stupidly he'd admitted as much to her last winter, at Mayor Ryan's Christmas party. In the sorry list of mistakes made in his lifetime, the alcohol-drenched confession rated as one of the biggest.

His thoughts strayed to Mary Chance. Unlike the woman trotting up his front steps in crisp linen shorts and expensive jewelry, the new woman in town was . . . nice. Sexy in a subtle way. Assuming he *did* have the courage to find a woman, he'd prefer to take a shot with someone down-to-earth like Mary.

"Oh, coffee! May I have a cup?" Meade asked.

"Sure." Anthony nearly tripped over Melbourne in his haste to reach the safety of the house. "Cream, no sugar. Right?"

She brushed past. "I'll fetch it myself." Melbourne dogged her three-inch heels.

Speechless, Anthony followed. Entering his house without an invitation was a new and disturbing escalation of her tactics. He wasn't sure what to do about it.

In the kitchen, she asked, "Using the beans I bought at Starbucks?" She frowned at the pizza box and the red sauce dribbling across the counter. "Where's the coffee grinder?"

Anthony stuffed the pizza box into the garbage. "Not sure." She'd given him the grinder and beans last week. The gift didn't mean they were going steady but the gesture brought an image of foxholes and bullets flying. "Let me look."

"You haven't been making fresh?" With a silvery laugh, she helped him rummage through the cupboards. "Ah, success."

She placed the grinder on the counter with a self-congratulatory smile. Blossom trudged into the kitchen with her golden retriever, Sweetcakes. The pooch noticed the much smaller Melbourne. Meade's runt bared his teeth and offered a low, rumbling growl in greeting.

Anthony sent his daughter a warning glance. Snickering, she pulled Sweetcakes into a sitting position before the dog made a snack of Meade's poodle.

Blossom flopped into a chair. "I wouldn't use the grinder if I were you," she told Meade. "The blades are screwed up."

Popping off the lid, Meade peered inside. "Goodness—they are." She gave Blossom a glittering stare. "What happened?"

"I was grinding stuff."

"*What*, exactly?"

Blossom licked her fingertips then dunked them into the sugar bowl. "Peppercorns. Some of my dog's biscuits. Rocks." She licked off the sugary mess. "I was experimenting."

"With the limestone Uncle Nick gave you?" Like his older brother, Blossom had a yen for experimentation that made Anthony proud. "Or the quartz?"

"Both."

He dared a glance at Meade. She was past simmer on her way to boil. "You should've asked first," he said in a suitably firm voice. "The grinder was a gift."

"Oops. I forgot."

Meade banged the grinder down. "You don't sound sorry." She scooped up Melbourne and stalked across the kitchen. "Anthony, I really don't have time for coffee. I have an appointment this morning."

He launched into an apology for his daughter's impolite behavior—too late. Meade sailed through the house and down the front steps.

When he returned to the kitchen, Blossom surged to her feet. "Do something about Meade." She fetched a cereal bowl then jangled through the silverware drawer. "She's on a mission, Dad. *You're* the mission."

He swigged down the last of his coffee. "Stop, all right?"

"This is serious. If she makes you marry her, what about me and Sweetcakes? We aren't into glam, and we hate Melbourne. If he sneaks upstairs and pees in my room, consider it an act of war."

"Stop with the theatrics. I'll handle Meade," he said, having no idea how. She possessed the tactical advantage of feminine wiles and the cunning of a savvy businesswoman. Without thinking, he added, "Don't blame her. I'm at fault for the way she's acting."

Blossom stopped pouring cereal. "Geez, what did you do?"

He stared at her as his brain emptied out. At a loss, he pretended to drink from his empty cup.

"Tell me!"

To punctuate her angst, Blossom stuck her hand inside her shirt. Red-faced, she looked away. Maybe she'd put the bra on so tight she was having trouble sucking in air.

The possibility sent his thoughts fleeing in another direction. Not that a stroll down memory lane to the drunken debauchery of Mayor Ryan's Christmas party gave any comfort. Had Meade set him up? She'd arrived with punch laced so heavily with alcohol, diesel fumes wafted from the bowl. Several of the shop owners on Liberty Square broke into song. Soon after, the mayor lured the county commissioner into her den. Other guests paired off.

Hammered after two cups of punch, Anthony grinned with drunken delight as Meade crowned him with mistletoe. When, exactly, did she lead him to a bedroom upstairs? More importantly, did she have a dragonfly tattoo above her left breast? Or was it a birthmark?

Blossom poked him in the ribs. "Spill, buster," she demanded. "If you can't talk to me, what will you do? It's not like you have friends."

"Who has time for friends? I have a garage to run, bills . . . and a nosy daughter."

"This concerns me too." Returning to the table, she dug into her cereal. "You need my blessing to marry. Skip the ritual and you're excommunicated."

"I'm not getting married."

Regrettably Meade received a different impression when they'd wrestled in the sheets. He'd always found her attractive if too slick for his tastes. He considered her a friend. She lived life on the surface, which he didn't like, but she was long-legged and shapely, which he did. For a woman nearing middle age, she stayed in great shape through merciless exercise and a Spartan diet. And who wouldn't admire her business acumen or her ability to get what she wanted from life? His days were a struggle. A shotgun marriage, Cheryl taking off, Blossom's leukemia—by the time Anthony reached his thirties, he'd felt beaten down by too many challenges. He'd nearly lost his child before the cancer was brought under control. Even now, worry poured into his gut if Blossom caught a cold or looked unusually pale.

Was the party's Christmas music to blame? The familiar tunes made him maudlin. And seeing couples together made him feel sorry for himself.

Eighty-proof punch would loosen anyone's tongue. By the time Meade steered him into the mayor's guest bedroom, he'd admitted he was tired of single life, of raising a daughter without a woman's influence to soften puberty's harsh edges. He'd gone soupy in an embarrassing, inebriated way, admitting the worse part of his day was the moment he climbed into bed alone.

Of course, the disclosure to the attentive Meade wasn't the worst transgression. The other issue? Too embarrassing to consider.

He'd always been hot-blooded. Years of celibacy took its toll in sports injuries from too much jogging and pick-up games of basketball. He'd only had a sampling of marriage before Cheryl left a cryptic note on the dresser and a dime store doll in Blossom's crib. At thirty-four he was at risk of reaching middle age as an abstainer. A real humiliation.

Which explained why he'd nearly slept with Meade before shame eroded his lust. He'd pinned her willingly against the pillows, her platinum blond hair spilling across his fists and her eyes dark with need. But he'd never used a woman. It took every ounce of self-control to get off the bed and leave.

He dispelled the embarrassing memory as Blossom said, "You need to think outside the box, Dad. There *is* someone else you can date."

If nothing else, his kid was persistent. Not that he was prepared to ask Mary Chance out. His dating skills were rustier than his '69 Mustang.

He found his keys. "Are you coming to the gas station?"

"You're avoiding the question."

"I'm not ready to date, all right?" He stopped from mentioning cancer, or remission, or any of the crap they usually discussed. They were both tired of a conversation that went circular, since there was no guarantee the leukemia was gone for good. "Stop bringing it up. When I decide to hang out my shingle, you'll be the first to know."

"Geez, you're touchy."

"Damn right."

"You shouldn't swear."

"You shouldn't make me." He shrugged on his jacket. "Well? What'll it be?"

"I'll hang with Tyler while you work."

Recalling the conversation he'd overhead about Tyler's cute butt, he wavered in the doorway. *"Where* are you hanging out?" If a childhood friendship was becoming something more, he'd ask Mary to write a script for Valium.

"At Tyler's house." When his eyes narrowed, she snapped, "Chill, Dad. His mom is home."

"She'd better be."

"Go to work already." She waved dismissively. "You're getting on my nerves."

There was no gain in responding to the hostile retort. At least she didn't plan to torture him at the Gas & Go with dating schemes.

Traffic on Liberty Square was light. Driving past the courthouse, he eased off the accelerator. There wasn't a single car parked before The Second Chance Grill. The tables looked spotless with their red, white and blue tablecloths. Small vases of carnations dyed in the same patriotic colors lent the lonely dining room a bit of cheer. By the long counter in back, Delia held her fingers up in the sunlight. Then she blew on her nails to dry the coat of polish.

By the picture window, Mary stood gazing at the center

green. Disappointment rimmed her mouth, a puckering at the corners of her pretty lips. She'd bound the rich mass of her hair at the base of her skull but tendrils fell loose by her ears in a fetching display. Driving past, he glanced in the rearview mirror in time to see her lower her face before disappearing from view. Now *there* was a woman worth gambling on.

Jarred from his thoughts, Anthony blinked. Why even consider it?

Chapter 3

The kitchen's turbulent atmosphere did *not* resemble the sanitized sanity of a hospital.

Unsure how to bring order, Mary closed her eyes and imagined Cinci General. She'd despised how the constraints of a patient's insurance controlled the amount of time allotted to administer care, how the long hours destroyed any possibility of a private life. But she'd enjoyed the nurses and the patients, and the air of civility pervading a hospital even on the busiest days. No matter how dire the emergency, medical professionals never resorted to childish tantrums. They never raised their fists or shouted oaths. Even when the ER brimmed with sports injuries and whimpering children, the doctors and nurses worked with steely-eyed calm.

Now, regarding the mayhem, Mary was swamped with a feeling much like homesickness. The kitchen was officially a war zone.

Muttering furiously, Finney stalked in a circle like a panther bearing down on its prey. Ethel Lynn cowered in a vintage lemon colored dress and a pillbox hat that would've done Jackie Kennedy proud. Getting the two women on anything resembling civil terms would prove difficult. Or impossible.

Silently Mary counted to ten. Pity she didn't have a weapon. Finney did, and she whipped the ladle past Ethel Lynn's shoulder. A joggle of old woman ankles, and Ethel Lynn scuttled to safety.

The cook stalked into the walk-in cooler. "What happened in

here?" She surveyed the shelves of fresh produce and meat. "Broccoli has no business cozying up with beef brisket. And I don't know what to make of collard greens sitting by the cottage cheese."

Mary said, "We can rearrange the cooler if you like." If anyone in town took the gamble on dining in the restaurant, at least they had ample supplies.

Finney muttered choice words, adding, "I don't want my cooler rearranged. It was perfect the way it was. Who's been messing around in here?"

"Why, I don't know . . ." Mary's voice drifted away. She looked to Ethel Lynn.

The old woman tottered on her orange pumps. "I alphabetized," she squeaked.

The cook rounded on her. "You what?"

"I wasn't sure how to find ingredients. Paprika and parsnips. Fresh meats and all the dairy. I spent more time searching the walk-in cooler than working the stove. Putting our supplies in alphabetical order saved lots of time."

"Are you nuts?"

"Heavens, you're agitated." Ethel Lynn waved a handkerchief before her delicately perspiring face. "Do have your blood pressure checked. Mary can help."

Finney backed her against the wall. "Here's a prescription. March your silk stockings out of my kitchen right quick."

"Why, the nerve!" The pillbox hat nearly tumbled as Ethel Lynn scurried back. With fussy impatience she righted the hat. "Must I point out you'd left this fine establishment for greener pastures?"

"I left because you fired me!"

Mary stepped between them. "Let's return everything to the way it was."

"How about if I put Ethel Lynn out of her misery instead?" For emphasis Finney sliced the air with her ladle. "Use your doctoring skills to raise her from the dead."

Delia crept into the kitchen. "Uh, Mary . . . someone out front wants to interview you."

"Interview me? I already have a job." One she'd gladly quit. Pity she'd poured her meager savings into the place.

"Better get out here," Delia replied.

"Hold on." Channeling her Inner Zen, she regarded the others. "I forbid you to kill each other. Finney, work on the cooler. Ethel Lynn, check out the storage room. I haven't finished digging through the antiques. See if there's anything we can add to the dining room's décor."

She followed Delia through the swinging door. "FYI, I've hung up my stethoscope for now," she pointed out. "If someone's looking for a doctor, I'm not in the market."

"This isn't about your last job."

"My *real* job."

"Yeah? Looks like you're a waitress now. Welcome to my nightmare."

Mary smoothed down her apron, noticed a smudge of grease. "*What* is this about?" She tried rubbing out the stain then gave up.

"You're in deep with the one person you should never cross. Grown men hide when she's on the rampage." The waitress eyed her sympathetically. "Do you pray?"

Mary skidded to a halt. "Someone wants to *interrogate* me?" She considered dashing back through the door, which slowly squeaked shut. "Who, exactly?"

"Theodora Hendricks wants answers. On opening day? She thinks you intentionally tried to kill half of Liberty." The waitress shrugged. "Or that you're incompetent."

"Tough choices. Is there a door number three?" If so, she'd escape through it. Ditching the thought, she lowered her voice. "In point of fact, Ethel Lynn did the poisoning—I mean cooking."

Delia smirked. "Sure, blame the old bat. The minute she learns Theodora is on the warpath, she'll sell you down the river."

"She'll let me take the fall?" And to think, Mary was beginning to like the old traitor. Ethel Lynn was strung tighter than a violin but she had a sweet side.

"Don't let her ditzy personality fool you. She's got the survival instincts of a Great White Shark," Delia said. "If I were you, I'd take Theodora's thumping like a man."

To punctuate the warning, she grabbed Mary by the shoulders and swung her around.

A petite woman was rooted at the counter's far end. Raisin-skinned, with a deeply lined face, she sat ramrod straight. The retro flowered dress covering her petite frame could've come from Ethel Lynn's closet.

She looked peeved. Which was odd, given her jaunty straw hat, a fruit festooned number reminiscent of Carmen Miranda headgear.

Theodora hurled her beady gaze on Mary. "Get down here, missy."

From behind, Delia whispered, "Let her give you an earful."

A mysterious force glued Mary's feet to the floor. "No thanks." Her throat was drier than Phoenix in July.

"If you don't get moving, she won't leave. She'll sit there all day complaining and demanding fresh cups of coffee. You were a doctor, right? Want me to get an ulcer? I'm too young for that shit."

"I *am* a doctor." And she wasn't about to suffer a verbal thrashing over something she hadn't done. Cowardly, sure, but Theodora had bared her false teeth in a threatening display of geriatric rage. Pulling Delia close, Mary hissed, "Get Ethel Lynn. This is her problem."

"You're on your own, boss. May I have your car if you don't survive the skirmish? My jalopy has chipmunks under the hood."

She squared her shoulders. "Remind me to fire the bunch of you after I'm skinned alive."

Mary hurried forward, grateful for the counter separating her from the intimidating, gnat-sized nemesis. Enduring a verbal lashing wasn't a keeper for the bucket list. At least she was spared the embarrassment of onlookers. There wasn't another customer in sight.

She'd barely come to a standstill when Theodora sputtered, "How dare you poison the fine people of Liberty. The drugstore is clean out of tonics. Do you know what you're done? The Spanish Flu of 1918 didn't give this many people the runs."

"I'm sorry for the inconvenience." Mary swallowed. "Everything is fine now."

"Like hell. Why should I believe you?"

"Finney's back."

The news didn't snuff the disgust in Theodora's expression.

"You mean she's promised to keep you out of the kitchen? How 'bout you put that in writing? I'd like a guarantee the town's no longer in jeopardy."

"Wait. I wasn't—"

Ethel Lynn flew from the kitchen. "Mary meant no harm," she cried.

Stunned, Mary let her mouth hang open. How could Ethel Lynn betray her like this?

The fluttery culprit scrambled for the coffee pot. "She's new to the culinary arts." China rattled as she placed a steaming cup before Theodora. "Don't worry. I can assure you, Finney will keep her on a short leash."

"You bet I will," Finney called from the kitchen. A banging of pots, then, "Damn it! Of all the—why are peaches stacked on top of pork chops? Ethel Lynn, I'm putting out your lights!"

Theodora leaned across the counter. "Get the tart out of your mouth and add sugar," she shouted back. "Your first customer has arrived. I won't tolerate foul words peppering my eggs."

Mary's eyes widened. "You're staying for breakfast?" Maybe a verbal thrashing wasn't so bad. Not if it put a few dollars in the till. "Would you like a menu?"

Theodora screwed down the brim of her hat. "Do you have ipecac? Just in case?" She waved her hand at Ethel Lynn, as if shooing a fly. "Get her away from me. My patience has worn thin."

"Right."

She gave Ethel Lynn a gentle push, which sent her dashing from danger. She flattened against the wall like a criminal in a lineup. Delia was correct—Ethel Lynn *had* sold her down the river. Mary sighed. Did everyone in Liberty blame her for the opening day fiasco?

There wasn't time for a private pity party. Theodora snapped her fingers. "Delia, pour my tomato juice," she commanded.

Delia grabbed the pitcher.

"Don't forget the stewed prunes or the grits. Eggs are worthless without grits on the side."

The waitress swished through the swinging door to ferry

the order to Finney.

After she'd gone, Mary tipped her head to the side. "What are grits?" she asked Theodora.

The old woman banged her flea-sized fist on the counter. "Now you have me wondering if you're as big a fool as Ethel Lynn. How can the owner of this historic restaurant have no familiarity with an American staple? Grits have been on the menu since The Civil War."

"What are they exactly?"

"A fine Southern dish made from corn. Brought to these parts by the restaurant's founder, Justice Postell. She was from South Carolina, in case you're wondering." Theodora switched topics. "Is it true, what they're saying? You were a doctor?"

"I *am* a doctor. I'm on sabbatical."

"How high was your malpractice insurance?"

From the wall, Ethel Lynn gasped. "Have you poisoned anyone outside of Liberty, dear?" she asked, buying her own lie.

Mary folded her arms. "My medical record is unblemished."

Theodora retrieved a smartphone from a white patent leather purse that was the height of fashion in 1962. "Let's Google her. See if she's run afoul of the law."

Ethel Lynn struck an obliging pose. "Let's do."

Mary readied a hearty defense. The words died in her throat as Finney barreled from the kitchen with a plate of eggs, sunny side up, and a mound of grits on the side.

"There'll be no poisoning today, not with me in charge." She placed the food before their feisty customer before regarding Mary. "All the doctors I know are high and mighty. Bedside manner, my ass. They give you five minutes and what do you get? A bill you can't pay."

"Insurance covers most of a standard visit," Mary said. Where was her laptop? Now was an excellent time to escape from Theodora and drum up business. Liberty didn't have a local newspaper but surely there were other places to advertise. "Co-pays are usually negligible." It was that, or contact Aunt Meg in Tibet and admit the townspeople had branded her a quack that couldn't cook.

"*If* you have insurance," Finney said. "Which I don't."

Theodora balled her fists. "Must I listen to this babble?

You're spoiling my meal."

Mary followed the cook back into the kitchen. "Didn't my aunt supply insurance?" she asked.

Finney ran impatient fingers through her hair. "Once Meg slowed down, business did, too. She made cuts to keep the restaurant afloat. Including health insurance."

"But you stayed?"

"You don't give up steady work."

"Well, don't worry. You *will* have health insurance." She couldn't imagine offering anything less. Full-time work deserved full-time benefits. "Give me a few days to set it up."

"You're serious?"

"Of course."

She spotted her laptop beside a bag of lemons. Maybe she'd run a promotion on Groupon. The restaurant, with its anemic grand opening, needed a transfusion of good publicity.

Finney's return gave The Second Chance Grill a fighting chance. With a bit of luck and enough advertising to draw in crowds, the place could become an investment in the future. Mary flipped open her laptop and glanced around for a chair. She had only to stay in Liberty for a year, long enough to make the restaurant profitable. Long enough to deal with the sorrow of losing Sadie and the dream they'd shared of taking over the free clinic serving Cincinnati's poorest citizens. She'd hire someone responsible to manage The Second Chance—not Ethel Lynn, God forbid—and grow a nest egg from the profits. Afterward she'd make good on her promise to Sadie's father, Dr. Abe Goldstein, and take over the free clinic he managed.

"I do appreciate the health insurance," Finney was saying. "You sure are something."

"Thanks." At least the cook wasn't accusing her of *not* being a doctor. It was a start.

"You sure are special." The cook beamed. Her attention bouncing past Mary, she added, "Isn't she a good woman, Anthony?"

Mary snapped shut the laptop. In the back doorway to the kitchen, Anthony casually swung the toolbox in his fist. Their gazes merged and warmth climbed her cheeks. She tamped it down.

The reaction was nothing more than common sexual attraction for the handsome mechanic. The jumble of hormones singing through her veins had everything to do with propagating the species and nothing to do with the human heart. Mere chemistry, she silently reminded herself. The deduction might have lent a feeling of satisfaction if not for the color rising on Anthony's face. His mouth thinned. The supercharged air zinging between them unnerved him too.

Finney spoke up. "Hey, Anthony." She thumped him on the shoulder, which started him blinking. "Get this—Mary doesn't know the first thing about running a restaurant. Isn't that the dumbest thing you ever heard? She's a doctor."

He placed the toolbox beside the sink. "You are?"

She dragged her attention from the dark lights warming his gaze. "I never thought I'd manage a restaurant. Thank Aunt Meg. She's full of surprises. I thought the only thing I'd inherit from her was my great-grandmother's pearls."

Finney said, "I'm glad you took over. Nice of you to bring back health insurance."

Anthony gave an appreciative nod. "You're insuring your employees? Good deal."

The cook looked up expectantly. "Our kids will be covered, too. Won't they? I don't suppose you'll add dental right away. My Randy has cavities in his back molars."

Mary smiled. "We'll see."

Catching the subtle evasion, the cook shrugged. "Dental can wait." She gave Anthony another thump. "Guess what? Mary here is single."

The corners of his mouth lifted but the smile he tried to produce misfired. The look he gave Mary was one shade from maniacal. She dropped her gaze to the floor.

"I'll bet she's been out of commission for as long as you, too," Finney was saying. "Must be hard on you both. I'm middle-aged. Makes the frustration easier. Not that I'd stop a man from sweeping me off my feet." She studied her size 10 shoes. "I like big men."

Her sexually charged commentary stamped pallor on Anthony's face. For reasons beyond logic, his embarrassment landed his attention back on Mary. She squirmed beneath his appraisal, his pallor melting beneath ruddy splotches of color that bled from the corded muscles of his neck all the way to his hairline. The rarity of the site, a grown man blushing like a vulnerable boy, snatched her breath away. With jerky movements, she wiped her brow. Was it hot in here? The kitchen felt like the Sahara.

From beneath the blistering flush, he managed to say, "I'll check the electric to the walk-in cooler." At her questioning look, he added, "Finney asked me to stop by. The motor's running hot."

Like me. And from the looks of it . . . you. Her thumping heart sent spots of grey before her eyesight. "Do you always handle the repairs?" Mary heard herself say.

"Whenever Finney calls."

"Our Mr. Fix-It is the best handyman in Liberty," Finney added.

"Which isn't saying much." He grabbed a wrench from the toolbox and tossed it from hand to hand. "This isn't a big town. I don't have much competition."

The cook swatted air. "Now, you know you're the best. I wouldn't trust another man in here. You can fix anything."

Mary laughed, a nervous bubbling of emotion. "Can you fix the business model for this establishment?" When he frowned, she added, "I'm having trouble bringing in customers."

"Look on the bright side," he replied lightly. "At least the town council hasn't condemned this place."

"That's what Delia said after Ethel Lynn did her best to poison our opening day clientele."

He grinned, which did something marvelous to his face. The tension at the corners of his mouth eased. His eyes sparkled. Mary sighed, entranced.

"How about if I make a few calls to drum up business?" He pulled out his smartphone. "What's today's special?"

They didn't have one. Between hunting down Finney and being sold out by Ethel Lynn, she'd forgotten.

Finney came to the rescue. "How about my special trout? I'll have my supplier bring all I need. Call the Rotary Club—those men love my trout." She sorted through the vegetables and meats that had arrived in the morning shipment. "And Veal Piccata."

"Got it." Pivoting away, Anthony spoke into the phone.

"Sam? Yeah, hi. Hey, Finney wanted me to tell you today's specials. Tell the men to bring their appetites."

Distress wove through his expression. Mary approached. "What's wrong?" she mouthed.

Sheepish, he lifted his shoulders to his ears. Turning away, he lowered his voice. "No, Sam. Mary isn't cooking."

She planted her hands on her hips. Where was the justice?

He hung up, and she said, "I'll never live this down, will I?"

"Not right away," he joked, dialing another number. "Bill? Yeah, I'm calling from The Second Chance. Finney's back. No, no—Mary isn't running the kitchen . . ."

Despite her bruised ego, she experienced growing amusement as he made a series of calls. When he'd finished, the cook said, "I'll call the bowling alley. The women's league plays this morning. They'll be hungry afterwards."

"Should I get on the line?" Mary asked. "Swear I won't do any of the cooking?"

Finney thumbed through her phone. "Like I'd let you." She found the number. "Stay off my turf and I'll draw back the crowds. Seeing we're becoming friends and all."

Mary chuckled. "Thanks."

"Least I can do. You're new to town and need my help. When you're ready to buy a house, I'll help with that, too. I know a good real estate agent."

Real estate? She wasn't staying long enough to put down roots. The Second Chance Grill was an investment, not a life's calling. Admitting as much to Finney seemed unwise.

Awareness tickled her spine. From over her shoulder, she discovered Anthony quietly studying her.

Nearing, he asked, "What's wrong? You look upset."

She took a self-defensive step back. It was that, or give into the urge to run her palms across the front of his work shirt, a thoroughly unwarranted thought. He smelled soapy and clean, and the compassion burnishing his features was its own form of temptation.

"Oh, I'm fine," she finally got out.

He nodded good-naturedly. "I'll mind my own business." He ducked into the walk-in cooler.

Wordlessly, she watched him disappear inside. Her

thoughts turned to his daughter, a girl with a mischievous grin and a crown of corkscrew curls. Who wouldn't feel affection for a child so full of life? Yet Anthony had nearly lost her to leukemia.

He'd suffered enough hardship.

The last thing he needed was a short romance sure to lead to disappointment. She liked him more than was sensible, which made the situation precarious. She'd enjoy his companionship. But she'd dread the sadness sure to follow once she handed off management of the restaurant and resumed her career in medicine.

Resigned to her choice, she buried her emotions beneath a physician's calm and got back to work.

Chapter 4

Throughout the week, the tables filled and the cash register sang as news spread of Finney's return.

Simmering broths and steaks seared to perfection lured in customers by droves. Finney retook the restaurant's kitchen with the skill of a conquering general, barking orders that sent her minions fleeing to slice potatoes and toss salads. Fresh basil perfumed the chopping block and homemade puddings bubbled on the stove. Mary put on five pounds in as many days, all the while standing in awe of the cook's culinary gifts.

The increasing business was enough to give hope. Yet as the days passed, other concerns mounted.

Health insurance, for one. Through Medicare Ethel Lynn enjoyed coverage, but Mary had promised to provide Finney and Delia with insurance. Finding a plan on a limited budget was difficult. During her residency at Cinci General she'd treated patients with only a passing thought of co-pays and deductibles. The hurdles small businesses leapt to insure employees had seemed inconsequential. Now, as she tried to negotiate an affordable rate, the mind-boggling intricacies of the various plans laid heavily on her mind.

The other worry? Blossom. The preteen was up to something, which sent anxiety through Mary like a cold virus. Getting to the bottom of it became a priority.

The girl now appeared at the counter every afternoon. Today she ordered a milkshake before launching into conversation, twirling her mop of curls for emphasis. Her unspoken questions pricked Mary's heart, the hint of entreaty mixed with a child's eagerness. Was Blossom gearing up to ask a favor? Whatever she wanted, a niggling unease warned there was more to the girl's sudden friendship than a desire to clear the restaurant of cherry sprinkles and chocolate sauce.

The bell above the door jingled. A tiny dog's *yip* followed. Blossom stopped drinking mid-slurp.

She gave a mock shudder. "Tell me it isn't Meade and her nasty dog."

Mary scanned Meade's stylish silk suit and platinum hair with more than passing envy. "Who else stops by for an early dinner with her dog in tow?" She returned the woman's brisk wave.

"Animals aren't allowed in here."

They weren't, but Mary couldn't afford to turn away business. "FYI, Meade tips well. She's one of Delia's favorite customers."

"She's rich, you know. Rich as rain. Rich as radishes."

"Radishes?" Mary reached across the counter and flicked one of Blossom's curls. "Aren't they tart or peppery?"

"We're studying alliteration in school. I'm giving it a test run." Blossom planted her mouth back on her straw.

Mary leaned against the counter, drawn close by the girl's quirky personality. "Do you enjoy school?" she asked.

"The biology teacher is a dirt bag. He picks his nose. Mrs. Martyn is nice. She's the new social studies teacher."

"I loved school."

The disclosure furrowed the girl's brows. "Meade loves my dad," she confided. "The way she acts around him gives me the creeps."

"He's a nice man." Mary banished the wistful notes coloring her voice. Quickly, she added, "No wonder she likes him so much."

"My girlfriend, Snoops? She says he's hot for an old guy." Blossom swiveled back and forth on the barstool. "What do *you* think?"

The trusty physician's expression, the one Mary employed whenever a patient revealed something bizarre or embarrassing, refused to materialize. What did she *think?* Anthony Perini was six feet of prime male packaged with a sweet personality and an admirable devotion to his daughter. She'd gladly dive into his earthy brown eyes and swim a few laps. Not that admitting as much to his daughter was appropriate.

At length she quipped, "I think your father is handsome for an old guy." Needing to steer the conversation to neutral terrain, she tapped the side of Blossom's glass. "Another milkshake? I wouldn't normally suggest a refill but it wouldn't hurt if you gained a few pounds."

The ploy didn't work, and Blossom said, "I'm serious, Mary. Tell the truth. Do you think my dad is dating material?"

"For many women, yes."

"Would *you* go out with him?"

The query revealed the reason for the girl's sudden friendship. Sure, she had a yen for ice cream and enjoyed Mary well enough. Trivial enjoyments compared to her bigger desire: finding someone for her father to date other than Meade.

Mary chose her words with care. "Blossom, it isn't polite to ask such questions," she gently replied. "I'm a newcomer to Liberty and he's been very kind. He fixed the motor in the walk-in cooler but refused pay for his time. I only paid for parts. We've become friends. Isn't that enough?"

To her distress, the prim response stamped glee on the kid's face. "You're as pink as a pomegranate. You *do* like my dad." Sobering, she patted Mary's hand. "Don't be scared. From what I've seen, he's got a crush on you too."

Drumming up a reply proved impossible. Thankfully Meade's dog *yip, yip, yipped,* drawing Blossom's ire. Swinging around on the barstool, she glowered as Meade chose a table by the window.

Blossom nodded at the box clamped beneath Meade's arm. "What is that?" she asked Mary.

"Don't know, don't care. I'm more concerned about her dog," Mary replied, glad for the diversion. The revelation about Anthony's crush had planted a woozy pleasure in her chest. "Melbourne's small but he's feisty. Does he bite?"

"Nope. But Meade does."

At the table, Meade battled the squirming canine. She

lowered him to the ground before depositing the box in Ethel Lynn's hands. Curious, Mary went to investigate.

Ethel Lynn brightened. "Isn't this wonderful? Thanks to Meade, we'll soon redeem the reputation of this fine establishment."

Meade handed Mary the receipt. "Theodora and I thought the message would reassure your customers. My printer was happy to make the banner at cost."

"What banner?" Mary said, astonished by her misplaced curiosity.

Darting past, Blossom rifled through the box. "Wow. This is embarrassing." She unspooled the banner for all to see.

Written in flowing blue script were the words, *Finney is back. Mary isn't cooking.*

Cringing, Mary opened her mouth to form a defense. Nothing suitable came to mind. This late in the game, was there any sense in revealing the culprit? If exposed, Ethel Lynn would faint dead away at Meade's stylishly clad feet.

Ethel Lynn opened the banner wide. "This is marvelous," she said, cheery with the reprieve she didn't deserve. "Let's hang this on the picture window."

"Like hell you will," Blossom said.

Mary gasped. "Blossom!"

"Sorry." The kid faced off before Meade. "You're as mean as mice. Mean as mercury." She hesitated. "The planet, not the chemical."

Intently Meade studied the girl. "Blossom, are you on drugs?"

"She's high on alliteration," Mary said.

"Aren't we all," Ethel Lynn agreed, trying to keep up.

Meade wagged a finger at the furious preteen. "Theodora *insisted* on the banner." She regarded Mary with faint misgiving, adding, "Liberty is a small town. Theodora can throw her weight around whenever she pleases. Frankly, I agree with her on this matter."

Blossom's shoulders trembled. "Why don't I throw *you* around?"

Mary steered her away from the impervious blonde. "I'm not hanging the banner," she said, warmed by the girl's defense.

Ethel Lynn was clearly sold on the idea but at least the kid had come through. "Everyone knows Finney is back. Isn't that enough?"

Meade ignored the poison-tipped darts zinging from Blossom's gaze. "You don't understand," she informed Mary. "The town deserves reassurance your entrees don't pose a health risk. You were once a doctor, I presume? Surely you understand."

'I *am* a doctor. And, no, I don't see why I should do this."

Blossom surged forward. "If people are still mad about Mary's opening day, I know how to make amends. Let's hand out free stuff." She grabbed Ethel Lynn's arm, which was encased in purple brocade—today she'd worn a cocktail dress straight from the 1950s. "Remember the Fourth of July decorations you bought last year?"

The old woman frowned. "Last year?" It was up for grabs if she remembered last week.

"The parade flags," Blossom prodded. "There are lots of them left. We'll hand them out."

Mary recalled the boxes of small flags in the storage room. The flags certainly fit the restaurant's Americana decor. Why not add flags to flower arrangements and give them to children when they arrived?

"Blossom, you're on to something," Mary agreed. Turning to Meade, she layered ice on her voice. "I'm sorry you went to such trouble. Your banner isn't necessary."

"Oh, you think so? Take your complaints up with Theodora." Meade paused as Delia approached to pour her a cup of coffee. "She's made her decision."

Ethel Lynn shuddered. "Theodora has a temper. Might we hang the banner *and* hand out flags? A dual promotion?"

"The flags will be my job," Blossom chimed in.

"Your job?" Mary asked, taken aback.

"Why not? Finney's cooking is making this place busy again. You'll need more help."

"Eventually, sure." She searched for a way out of the impasse. Her mind went blank.

"Summer vacation is right around the corner." The girl composed her features in a fetching display of entreaty. "Hire me. I'm definitely worth it."

On an intake of breath, Mary hesitated. The girl's face brimmed with pride and something else, something immensely warming.

Which made it all the more imperative to let her down gently. "Honey, you're awfully young. Holding a job is a grown-up affair. Why not spend the summer hanging out with your friends?"

"I'll see them at the end of my shift. I don't have to come in for work too early, do I?"

Meade laughed with derision. "Be serious. You need a summer regimen that doesn't involve swabbing down tables or scrubbing pots. Tennis lessons. Equestrian Camp. Something to keep you out of trouble."

"I'm not into tennis or horses. I'm working here."

Meade set her cup down with a bang. "Of all the nonsense! You can't work. You're *eleven*."

"Shows what you know." The girl planted her attention on Mary. "We're friends, aren't we? Tell her you can't wait to hire me. The Second Chance Grill's official flag girl. I'll make sure every kid that eats here doesn't leave without a flag."

She gave a look so imploring it would haul any adult onto The Guilt Train. Not that hiring a preteen made sense. The Second Chance was a restaurant, not a summer camp.

"Sweetie, let me think about it," Mary prevaricated.

Meade studied her with palpable outrage. "You aren't considering this, are you? She's a minor. The law forbids you from hiring a child. Do you want to lose your operating license?"

Mary stiffened. Was this a threat? Evidently if she didn't steer clear of the girl, Meade planned to cause trouble.

In a chilling flash, she understood the real stakes. Meade viewed her as a rival for Anthony's affections. His daughter was off limits.

The danger of two women locking horns went right over Blossom's head. "Since when do you care about the law?" she asked Meade. Her bravado slipped and her voice wavered. "If I want to work, my dad will agree. He lets me do whatever I want."

Mary offered an encouraging smile. "How about this. When you're fourteen years old, I'll hire you. Guaranteed."

Betrayal darkened the girl's perilously moist eyes. "Why

aren't you sticking up for me?" Somehow she coiled in the hurt, washing her expression clean of everything but fury. "I thought we were friends."

"Of course we are."

"Stop pouting," Meade put in with cruel disregard for the girl's feelings. "Children don't hold down jobs. What a ridiculous notion."

The urge to strike the woman was nearly overpowering. Mary was about to tell Meade to stay out of it when the door to the kitchen swung open. Finney stuck her head out.

"Mary, I hope you don't mind I picked up. There's a Dr. Goldstein calling on your cell." The cook's expression softened. "Isn't he the father of your late friend?"

"Ask him to hold on." Searching for a way out of the impasse, she brushed her knuckles across Blossom's arm.

The gesture, a simple request for understanding, propelled the girl out the door.

The rumble of Dr. Abe Goldstein's voice carried across the line. "Mary, my dear! How are you?"

If not for the disagreement with Blossom, hearing from the father of her late friend would've been a welcome surprise. He'd encouraged her friendship with Sadie, which began in junior high biology class. Throughout high school and college, the gregarious physician piqued their interest in anatomy and regaled them with stories of the working poor he aided at his free clinic in Cincinnati. He urged them both to attend medical school. When they'd approached him with the notion of joining his practice after completing their residencies, he'd agreed on the spot.

"Abe, what a surprise." With regret, she considered the bind she'd left him in. He never expected her to inherit a restaurant, or leave suddenly on sabbatical. "How's everything at the clinic?"

"Busier than ever. The Great Recession may have ended, but the consequences haven't. We're caring for patients who used to be solidly middle class."

"Are you managing?"

"We have two new physicians on rotation from the hospital." Pride laced his voice. "We also just received a grant from the Women's Network of Southern Ohio. Not a moment too soon."

"A large gift?" The clinic was perpetually in need of donations.

"Fifty thousand." He chuckled. "We have Jillian to thank. She hounded the Women's Network for months."

For privacy, Mary tiptoed into the hallway behind the kitchen. "How is she, Abe?"

Her daughter's sudden death had devastated Jillian Goldstein. She possessed a fragile temperament. She'd always reminded Mary of spun glass, her lithe figure and long neck, the way emotion broke through her reserve. When Sadie and Mary left for college at Ohio State, her constant vigil through email and text message became a source of amusement. Losing Sadie to a drunk driver's negligence had sent Jillian into a nearly inconsolable grief.

"She's managing." Abe's voice caught. "She's in Hilton Head, in fact."

"Shouldn't you vacation with her?"

"Don't tempt me. Eighteen holes of golf each morning and cocktails with my wife at sunset. What's better?" He sent an uncomfortable silence through the phone. "Jillian's looking at condos."

"Are you thinking of retiring?" The prospect filled her with regret. "Listen, I haven't made a decision," she added in a rush. "I'm still interested in managing the clinic."

"You're worried you won't succeed without my daughter. What have I always told you? Sadie wasn't the only one with uncommon strength. You're just as strong."

"I'd like to think so." Without Sadie, her guiding light, she felt diminished. "I miss her."

"She'd tell you to stop hiding in Liberty."

"You're wrong. Sadie would find the idea of me running a restaurant hilarious."

"She was a cut-up." Sobering, he added, "Jillian may have found the perfect condo. I'm straddling the fence. Mostly because a young doctor in Liberty is straddling the fence, too."

"Abe, I needed a break from medicine. I really did."

"You need to resume your profession. Come to think of it,

there's a nice clinic in Cincinnati. The building's drab and the parking lot is one big pothole, but the patients are beyond compare."

Despite her sagging emotions, she said, "Sounds great. I'll look into it."

As he made small talk, she walked to the end of the hallway and flicked on the storage room's lights. Stacks of cardboard boxes and tall metal shelves hid the vast length of the wall, reminding her of sentries guarding the restaurant's illustrious past. Antique tables were scattered around the room. Upholstered furniture, old and impeccably kept, sat beneath filmy sheets of cellophane.

Mary found a chair and sank into it. "I know you'd like an exact date when I'll take over the clinic. I need some time to get the restaurant on sure footing."

He made a soft *tush-tush* sound. "You're stalling."

"I'm grieving." She closed her eyes.

"I am too, but not as much as my wife. She needs the condo and South Carolina's palm trees. She needs anything that'll keep her mind off the tragedy of losing our daughter." A pause, then, "I do understand why you took over the restaurant. The building alone is valuable real estate."

"Don't forget the antiques."

"Worth a fortune, I'll bet. Have them appraised."

"It's on my to-do list." She drew quiet for a moment before adding, "Give me a year—"

Cutting her off, he said, "Promise me something, young lady. Don't forget how much you love medicine."

She thought of Finney, waiting for health insurance, and Blossom, who'd work to feed her ice cream addiction. Ethel Lynn was of retirement age, but Mary sensed the restaurant provided a reassuring center for an otherwise dull life. Delia was just a few years past high school. The member of a large family, she methodically counted her tips each night, placing the bills in neat stacks and the coins in careful rows. Did she pitch in on the family grocery bill? Pay rent to help her parents make ends meet?

"Abe, I do love medicine but I have an obligation to the women I've hired," she finally said. "I can't let them down. When I conclude my stay in Liberty, I'd like to leave with the knowledge I've made their lives better."

"You've given them jobs. Isn't that enough?"

What would Blossom have given? She'd regarded Mary with a look of betrayal. *I thought we were friends.*

Any well-trained physician understood the delicate quality of relationships. Blossom wasn't merely seeking a job; she'd offered friendship with the faith that Mary was worthy of the gift. Which spoke to the reason why Mary dreamed of managing a general practice at Abe's clinic. Specialists viewed the people in their care as a compartmentalized set of problems: a heart valve blocked by thrombus, a fractured tibia. As a primary doctor, she'd care for patients in their entirety. Treat common viruses and offer comfort to the dying. She'd help them navigate their lives, year in and year out.

He broke the reverie. "Just remember you're a doctor," he said. "Don't fall in love with the restaurant or the town. You'll heal yourself, just as you'll heal your patients once you return to medicine."

She murmured her assent. If not for Sadie's death, she never would've accepted the generous inheritance of the restaurant.

Her life belonged in southern Ohio.

Chapter 5

During the following days the urge to follow Abe's advice and return to medicine became a nagging temptation. Despite Mary's objections, Ethel Lynn and Meade strung up the banner on the restaurant's picture window—*Finney is Back. Mary isn't Cooking.* Naturally they waited to conduct their sabotage until after Mary left to run errands. She'd returned late in the evening through the building's back door and gone directly to her apartment upstairs. Their treachery wasn't discovered until the following morning.

The embarrassing addition to the décor came down immediately—Mary *did* have her pride. But the banner had remained in full view long enough to cement her reputation as a quack who couldn't cook.

The barrage of embarrassments didn't stop there.

In the drugstore, Theodora cornered her. Liberty's elderly matriarch demanded to know if she'd so much as flipped a pancake during the restaurant's hours of operation. Jogging through the Square's center green, she discovered three members of the town council dogging her heels and seeking assurance that Finney alone manned the kitchen.

Now, with the dinner rush in full swing, the restaurant brimmed with customers. In the air the succulent aroma of Martha Jefferson's pork loin with orange glaze competed nicely with the delectable fragrance of Dolley Madison's vanilla pudding. Every barstool was occupied. The tables in the dining room were packed. Sprinting back and forth taking orders, Mary plastered on a pleasant expression. Diners eyed her with unmistakable suspicion.

Beneath the counter, two boxes of patriotic flags sat neglected. She'd hauled them from the storeroom even though she didn't have the heart to put them out. Handing out the flags had been Blossom's idea.

For days now, she hadn't stopped by. Her absence was proof of the staying power of adolescent fury. Short of offering a job, there was no simple way to make amends.

Startled from her thoughts, she found Anthony standing before the busy counter. Mayor Ryan rose from a barstool. He quickly sat.

Usually he arrived for a cup of coffee after Blossom left for school, or earlier still, if she spent the night with her grandparents or her girlfriend, Snoops. Although Mary always looked forward to seeing him, this was the first time he'd arrived at dinnertime.

"Is it true you can't cook?" he said, by way of greeting.

She brushed off the joke. "I can boil water." She regarded the wary businessman seated to Anthony's left. "But I won't, promise," she assured him.

The man nodded, relieved.

Anthony leaned across the counter, whispering, "Don't let them get to you." He surveyed the dining room and the packed tables. "People in small towns are suspicious by nature. They'll come around, Theodora included."

"Yeah? This feels like a frat-boy hazing. Only I didn't sign up with the fraternity." Beneath the amusement in his expression, she noted distress. "How's Blossom?"

"I'm not ready for the teenage years," he admitted. He nodded toward the coffee station. "Would you mind?"

She fetched the pot. "You look tired." An understatement. He sported dark patches beneath his eyes and his shoulders sagged. "Would you like it intravenously?"

"Sure."

"Want to talk about it?"

He shrugged as she slid the cup under his nose. "This is

more than I can handle. If Blossom doesn't snap out of her funk, I'm having her strung up and shot."

Rarely did a man reveal a more vulnerable side, and his desperation *was* endearing. "I'm sure she's just out of sorts," Mary said, glad he thought enough of her to confide his worries. "Kids go through stages. Give her space and she'll come around."

"Optimism. I can't stand it." He covered his eyes with mock horror. "She stomps around the house like the queen of darkness. Moody silences, slamming doors—" He looked up suddenly. "It's a female thing, right? Not talking then torturing me when she shoots off her mouth."

"You've been married. What do you think?"

"I'm no expert." He toyed with the spoon she'd placed before him. "All I learned in two years was that raising a baby was expensive."

She pitied him—his marriage had only lasted two years? "Sometimes women need time to process their emotions." This sounded analytical and not nearly as friendly as she'd intended so she added, "Have you tried talking to Blossom?"

"A few days ago, sure. Since then? Hell, no."

"You shouldn't swear."

The suggestion put a mysterious delight in his gaze. "You shouldn't make me." Grinning, he lowered his eyes to his cup.

Something sweet drifted through her heart as her attention lingered on the five 'o clock shadow darkening his face. It was rather unsettling how the stubble on a man's chin made him altogether too attractive. She'd take him unshaven any day.

"I don't get it," he was saying. "Since when do sixth graders want to work? I can't even get the kid to pick up the crap in her bedroom. As far as I'm concerned she's rebuilt the Berlin Wall. Someone else can tear it down."

"She's your daughter. You have to try."

"Would you mind trying?"

The request took her off guard. "Anthony, your daughter has been ignoring me for days. She's upset because I can't give her a job."

"She has a fixation on you. Push hard enough and she'll spill."

"Blossom won't spill anything." She thought of Meade's

none-too-subtle threats. Evidently she wanted Mary to back off from Anthony, too. "It's not a good idea to involve me. I barely know your daughter."

"Then do something to get to know her better. I'll gladly pay." He reached for his wallet. "Take her to the movies. You don't do slumber parties, do you? I could use a full night of shut eye."

"I'm still living out of a box."

"Like the homeless, living in a discarded appliance box?"

"Hardly. I live upstairs. I've been here a month and still haven't found time to unpack. You should see my apartment. On second thought, you shouldn't. A condemned zone."

"Then the slumber party is off?" He appeared genuinely sad and she wondered if he'd been serious.

"Sorry, friend. The sleepover must wait."

"It isn't just you. Blossom hasn't been acting like herself. There's something else going on."

"Like what?"

"No clue. Whatever the problem, it's trouble." Rising, he tossed several bills on the counter. "I'll call my mother. Maybe she'll take pity and haul the demon away."

Mary pocketed the bills. "That's it? You can't handle her, so you'll dump her on the nearest woman?"

"Cut me some slack, will you? I've never raised a kid on the edge of the teenage years."

"You'll manage." A doctor's instincts prodded her to ask for the particulars of Blossom's leukemia. The longer the remission, the greater the chance the girl would remain cancer-free.

The niggling questions evaporated beneath the tension lining his features. Peppering the man for answers seemed an intrusion. She couldn't broach the subject until he brought it up—*if* he ever brought it up.

"You'll get to the bottom of her funk." She thought of something else. "Does Blossom get into trouble?"

His pirate's grin nearly took her hostage. "Woman, you have no idea."

"Why don't you get it?" Blossom said through clenched

teeth. "I need an iPad. I'm serious. Everyone has one."

Anthony ducked his head beneath the Mustang's hood. "Don't you have something better to do than torture Dear Old Dad?" he asked, unable to stop the frustration from rimming his voice.

"Not really. Not unless you'll stop being unreasonable and take me to the Apple Store."

"Dream on."

Seven days and counting, his daughter was still in a funk. Now she had it in her head that Life Would End if she didn't own an iPad. Recently her closest girlfriend, Snoops had received the pricey gadget for her birthday. Now his kid wanted one.

"I'm not asking for a hand-out." Blossom shot around the side of the Mustang, cornering him. "Give me a loan. I'll pay you back from my first paycheck."

"What paycheck?"

She looked at him like he'd gone brainless. "The one I'll get once Mary hires me. She's being stubborn but I'll convince her."

"No, muchacha. She's being realistic. No one hires a minor to wait tables."

"Hand out flags," his daughter corrected.

"Whatever." Straightening, he tried to wipe the irritation from his face. Let this escalate into an argument and he'd never get her to leave the garage.

"I'm getting a job as a greeter. I'll *greet* people when they come into The Second Chance." She frowned. "When did you get so stupid?"

Crackling tension followed the obnoxious query. They traded hostile looks for ten seconds before he said, "Fair warning, kiddo. If you don't let me get back to work, I'm grounding you. Summer vacation in jail. Comprendo?"

She flounced into the afternoon sunshine. "Fine. Don't lend the money. I'll ask someone else." She threw a backward glance. "Cheapskate."

The comment nicked his heart but he kept his silence. It was reward enough when she disappeared into the leafy shade of the center green. Best guess, she planned to stand outside Mary's restaurant in a state of pubescent rage. She'd stand there fuming in the sun until her strength gave out or Mary relented.

He didn't care.

Surrendering to a bout of self-pity, he slammed shut the Mustang's hood. He sauntered into the Gas & Go's parking lot weighed down by a host of unanswerable questions. The only certainty? The mysteries of a female adolescent would test the endurance of any man. *Why* was Blossom increasingly moody? Her sudden interest in bras and pig-headed desire to work—an eleven year old gyrated through so many moods, only a mystic could divine the contents of her heart.

Rocking back on his heels, he stretched his back. Cars wended around Liberty Square in the June heat. At the north end of the center green, a young couple chatted beside the sugar shack. The building became a focal point every March when local farmers boiled the county's famous maple syrup. Today the place appeared sweetly private as the dark-haired youth nuzzled his girlfriend's ear. Laughter bubbled from her mouth. They looked happy taking in the fine June air and trading kisses. The way their heads bent close, their conversation as intertwined as their arms, gave the impression they were planning their wedding. The possibility made him blue.

Lovers never used to bother him. When his older brother Nick married, Anthony had enjoyed the wedding with three-year-old Blossom glued to his lap. Sure, he'd felt awkward running into friends, the entire lot cocky with pride because they were finishing college. But he'd smiled encouragingly as they went on the hunt and quickly paired off with long-legged girls dressed bright as flamingos.

The moment Blossom began rubbing her eyes, he'd flocked to the coat check with the older guests.

Retreating from the memory, he let his attention stray to the opposite side of the Square. A row of cars hemmed in the planters of red geraniums flanking The Second Chance Grill's door. With Finney back at work, the locals were again frequenting the restaurant. Anthony was no exception, appearing for breakfast each morning. Recently he'd added a visit at midday for coffee and a snack, a bowl of fries or a shake. On nights that Blossom went out with friends, he found himself slipping onto his favorite barstool and ordering dinner. He understood that Finney's culinary gifts, marvelous though they were, didn't have him counting the hours before he could return. The restaurant's only lure was Mary.

He kicked the gravel at his feet. Did he have a crush on her? The likelihood was depressing. With Meade stalking his every move and Blossom practicing the dark arts of an adolescent, he had troubles enough.

Even if he found the courage to ask Mary out—which he wasn't prepared to do—he'd like to embark on a relationship in a cooler frame of mind. He'd like some assurance he wouldn't become lost in her moss-colored eyes before they were thoroughly acquainted. He'd like to take it slow. Not glacial-slow, but at a reasonable pace to allow a review of the dating playbook before he risked falling in love.

Problem was, he liked everything about Mary from her warm, inquisitive gaze to her throaty voice. She'd been a doctor. Had she despised the rat race of caring for patients? She was adaptable enough to quit the profession to take over her aunt's restaurant. If she'd yearned for a slower pace, she'd found nirvana in Liberty, Ohio.

Other qualities were also praiseworthy. Whenever Finney and Ethel Lynn crossed swords, she effortlessly steered them apart. Nor had she lost her temper with Theodora or Meade over the banner. Folks in town still viewed Mary with suspicion, but she treated everyone kindly.

Most of all, he liked the way she looked at him.

Seated at the counter, he'd battle a frothy excitement for seconds that ground into an eternity. After his patience was as frayed as his emotions, he'd throw caution aside and focus on her like a beacon. She always knew the precise moment he drew her into his line of sight. His breath grew choppy as her eyes lifted and found his. Yanking her attention away, she'd reward him with a slight pursing of her lips and a slow, subtle rise of color feathering across her cheeks. Which invariably sent her rushing to the opposite end of the counter. His chest would fill with something like victory, a wild emotion that put a bounce in his step when he slipped off the barstool and returned to the Gas & Go.

Yesterday, their interlude gained added depth. They'd engaged in an honest-to-God conversation about his daughter for seven minutes.

Anthony was sure of the time. He'd checked his watch on the way out.

That he'd measured—in a state of exhilaration—the exact duration of the conversation posed its own threat. For a man in his thirties, he was embarrassingly inept with women. He'd unbound the natural order clear back in high school by becoming sexually active with a series of girls.

The last in line, Cheryl, graduated from Liberty High three months pregnant.

If he reflected on high school at all, he did so with shame. During those careless years he wore arrogance as tight as his jeans, a flimsy barrier for the fear over what he'd done and the responsibilities lying ahead. On the altar of St. Mary's Church, he'd stood with Cheryl in a suit he wasn't yet muscular enough to fill. They treated the child growing in her womb like a prank easily dismissed once their parents calmed down and life resumed a thrilling pace of all-night parties and socializing with friends.

Soon life dashed them with icy reality. Trapped together at Fairway Apartments in Liberty's seediest neighborhood, they watched Cheryl's body transform at a fearful rate.

All his schoolboy bravado vanished the moment Blossom was placed in his arms. A wiggly mass of flesh with eyes identical to his, she carried a scent so tangy he'd pressed his nose to her belly with curiosity and delight. The wonders of new life were lost on Cheryl. She slept through Blossom's colicky whimpers and slipped off with girlfriends at every opportunity.

For Anthony, the change was profound. Instinct stirred him from the deepest sleep; he threw out the SAT Study Guide, opened a savings account and learned the mechanic's trade. At age two, Blossom found her way out of the apartment late one night. Somehow he snapped to consciousness as if someone had zapped him with current. Hovering in the doorway to her empty bedroom, he battled a sensation like suffocation. He bounded down the apartment stairwell screaming her name and waking all their neighbors. In the parking lot, he'd found her shivering. She was peering through a rust hole in his Ford. Frost trimmed her curls.

Now, a decade later, he understood the map of fatherhood with some confidence. But he'd lost something in the bargain, those years other men spent practicing the art of courtship. Embarking on a relationship with a woman like Mary was daunting. Why even try?

Head hung low, he returned to the garage. There was a tire rotation scheduled for the afternoon with an oil change soon after. A light day of work, yet he was spent. Between his daughter's funk and his attraction to Mary, rest was becoming elusive.

Climbing into the pit, he battled self-pity and a clamoring defiance. A seed lodge in his brain, a fertile, fledgling hope. Caught by the notion, he sat heavily on the cement steps.

If he ignored common sense and asked Mary out, would she consent?

Chapter 6

Summer blew into northeast Ohio on a deliciously balmy breeze. Children counted down school days now in the single digits.

In an effort to fit in, Mary merged her routine with the town's activities. She underwent the local ritual of jumping out of the way when Theodora zoomed by in her sky-blue Cadillac. She filled her car at the Gas & Go on her way to the community pool, where she swam laps. When The Second Chance slumbered during the afternoon lull, she strolled the streets that unfurled from the green, grassy nexus of Liberty Square.

North Street became her favorite. Most of the houses were built in the 1800s. Many were lovingly restored, an amazing feat given the town's sluggish economy. North Street boasted pillared mansions built in the Greek revival style, huge saltbox Colonials with simple lines, frivolous Victorians with filigreed porches and whimsical cupolas. Anthony's large, rosy pink Victorian, a gorgeous structure, lay midway down the street.

Today she found herself wavering on the sidewalk before his house. Tamping down her nerves, she squared her shoulders. She was a doctor, after all, and the nerves bounding beneath her skin were a mere inconvenience. With that thought in mind, she strode up the stone path to the porch with its gingerbread latticework and pots of impatiens spilling petals across the welcome mat.

At the restaurant, Blossom was now as scarce as emeralds.

Naturally she was still angry because she'd been refused a job. Though her absence was upsetting, it wasn't the galvanizing force that propelled Mary across Anthony's front porch. Yesterday she'd stepped out of the restaurant and glimpsed the girl in the center green.

With a practiced eye, she'd assessed the shadows beneath Blossom's eyes. Her skin appeared frighteningly pale. She'd seemed lethargic, seated on a picnic table staring into space.

Like any good doctor, Mary understood the emotional toll wrought by cancer. Even with a successful remission, a child who'd undergone the rigors of treatment became easy prey for depression. Uncomfortable with the prospect, she believed the time to broach the topic of Blossom's health with Anthony was long overdue. They'd become friends despite their mutual, and blessedly unspoken, attraction. She owed him nothing less than her professional opinion.

The other reason for her visit? She hoped he'd agree with her plan.

The doorbell's chimes echoed through the house. Wedged beneath the sink, Anthony muttered a curse. He'd fixed the leak in the faucet. Other chores lay ahead, from caulking the master bath to dealing with the lawn, which was beginning to resemble the Missouri prairie. He didn't relish the interruption. In fact, he was doing a damn fine job keeping busy.

Each day Blossom grew more churlish, spouting tears and rage in equal measure. With his once-sweet kid morphing into a monster, why consider asking Mary out? No one in his right mind dropped a woman into hell's inferno. Far better to nix the idea of dating. Mary had become important to Blossom but they'd had a falling out.

Another series of chimes, and he clenched his teeth.

"Nick, come in!" On hands and knees, he mopped up the water by the sink. "I'm in the kitchen, you lazy ass. The leak's fixed, no thanks to you."

"This isn't Nick." A perilous silence then, "Is this a bad time?"

He shot to his feet, banging his head on the way up.

Mary.

Cradling his throbbing skull, he swung in a mad circle. The kitchen looked like marauding Vikings had invaded. Dishes everywhere—Blossom had been trailing pizza and bad vibes through the house for days. Neither one of them cared much about cleanliness after she went into her funk and they broke trade relations.

"Be right there." He launched toward the pizza sauce spattered across the microwave. Snatching up a rag, he groaned. More sauce covered the cupboards, a real spackle-art display. What would Mary think if she saw the place like this? He couldn't spruce up the house in ten seconds flat.

Surrendering to embarrassment, he stalked to the foyer.

He found Mary on the other side of the screen door at the precise moment he remembered he'd used his tee-shirt, an old Cleveland Indians number, to wipe up the water leaking from the sink.

Aw, man.

Mortified, he rubbed his hands down his naked and slickly perspiring torso. Which, come to think of it, Mary assessed with more than a passing appreciation. He was still in a crappy mood but her expression was an ego boost.

"I was walking by," she said, too quickly. "I need to talk to you."

He joined her on the porch. "Yeah? About what?"

He didn't mean to sound challenging even if she *was* stirring up trouble in his life. Not that she could reasonably give his kid a job. But, still.

His determination to get back to work was eroded by her fetching vulnerability. She took in the porch, his shoes—everything but the scowl he'd inadvertently stamped on his face.

She rubbed her lips together. "I'm here about Blossom," she finally said. "How is she?"

"Barricaded in her room. Snoops is helping trash the bedroom with craft projects. Tyler is probably sulking in a corner, wondering why puberty turns girls into demons."

"Nice she's with friends. Seems you're thin on patience."

He winced at the statement's accuracy. "And you're an expert on raising kids?"

To his dismay, hurt flickered across her face. "I know how lonely it is growing up alone," she replied. "Like Blossom, I'm an only child. From what Ethel Lynn tells me, you come from a large brood."

He brandished a genuine smile, his first in days. "Aside from my brother, Nick, I have three sisters. Add in my parents, spouses and grandkids, and it turns into a mob."

"A wonderful mob, certainly."

He opened the door. "Why don't you come in?"

He placed his hand on her back, to usher her inside. Immediately he withdrew his touch. Less-than-stellar conversational skills were bad enough. Why hadn't he donned a shirt before answering the door?

Cringing, he gave her a wide berth as she entered the foyer. She looked pretty in the blue tank top and yellow running shorts, her thick hair piled high on her head. Her eyes danced across the floor and his feet; droplets of sweat dotted her thin, prominent nose. It dawned she might've been jogging before stopping by.

"Want a glass of water?" Whatever the reason for the visit, he sensed it wasn't pleasant. Fetching a drink for her was as good a stall tactic as any.

The question went unheard. She came to a standstill in the center of the spacious, curved-wall foyer.

"My God," she murmured, "what a gorgeous space." To his relief, she ignored the board games strewn across the living room and paused at the wide stairwell instead. "Your home is enormous."

"A work in progress," he said, unable to keep the pride from his voice. "It'll take decades to fix everything." When she glanced at him, he added, "This place was a foreclosure. I bought it for a song."

She turned slowly to take in the rooms spiraling off the foyer. "It's beautiful." With evident delight, she lowered her hand to the banister.

He liked the way she smoothed her palm across the golden oak he'd worked hours to refinish. "Want the grand tour?"

She snatched her hand away. "You're busy. I merely stopped by to discuss Blossom for a moment. If you have time."

He felt uncomfortable beneath her sudden formality.

"You're right. The place looks condemned. I should call a Hazmat crew."

"That's not what I meant. There's nothing wrong with a lived-in feel—it's cozy."

The amusement sparkling in her eyes drew him closer. "Then how 'bout a tour?" She appeared eager for one, which buoyed his spirits. "If you don't mind, we'll skip Blossom's room. She's upset with both of us."

The comment dashed the pleasure from her eyes. "I'm sorry."

"Don't be," he replied, mentally chastising himself for upsetting her. He started up the stairwell. "Give me a sec to grab a shirt."

Returning in a flash, he walked her through the dining room where his mother had assisted in hanging the shimmering gold wallpaper. The living room came next, the pine floors eager for a thorough sanding and a coat of polish. They hurried through the library, a catch-all room for building supplies, to savor the kitchen's tall windows and the sweeping view of the acres out back.

Upstairs they toured bedrooms resembling work sites with lumber stacked in corners and paint cans blocking entry to the closets. The medical expenses for Blossom's care meant there was never money enough to do things right. Apologizing for the mess, Anthony steered her past his daughter's bedroom. Inside, three voices mingled.

Returning downstairs, he grabbed glasses of ice water and led Mary to the veranda on the south side of the house. She'd grown quiet, increasing his nervousness. Together they sat on the porch swing.

She took the offered glass. "About Blossom working at the restaurant," she said, gauging his reaction. "I have an idea."

"She's too young for a job."

"She can't actually work, not for money. But she *can* help. I don't care what she does as long as she behaves."

"Which is up for grabs on any given day."

"Anthony, I'm worried she's depressed. She has nice friends, but her childhood has been anything but normal. Believe me, I understand the challenges of dealing with a serious childhood illness. Frankly I'm worried about her health, how pale she's become."

"She's fine," he said, with heat. The defensive reaction was unwarranted, the sickly fear barreling through him in waves. "There's nothing wrong. If she'd stop living on pizza and make friends with vegetables, she'd look better."

The outburst would've raised the cackles of most women. Not Mary. She seemed to understand every demon stalking him, every fear he harbored about the cancer coming back and claiming his daughter.

She smiled encouragingly. "If Blossom helps out at the restaurant, I'll take her shopping in trade. A girl her age would enjoy new outfits to show off to her friends."

He set down his glass. No matter how much he'd like to spoil Blossom, he couldn't afford a new wardrobe. Did Mary think he needed a . . . handout?

"When did you think all this up?" he finally got out.

Considering, she took a sip of water. "It's all I've been thinking about even if I'm not sure this is sensible." She regarded him with cool detachment that made it easy to see her for what she'd been—a doctor. "A child who has survived cancer needs encouragement. She's been through quite an ordeal."

"Everyone in my family says the same."

Mary patted his knee, the gesture melting the defensive wall around his heart. "Discussing her illness must be hard for you," she murmured.

No topic was more excruciating.

Instantly he knew Mary had been a very good doctor. She'd gracefully navigated the most difficult subjects with her patients. Did she measure her affection for his daughter against the cost of allowing a child into a business not yet solvent? She liked Blossom enough to take the risk. His esteem for her increased.

Her expression grew impish, lightening the conversation's heavy tone. "By the way, a young lady shouldn't hide in her bedroom for days. Shouldn't Blossom entertain Tyler downstairs? When I was growing up, my parents never allowed boys in my bedroom."

Speechless, he canvassed her face. What was the big deal? Blossom was still a kid. So was Tyler. Where they played computer games or hung out didn't matter. Anthony had years—eons, really—before his daughter matured. The steep climb to womanhood, with all the mysteries and dangers, was too far off to contemplate.

Something in his expression must've become transparent because Mary said, "She *is* growing up. Have you noticed her shirts?"

He crossed his arms, needing to protect himself from her incisive mind. "Blossom picks out her own clothes," he said, recalling her recent purchase of the bra. He was grateful she handled shopping without help. "I'm just the banker."

"Her shirts are baggy for a reason."

"What?"

"She's developing, hiding the changes from you. Girls often do. In fact, she's probably close to having her first—"

She cut off. Anthony raked his hand across his scalp. For the love of God, where was the conversation headed?

She leaned close, undoubtedly to gauge his reaction. Having a woman presume you needed advice was no picnic, but Mary had drawn near enough for him to catch the scent of flowers lingering on her skin, something light and fresh. The urge to take her hand in his nearly overpowered his common sense. And she appeared to think she'd gone too far, which made her eyes soft.

"I don't mean to embarrass you," she said. "I wondered if you'd noticed how Blossom is changing. Puberty is an awkward stage for kids *and* parents."

He considered everything his daughter required in the coming years. Advice on dating and clothes. Someone to listen when she experienced first love. Naturally she'd prefer a woman to her blundering dad. What did he know about fashion or modern dating, for that matter? No wonder Meade was targeting him for marriage. Any fool could deduce that his family lacked a critical element.

A woman.

Uneasy with his thoughts, he stirred on the porch swing. His daughter didn't want Meade. She wanted Mary.

Confusion tangled in his gut. "Mary, I know you mean well. You don't need Blossom hanging around the restaurant from dawn to dusk. She's already too attached to you."

"I'm attached to her, too." Rising, she stared at him pointedly. "Your daughter is maturing. Are you suprised she'd seek out a woman to bond with?"

"Meaning she wants you in *her* life, not mine."

"I'm not following."

He struggled to his feet. "Now it all makes sense." He rubbed his forehead. "I can't believe I'm this dense."

He might be slow on the uptake but he wasn't stupid. It was just a matter of deducing *why* Blossom was determined to cook up a romance between him and Mary. Which, in a perfect world, was a great idea. His world, however, was far from perfect.

She rested her fingers on his arm, drawing him from his musings. "What makes sense?"

"Blossom wants a mother."

"Most kids do."

"Yeah, but the way she's going about it . . ." Embarrassed, he tried to laugh, and failed. "Mary, here's the deal. She's on a mission to make us fall in love."

"She . . . what?"

"Crazy, right? She's even stuffed a bridal magazine behind the john upstairs."

"She has?" Mary picked up her glass and chugged.

A surge of pride ate through his embarrassment. He'd solved the mysteries of the universe. Hell, someone should give him a medal for unraveling his daughter's machinations.

"I should've picked up on this faster," he said with growing animation. "I should've put it all together when you moved to Liberty. Blossom started right in. I thought she was looking out for me. She isn't. *She* wants you—for her mother."

Triumphant, he grinned. It wasn't every day a man figured out the female mind. Once in a lifetime odds, that bet.

But his satisfaction was short lived. Mary angled her head back, the shock and astonishment battling in her eyes. It was anyone's guess which emotion would win.

He raised his hands with contrition. "I didn't mean to rattle you." When she remained silent, he added, "Stop looking at me like I'm an idiot."

The comment was rude in the extreme. Adolescent. A real dip-shit remark.

In response, she swiveled her neck and spotted the door off the veranda. "I've bothered you enough for one morning." She hurtled toward it.

"Hold on." He sprinted down the driveway after her, certain she was thinking, *You, my man, are a smooth operator. A primo idiot.*

From over her shoulder, she nicked him with a glance.

"Wait! I'm on board with the idea of Blossom working for you."

The entreaty in his voice brought her to a standstill. Jogging to catch up, he searched for a way to put her back at ease. Capturing her skittish gaze proved impossible. On impulse he grazed his finger beneath her chin, stopped, moved back.

"I like the idea," he said, stunned by his acquiescence. "Blossom will be thrilled."

"Maybe I've overstepped. What business do I have telling you how to raise your daughter?"

He glanced skyward at the clouds drifting past. "Your input is appreciated."

He looked down precisely as Mary looked up. His heart lost its rhythm for a stunning moment. Dizzy, he felt his attention narrow on the woman before him, an exhilarating pursuit.

Mary was nearly a head shorter, coming up dead even with his shoulders. For reasons he didn't care to examine, this pleased him. It also made him hungry to draw her into his arms, a tempting thought he dismissed as her attention swept to the house.

Blossom came down the steps with Tyler and Snoops close behind. Sweetcakes ran a tight circle around them barking for the world to hear. The dog barely registered. Anthony saw only his daughter, the movement of her head as her chin lifted, the dullness in her eyes vanishing. Her face was given over to light as she connected with the woman at his side. Then he heard the sound, a soft note of pleasure that was nearly inaudible. Slowly he turned back to Mary as the low and spontaneous sigh drifted from her lips.

A golden cord joined them. *I only have eyes for you.* It was a song, wasn't it? He couldn't recall. Besides, it didn't matter.

His daughter hurried forward. Mary greeted her with an

intense familiarity that might've made him jealous if it hadn't already struck him dumb.

"Hey." Blossom's voice, thin as dreams, increased the joy on Mary's face. They were twin moons, basking in each other's reflected glow. "What are you doing here?"

Mary clasped her shoulders. "You haven't been dropping by The Second Chance. I wanted to see if you were okay."

"I'm all right."

"I'm sorry," Mary said, and Anthony wondered why he'd never thought to do that, apologize for the hardness of life. "You've had it pretty rough, haven't you?"

A weight settled on his heart. She wasn't talking about Blossom's quest for a job. She was talking about luck, or the lack of it. She was talking about cancer.

Blossom understood. "Sometimes life stinks." She nudged him, prodding him to drape his arm across her shoulders. "Why didn't you tell me that Mary was here?" she asked him. "Can't you share, or what?"

He pressed his daughter tight to his side. "My mistake." He pivoted her back around to face Mary. His voice gruff, he added, "Guess what, kiddo. Your wish is about to come true."

"Yeah?" Blossom said. "Which one?"

Chapter 7

Ferrying the tray to the kitchen, Mary let her thoughts wend back to Blossom. Did the girl actually hide bridal magazines in her bathroom? She considered Mary "mother material?" Which meant she considered her worthy of Anthony. The notion was heartwarming—Mary was tempted to date the girl's father. Distressing too. In less than a year, she'd return to Cincinnati.

Wearily, she set the tray beside the sink. Anthony was a good man. She hadn't enjoyed a durable relationship since her first year of med school. Blossom was an added bonus with her sudden bursts of maturity peppered by more childish pursuits, like her fixation on ice cream. Who wouldn't be tempted to become part of their world?

Of course, she *could* help Blossom. Abe wasn't expecting her at the free clinic just yet. He understood the demands of putting The Second Chance Grill on sure footing. There was time enough to forge a friendship with the girl.

The kitchen buzzed with activity for the upcoming breakfast rush. Finney danced between the stove and the grill with sweat glossing her brow. Ethel Lynn worked at the sink, polishing an antique pewter tray. Beside her, Delia stood rubbing her jaw.

Finney slapped a pork chop on the grill. "Mary, about health insurance." She gave a questioning look.

"I still haven't found an affordable plan." Not for lack of trying. She'd spent days calling insurance companies to compare rates.

"Figured you'd come up empty so far."

Delia slipped an order pad into the pocket of her apron. "I can't wait much longer. I need a doctor."

The healer's instinct had Mary assessing the waitress. "What's wrong?" Delia appeared fine. Of course, assuming good health based on a surface appraisal wasn't wise.

Wincing, Delia tugged at her earlobe. "My ear has been bothering me for weeks. The pain is becoming unbearable."

Finney slapped her spatula down on the pork chop. "Ask her when she last saw a doctor, Mary. Go on. Ask her."

Mary brushed her knuckles across the waitress's forearm. "How long?"

"Three or four years, I guess." A blend of resignation and pride filtered across Delia's face. "I don't remember exactly."

Mary pursed her lips. She knew little about her employees. They were hardworking women who arrived on time and never called in sick. Finney drove a truck pockmarked with rust. The rumble from Delia's Mustang shook the restaurant's windows when she arrived for her shift. Ethel Lynn seemed more financially stable, but her vintage outfits surely came from Goodwill. None of the women complained about a difficult lot in life.

"Delia, wait here." Mary went to Ethel Lynn and gently took the silver polish from her hand. "The tray can wait. We'll have customers soon. Cover the dining room while I finish here."

After she hurried out, Mary slipped into the hallway and climbed the stairwell to her apartment. Moving boxes were strewn across the tiny kitchen. More boxes stood in stacks by the living room's plaid couch. Sweeping past, she retrieved her medical bag from the bedroom.

Black leather, the weight was deliciously balanced in her hand. The bag looked glossy and new, the instruments in pristine condition. A rush of memories cascaded through her on the way back downstairs, the pride she'd felt after receiving the present from Sadie's parents upon graduation from Ohio State School of Medicine, the nerves she'd experienced treating her first patient during her residency. The seven-year-old boy had arrived in the ER with a sprained ankle.

She ushered Delia into the storage room and coaxed her

into in a chair.

"There's inflammation," she said, removing the scope from the waitress's ear. Next she checked her temperature. "You're running a low-grade fever. How long have you been ill?"

"Oh, a few weeks. My jaw hurts, too."

"You have an ear infection."

"I thought only kids had trouble with their ears."

Mary wrote out two prescriptions, one for ear drops and the other for an oral antibiotic. "Fill these immediately," she said, with unexpected satisfaction. How long had it been since she'd cared for a patient? Too long, clearly. "Get in the first dose and stay home to rest. Don't come in tomorrow. We'll manage without you."

Delia followed her into the kitchen. "I'm taking the day off?"

"With pay." Mary smiled at the wonder on her face. "You need to recuperate."

"If I skip tomorrow who'll wait on customers?"

"I will," Mary tied on an apron. "Ethel Lynn will help."

Finney snorted. "You're setting that crazy bat loose in the dining room? Danger enough when she works the counter. Yesterday she dumped prune juice instead of chocolate sauce on the Girl Scout troop's sundaes. Delia stopped her from serving the mess."

A vision of distressed Girl Scouts racing for the bathroom accosted Mary. "I'll watch Ethel Lynn," she replied, chuckling. "Don't worry."

"I save my worry for bigger stuff." The cook flipped the pork chop with sizzling impatience. "Like health insurance. You aren't giving up now, are you?"

Defeat sagged Mary's shoulders. "I'll keep looking," she promised.

"Anthony? Sugar? Where are you?"

Wiping the motor oil from his hands, Anthony climbed from the pit. By the garage's wide double doors, Meade stood with sunlight cutting triangles across her linen suit.

"I have the tickets." She placed her briefcase on the workbench and snapped it open.

Silently he chastised himself. He'd forgotten about Mayor Ryan's fundraiser for the high school athletics department. "Is the benefit Saturday night?" he asked.

Meade held up the tickets. "You're picking me up at eight." Her face fell. "I invited you weeks ago. Did you forget?"

"I'm sorry."

Hurt bloomed on her face. "If you'd rather not go . . ."

"We'll have a great time." Remorse brought him close. He clasped her hands and silently chastised himself for appearing callous. "Count on me to pick you up five minutes early."

A watery smile lifted the corners of her mouth. "I'll be ready."

He let her go, looked around. "Where's your dog?" She never went anywhere without Melbourne.

"Outside courting a fire hydrant."

He spotted Melbourne on the grass. The tiny beast had wrapped his front paws around the fire hydrant. The poodle gyrated wildly, his hindquarters moving like pistons gone berserk.

"I hope they've been properly introduced," Anthony said.

Meade sighed. "As if Melbourne cares."

"Get him fixed. I'm nervous whenever he nears my legs."

"Put my baby through an unnecessary surgery? Never." She called to her dog, which effectively stopped his thrashing. The poodle trotted across the pavement and leapt into her arms.

Cooing softly, she ruffled Melbourne's ears and murmured to him like a child. Which made Anthony wonder: *why* had Meade remained single?

The question barely cleared his brain when he found the answer. For years now, she'd lavished her attention on her cosmetics business. Now she'd approached middle age, but barely. There was still time before the door to motherhood closed. Was she trying to chase him into marriage because she wanted to bring a child into the world? Meade often remarked that he was an exceptional father, her expression tender as she studied the photographs of Blossom he kept in his wallet, the hard-won trophies of parenthood. She favored the pictures of Blossom in pink tutus, those precious years when his daughter bounded through first and second grades full-cheeked and sweet with baby fat. The years before cancer.

"Meade," he said, brushing the memory away.

She looked up and his throat tightened. He didn't want to hurt her. Yet silence was its own form of deceit.

She didn't know about Mary stopping by his house, how one event had altered his life. When Blossom came down the steps and moved into Mary's embrace, something shifted in his world. Something else clicked into place, his awareness that he'd try for Mary, reach high, as if she were the locus of dreams he hadn't known he'd harbored. He'd try for her. Win or lose, there'd be no one else.

"Listen, Meade," he said, but he saw Mary. The joy on her face as she'd regarded Blossom, the intensity of her affection. Was there room enough in her heart for him too? "We'll have a great time at the benefit. I'm looking forward to it, but there's my daughter to consider and she needs something else. Someone else, actually—"

"You didn't lose her," Meade broke in. The comment, strange and startling, left him battling vertigo. "She's safe. Her leukemia has been in remission for, what? Two years now?"

"Almost two years," he said, ungrounded. Fear rolled through him too swiftly to repress.

"Stop waltzing with death. Sometimes when I see you with your daughter—Anthony, stop being so vigilant."

"I'm her father. I'm supposed to protect her."

"Yes, and she'll survive. She's a fighter. Cancer won't cut her life short."

She startled him by taking his wrist in a firm hold. Hell, he was trembling. He was shaking like a child caught in a thunderstorm. The tumble of memories jarred his senses: Blossom seated on the exam table at St. Barnabas, Blossom at seven years of age, and eight. At ten. His daughter last month when he'd driven her to the oncologist, his chest tight with the sickening, fluid worry that never abated until Dr. Lash announced her remission was holding.

Meade let him go. She appraised him with more compassion than he deserved given that he was trying to nix their relationship.

"Anthony, we don't have perfect chemistry." She laughed

softly, a reassuring sound in the center of an awkward moment. "But we *do* have chemistry. At Mayor Ryan's Christmas party . . . I wanted you to make love to me."

"We drank too much."

"Christmas revelry. No harm done."

"I almost took advantage of you."

"Stop being so honorable." She lifted her shoulders in a careless shrug. "Time for you to join the land of the living, don't you think? You're still engrossed in some kind of vigil, putting your life on hold as if doing so protects your daughter. Start thinking about your own needs. Stop worrying about Blossom's."

She was mistaken. He despised worrying about Blossom's next blood test, the endless series of exams. He wanted to unburden his heart. Seated on the veranda with Mary, he'd sensed a host of dreams bubbling up in his chest. It was too soon to glimpse their future. But for once, he wanted to put himself first. He wanted to forget the heavy demands of parenting an ill child long enough to enjoy a woman's company.

"You look like you're about to bow out of Saturday night," Meade said. "Say we'll have a great time at the benefit. We will, you know."

"Sure," he replied, too much of a gentleman to disagree.

In the four days since commencing work, Blossom's halo remained firmly in place.

Mary paused beside a table as the girl offered a parade flag to a freckle-faced boy dining with his parents. Blossom now appeared daily to hand out flags and greet customers. During the busiest hours, she scooped ice cream for Delia and ferried soft drinks for Ethel Lynn.

Would the new state of affairs bring more threats from Meade? It was too soon to tell. Mary comforted herself with the knowledge she'd granted a young girl's wish without, exactly, hiring her. Soon she'd take Blossom shopping as a 'thank you' for the hours spent pitching in.

Confident she'd made the right decision, she walked outside with a sense of self-congratulation. Traffic moved past the courthouse. On the other side of the Square, several cars were parked in front of the Gas & Go. On tiptoes, she searched for Anthony. His frequent appearances were now a welcome part of her day. He stopped in regularly—ostensibly to check on his daughter, but she knew better. If he hadn't come up with excuses to visit, she would've been drawn to the Gas & Go on the flimsiest of excuses.

Blossom joined her on the cobblestone walk. "What are you doing?"

"Enjoying the sunshine." Mary dragged her attention off the Gas & Go.

"It's slowing down inside." Blossom peered into the picture window. "Ethel Lynn's taking a break."

"Is Delia in the dining room?"

"Yeah, but she doesn't have many customers."

In a new habit—one that still surprised—the girl looped her arm around Mary's waist. They stood admiring the bright June day.

Warmed by the affection, Mary dipped her head to brush her cheek across Blossom's curls. Lavender, sharp and sweet, enveloped her. Yesterday, the scent of coconut shampoo had trailed the girl. Before that? A concoction of rose and citrus. Perhaps Anthony bought all manner of shampoo in defiance of the chemo treatments that had taken Blossom's hair several years ago. Mary hoped so. The gesture was a lovely way to demonstrate their triumph over leukemia.

And yet . . . she lifted her head to study Blossom with a practiced eye. The girl was disturbingly pale, her skin a near-translucent sheath. Bluish veins wove across her temples and down the delicate column of her throat. Often she tired easily. She'd rest at the table in the back of the kitchen, lured by the fashion magazines Finney purchased for her. The cook, like everyone else in town, understood the battle Blossom had waged, and the fragility of her recovery. She plied the girl with beef stew and fresh salads, and the servings of ice cream Blossom adored.

Yesterday Mary was relieved to learn Blossom was prescribed iron supplements. Was her remission progressing well? She wished for the authority to quiz the oncologist.

Blossom's expression clouded. "Uh, Mary? Almost forgot.

I'm supposed to ask you something." She pointed toward the center green. "About Mrs. Hendricks."

Theodora Hendricks marched toward them in a Davy Crockett hat and a herringbone suit reminiscent of Prohibition and Al Capone. She launched into traffic at an impressive gait for a woman her age, seemingly impervious to the danger. Tires squealed and cars ground to a halt.

Mary steeled herself for the impending confrontation. "I hung the stupid banner for an entire morning. What more does she want?"

"She needs a favor."

Theodora narrowed her sights, and Mary's heart jumped with trepidation. The hat's raccoon tail fluttered as the town matriarch hopped the curb.

"If I'm late for my appointment, blame Anthony," she said. "He's a pain in my behind. Still holding my trusty Cadillac hostage at the Gas & Go."

Blossom asked, "What did you hit this time?"

Theodora drew herself tall. The effort got her to nearly five feet in height. "I'll ask you to mind your beeswax, young lady." Hitching up the hem of her skirt, she stabbed a finger at her knee. "Mary, is it true? Your doctoring is first-rate?"

The flesh was bruised and purpling. "Shouldn't you have your primary doctor look at this?" Mary asked.

"The nearest clinic is thirty minutes away. I have a bridge tournament this afternoon. Hell and damnation—will you help or not? Blossom promised you would."

The eager child promised medical care? Theodora was the type of patient physicians dreaded, a demanding woman with a willful temperament. If the rumors were true, she carried a pistol in her buckskin satchel. Finney believed the firearm contained rock salt but Mary had her doubts. In her estimation, Theodora was no one to tangle with.

"Let's get your leg elevated." Turning the restaurant into a makeshift clinic was a ridiculous idea, but was there a choice? After the fiasco with the banner, she didn't dare disappoint. "I can't examine you here on the street."

"Then do it!"

Without further prodding she led Theodora through the

dining room. Patrons stepped back in deference to Liberty's town matriarch. A farmer in coveralls whipped off his cap, drawing a *harrumph* of satisfaction from the old woman. Mary recalled the stories she'd heard of Theodora's largess, the stadium built for the high school, the church dinners she generously funded. Her marksmanship was reputed to equal that of a sharpshooter half her age; Delia swore the old woman's recipe for squirrel stew was famous in three counties. Whatever the particulars of Theodora's generosity—not to mention her culinary habits—Mary determined to avoid her fiery blasts of temper.

Reaching the storage room, she drew a startled gasp. The cellophane was removed from several of the chairs. A coffee table gleamed from a recent polish. The furniture lay in a hasty seating arrangement. On a hunch, she cast a sidelong glance at Blossom.

"I did a good job, didn't I?" Blossom said, helping Theodora into a chair and scooting a stool beneath her leg.

"How long were you in here setting up?"

"Oh, it didn't take long."

Theodora winced. "Enough chatter. Get the show on the road."

"Let me fetch my medical bag." The words barely out, the bag landed with a thud at her feet.

Blossom splayed her hands wide. "Delia told me where to look."

"Perhaps you should help in the dining room." She grinned as the girl slunk past. "And give me a head's up the next time you're sending in a patient."

Blossom saluted. "No problemo."

After she'd gone, Mary washed her hands in the sink. Returning, she pulled a chair close. "How did you injure your knee?" she asked Theodora.

The webwork of lines on Theodora's ebony skin deepened. "A tree hit me."

"On purpose?" She tamped down a smile.

"Blasted thing. I was hunting quail in the marsh. Damn oak tree jumped right in my path."

Mary felt around the purpling kneecap. "Probably just a bruise, but we need an X-ray to be sure. Why don't I drive you to the clinic in Mentor?"

"Are you suffering hearing loss? I said I can't go anywhere today."

"Theodora, you're elderly. The joint feels sound but I can't be sure without diagnostics."

"Nothing's broken. Don't you think I'd know if it were?"

Mary drew back, frustrated. "What about a hairline fracture or a blood clot? You can't know everything that occurs in your body. Be sensible."

Theodora leaned close, the raccoon hat sliding forward at a jaunty angle. "I've been walking around in my skin since before the world went crazy on computers, back when money was green and 'plastic' had to do with manufacturing. I know a sight more about my body than you do."

"At least promise you'll stay off your leg for the remainder of the day." From her bag Mary withdrew an ace bandage. "I'll call you tonight. If the pain increases, I'll insist on taking you in for diagnostics."

"What makes you think I'll listen to some fool who runs a restaurant?"

"You'll listen." Waffling between fear and amusement, she aped Blossom's language. "Comprendo?"

By the time the bandage was securely in place, Theodora's expression had lost its unnerving fire. The old woman felt along the edges of the bandage. Satisfied she rested her head against the chair's cushioned back, taking in the contents of the storage room, the long rows of boxes and the ruddy walls of hand-fashioned brick.

"How much did your Aunt Meg tell you about this place?" she asked.

"Not much." Mary snapped her bag shut. "I know the building is old."

"Built right after The Civil War by a freed slave. The restaurant has changed hands several times. Meg won ownership in a poker tournament that never should've taken place. We were all a bit younger and that fool, Ethel Lynn, got us drunk. She was in her martini phase."

The cryptic explanation brought Mary's head up. "Who owned The Second Chance before my aunt?"

"Did Meg tell you why she'd decided to give you the

restaurant?" Theodora shot back. She dug a long feather from her satchel and proceeded to clean her bluntly cut nails with the shaft. "I'm guessing she kept you in the dark."

"She wanted to retire."

"Oh, I'll grant she was toying with the idea. Wasn't the kicker, however. She was worried about you after your doctor friend died." Theodora waved a hand to encompass the massive storage room. "The freedwoman who built this place, her name was Justice Postell. She suffered losses too, mostly the loss of the man she loved."

Grief clouded Mary's thoughts as she settled back in her chair. "I wasn't ready to lose Sadie," she admitted. "She was like a sister, always after me to improve, to believe in myself. I relied on her self-confidence too much."

"You were gutless?"

"Insecure, I suppose."

"Finney mentioned she was killed by a drunk driver."

"Sadie never saw the car." Mary looked up suddenly. "Did Aunt Meg hand over the restaurant because I told her I was quitting medicine? I never would've, you know. After the funeral, I simply wasn't myself."

A whisper of amusement passed through the old woman's eyes. "Meg thought you needed a break," she said. "And I knew Liberty needed a doctor. You might say I greased the transaction to ensure you'd take Meg up on the offer."

"You *paid* my aunt to bring me here?" When Theodora, silent as a Sphinx, blinked heavy lidded eyes, Mary asked, "If you wanted me to take over, why give me a hard time with the banner? Half of the town thinks I'm a quack who can't cook."

"You *are* a quack who can't cook."

The insult dissolved her good manners. "You don't know the first thing about me," she snapped. "I'm not a quack. I'm a fine doctor. Sure, I've only been in practice a few years. Doesn't matter. I work hard to provide my patients with excellent care."

"If you aren't a quack, why haven't you set up shop? Seems foolish for a doctor to wait tables if she *is* any good."

"You don't understand."

"Enlighten me."

"I can't practice here. There's a free clinic in Cincinnati I plan to take over."

"Says who?"

Irritation jangled through Mary. "I feel an obligation to take over the clinic, all right?" Reining in her temper, she added, "I planned to manage the clinic with Sadie. Now that she's gone, I'll go it alone. I'm not sure how I'll manage without her, but I *want* to go it alone."

A snort of disbelief popped from Theodora's mouth. "How do you know *what* you want? You're in mourning. With your emotions gallivanting across the map, you aren't in the proper frame of mind to make life-long decisions."

Brows lifting, Mary searched for a response. Okay, she'd give Theodora the part about grief. Perhaps she was too heartbroken about Sadie to chart a plan. What about Abe? He was also grieving, and he was getting older. He needed to plan his retirement.

The silence prodded Theodora to her feet. "Why are young people fools? All that book-learning and nary an ounce of common sense." Screwing her raccoon cap on tight, she asked, "Have you told Anthony your plans? Stubborn as a bull, he is. I'll wager he finds a way to keep you in Liberty."

The chance to disagree never arrived. Finney stuck her head into the storage room.

"Enough doctoring already. Mary, I need you in the kitchen." She locked gazes with Theodora. "Did you thank her?"

Theodora brushed past. "She's a doctor. Has a sworn duty to aid the sick."

"Ungrateful old bag." The cook winked at Mary. "At least Delia's grateful. Your doctoring has her on the mend."

"Make sure she finishes the antibiotics." Mary paused beside the table in the back of the kitchen. Blossom sat doodling on an art pad. "I'm running a restaurant, not an ER," she informed the girl. "No more patients, okay?"

Blossom shrugged. "What's the big deal? You helped Mrs. Hendricks, right?"

"That isn't the point." She wasn't sure what to make of everything Theodora had mentioned. Anthony couldn't convince her to stay. And why hadn't Aunt Meg told her about Theodora greasing the transaction?

"Let the child be." Finney patted Blossom's shoulder. "Think you can wash and peel potatoes without flooding my kitchen, child?"

"No problemo."

"No working with knives," Mary put in. The last thing she needed was another injury to tend to.

Blossom tossed a potato in the air. "Where's the peeler?"

"Check the drawer by the sink." Finney wiped her florid cheeks with the back of her hand. "Mary, help out front. Delia and Ethel Lynn are swimming in orders."

The statement proved accurate. Over the next two hours, Mary ran enough miles to qualify for the Boston Marathon. Perspiration beaded on Delia's forehead and Ethel Lynn—a flitting hummingbird in a gauzy yellow dress—took to shouting *"Lordy!"* every time a new customer arrived.

Throughout the afternoon, the spindle on the kitchen's pass-through window spun with orders. Hanging another slip, Mary flinched as Finney bellowed. The sound of her desperation brought the dining room to a standstill for the briefest moment. Then pandemonium resumed.

At the grill, the cook wrung her hands. An unusual sight—Finney was unflappable.

"What's wrong?" Mary asked.

The cook grabbed her by the shoulders. "We're running out of supplies. Lucky Foods should've arrived by now."

Mary checked her watch. "They're never this late."

"I'm low on everything from tomatoes to chicken breasts."

Panic swept through her. "Call them. I have to get back to the counter. Ethel Lynn won't last ten minutes without me." At this rate they'd be serving toast by six P.M. "Tell Lucky Foods to get here immediately."

Finney made the call only to discover the answering machine picking up.

Chapter 8

Rubbing her knuckles—which throbbed after helping Blossom scrub twenty pounds of potatoes—Mary wondered if her emotions were as bruised as Theodora's knee. "I'm not a quack," she muttered to herself, tossing down the paring knife. True, managing a restaurant she'd inherited wouldn't provide sparkling conversation at a medical convention. Even Abe, though he kept his opinions private, surely thought she'd behaved foolishly by taking a sabbatical from medicine.

On leaden feet, she crept back to the counter. Dinner patrons crowded every barstool. Brandishing a hastily revised menu, she was sucked into the vortex of demanding customers, clattering dishes and frantic chatter that heralded the beginning of the dinner rush. Anxiety pitched through her. Even with half of the entrees struck from the menu, they'd run out of food.

In the dining room Blossom helped Delia clear a table. Guilt took a swipe at Mary's heart. She'd already asked Blossom to go home. The girl had refused. In a chirpy voice she'd explained that with her dad working late, sitting alone in an empty house didn't thrill.

Picking up the coffee pot, Mary refilled cups all the way down the counter. A balled up napkin whizzed past her ear. Ducking it, she stared pointedly at a boy seated on his mother's lap.

Delia stumbled to the kitchen with a tray of dishes, returned. "Finny needs you." She hurtled back into the throng.

Glad for the escape, Mary rushed through the swinging door. She was exhausted—they all were. The moment a table cleared, new customers arrived.

"If this keeps up, we'll need more help," Finney said, dealing hamburgers across the grill like a stack of playing cards. "Think about finding me an assistant. Delia needs help, too."

She hadn't solved the health insurance puzzle. How to add more staff? "I can't afford to put in an ad until we're profitable."

Ethel Lynn, waiting by the stove for an order, threw her hands into the air. "What am I, chopped liver? Don't I help?"

Finney whipped her spatula through the air. "You're a hindrance."

"And you're grilling hamburgers too close together. Look. They won't cook properly if you don't make room."

The cook whipped again, sending Ethel Lynn backwards with a yelp. "You second guess me so often I'm ready to pull my hair out. Or yours."

Ethel Lynn darted out of reach, a gnat in mortal danger. "This is the thanks I get? Good heavens, I came in to rescue you."

The cook grunted. "Not much of a rescue operation, are you? Go home."

"Fine. I'm going."

"Wait!" Mary leapt between them. "Please stay."

The plea didn't melt Ethel Lynn's resolve. "Finney, you're a hard woman," she snapped. "You've got meanness all the way to your bones."

She did a frilly turn and darted out.

Mary threw up her hands. Now what? The noise from the dining room was increasing by the minute. They'd never manage short-handed. Even if Ethel Lynn predictably dropped dishes and spilled drinks, at least she helped.

"Take a chill pill." Finney slapped a skillet down on the stove and tossed in vegetables. "That old woman may have run this place for your aunt but she doesn't know diddly-squat about cooking."

Mary stalked to the sink and turned on the tap. "We needed her tonight." She thrust a head of lettuce beneath the icy stream. "She's elderly. Give her a break."

"I'm happy to break her neck, if you're sending an

invitation." The cook opened the cupboard beneath the stove and rooted around inside. "Look how Ethel Lynn was handling the cooking after she fired me. Mary—come look. She's got an old pancake griddle down here and one of those George Foreman grills."

The items landed on the counter with a thud. Enough grease layered the grill to grow bacteria for medical research. The griddle was worse. Large spots of metal showed through the worn Teflon surface.

Horrified, Mary approached. "*This* is what she used?" No wonder they'd sickened patrons on opening day. "What about the stove? Are you saying she wasn't using the stove?"

"I have a theory about that."

"A theory?" More bad news she didn't need.

"This old stove has been twitchy for weeks." Finney jiggled the control knobs. Flames burst high on all six burners, then low. "Watch number four. Hardly moves at all. Flame just stays where it is. And six—" she cranked the knob clockwise, "—look how high it goes. This stove needs servicing. Something's punky in the gas line."

Mary leapt back. "Then stop playing with it! You'll blow us up!"

"How will I feed the hungry hordes with just a grill?"

"Turn off the stove. Cook whatever you can on the grill. Is the oven working?" From the corner of her eye, she noticed Delia at the pass-through window. *"What?"*

"Mary, get out here. You need to see this."

Behind the counter—which was now hemmed in by customers on every barstool—the ice cream freezer made an awful clatter. Somewhere inside the ancient innards, gears shifted with a grinding racket. They sputtered into silence. Delia slid back the door on top and craned her neck.

Mary lowered her voice for fear of alarming diners. "What are you doing?"

The waitress jabbed a finger at the tubs on the unit's floor. "The ice cream is melting, dufus." She cast a baleful glance at the girls in matching red plaid at table seven. "Know how many kids are finishing dinner? I've got three tables ready to order dessert."

Mary peered inside. With all the renovations she'd made,

why hadn't she replaced the contraption? The freezer was on life support.

"I'm no expert with appliances," she admitted. "Did you try jiggling the plug?"

"Yeah, that'll work. After we jiggle the plug, we'll call the ice cream fairy. She'll wave her wand and make this piece of crap work like new."

"Can it, Delia." Mary bent in farther, examined the glop on the floor. "Good grief. Who tipped over half of the tubs? There's ice cream all over the bottom."

"The floor inclines toward the front of the building. We could roller skate down the slant in here. When the tubs were frozen, who cared if they tipped or not?"

"It matters now! They're melting!"

"No shit, Sherlock. They don't even make replacement parts for a freezer this old." She picked at the strips of paint peeling off the front panel. Papery flecks drifted to the floor. "This thing was made when Nixon was president. Customers were eating banana splits and reading about Watergate in the *Plain Dealer*."

"You're nuts." At least Mary hoped she was. "The freezer isn't that old."

"It's ancient, pal. We'll have to eat the ice cream or throw it out."

The phrase, *eat ice cream*, reached Blossom's ears. She stopped swabbing down table six. Rapture suffused her features as she wandered toward them, a mummy in a trance.

Delia muttered a curse. "Great. If she makes herself sick on Toasted Almond Swirl, Anthony will have our heads."

"Just give her a bowl. It's going to melt anyway."

"A bowl." Delia snickered. "How 'bout a tub? That's more Blossom's speed."

"Oh, come on. How much ice cream can one child eat?"

"Mary, when it comes to kids you're a novice."

Approaching, Blossom grinned maniacally. "The ice cream's melting? Can I have some?"

Delia came forward, a Good Samaritan performing a desperate intervention. "Stop her—"

"Give it to me." Sugar lust compelled Blossom to reach inside the frozen space. "Just one tub. Oh. Wait. You ordered

Double Chocolate *and* Strawberry Cheesecake."

"Mary, do something!"

Mary pressed her fingers to her throbbing temples. "Blossom, hold on. I'll get you a bowl."

"Don't bother." Her head and shoulders disappeared inside the freezer. "I'll take this to the kitchen."

Delia threw up her hands. "Fine. Take a tub, Blossom. Take two."

Mary stood transfixed as Blossom hauled off two tubs. After the kid disappeared into the kitchen, she asked, "How will we finish the dinner rush without ice cream?"

From the kitchen, Finney shouted, "Forget about ice cream. Lucky Foods isn't coming."

"*What?*" Mary sprinted back inside.

Oddly calm, the cook returned the cell phone to her apron pocket. "Lucky's dispatcher said she talked to Ethel Lynn hours ago."

"Why didn't Ethel Lynn—" Mary cut off, deducing her own answer. In typically ditsy fashion, Ethel Lynn would've forgotten the call within seconds of hanging up the phone. "Why aren't they coming?"

"Truck accident on Cherry Street. There's stuff all over the road—meat, fruit, vegetables. I called my son, Randy. Told him to get his butt over there. I'd like a few sirloin steaks for the church picnic on Sunday." Aware she'd said too much, the cook turned a bright shade of pink. "Seeing that you're giving away free ice cream, I'm betting Randy will stop here afterward."

Mary fluffed off the news about Finney's freeloading son. Miserable, she cradled her head. "How could Ethel Lynn forget to tell us about the accident?"

"We'll kill her later."

"What about our dinner specials?"

"There'll be no trout on the menu. We won't have Martha Washington's veal stew, either." Finney rolled beef into patties and shrugged her meaty shoulders. "There'll be complaints, I'll grant you. When customers scream, just smile."

"I'll explain the truck didn't arrive. Play the honesty card."

"Like hell you will. I've got people coming back to the restaurant. You're not driving them off."

"Oh, God." Mary slumped against the counter. "We're doomed."

"Stop praying." The cook slapped the patties into a skillet. "You're a doctor. You've seen emergencies. Let the customers yell. They might forgive you tomorrow."

Or perhaps they wouldn't. Mary spent the next hours apologizing to patrons for the diminished menu the way she'd once apologized to patients for being late on rounds. Meade complained shrilly because fish—which she couldn't order—was on her diet plan. The mayor's nephew, chubby Buster Atkins, wept enough tears to float a rubber raft when informed a chocolate sundae would not be forthcoming. He'd valiantly eaten all the peas on his plate.

Bigger catastrophes loomed. Theodora chewed Mary out when told the veal special was off the menu. A sweet-faced tot—happy with her hamburger—flung herself across table six when told there was no ice cream for dessert. Chocolate milk and Diet Cokes flew through the air. Afterward, the rug made squishy sounds whenever Mary ran past. And a family of four stormed out without paying for their drinks after Delia gave up on reciting the dinner specials and rattled off the few entrees still available.

By nine o'clock, Mary was worn out and jumpy and just plain frustrated. Which was how Anthony found her when he came to fetch his daughter.

He'd been at the Gas & Go taking his time on a brake job, allowing Blossom more time to fool around at the restaurant. Strolling in from the street, he searched the throng for Mary. He caught sight of her behind the mobbed counter.

Her hair was a mess. Streaks of mascara ran down her cheeks, lending a clownish appearance. Rushing toward the kitchen, she didn't quite clear the swinging door. It swung back and hit her squarely.

He flinched. Unbelievably, she seemed oblivious to the injury. She disappeared inside.

Following her proved difficult. In his path, a woman in pink shorts argued with Delia. Beyond them a boy spun in a circle as his parents battled over a wad of bills. The little monster had toilet paper stuck to the heels of his sneakers. His hands were loaded for bear with sugar packets. He hurled them out in a circle, spinning like a Gatling gun gone nuts.

Dodging the kid, Anthony skirted around a mound of rice pilaf on the floor. A sugar packet whizzed past his shoulder and he dived for cover. He scooted behind the counter where a motley group of teenagers sat devouring hamburgers and fries. A boy with punk-style orange hair was deep into a lip-lock with the girl on his lap. If someone didn't stop them, they'd soon be doing the nasty.

For the love of . . . He hoped Blossom hadn't seen the teenagers in mid-grope.

"Knock it off," he growled. The teens sprang apart.

Delia materialized before him, throwing his heart painfully out of rhythm. It was one of the negatives of being a tall man. Women, many of them fairly short, leapt in front of him. He felt unnerved, like an elephant intimidated by mice.

She dug red-tipped talons into his arm. "Run for your life," she hissed. "It's not safe here. Don't blame me when you see Blossom. I tried to stop her. So help me, I did."

"You tried—" His foot slid a startling inch. Confused, he glanced down. "For the love of God, what's on the floor?"

He lifted his foot from the pool of pink goo. Slowly he brought his attention to rest on the ice cream freezer. Delia muttered something and ran off.

Ice cream. All over the floor. It was leaking out of the freezer.

Leaking. Out of the unit's bottom panel . . .

He charged the freezer. Grabbing hold, he hauled the appliance from the wall and yanked out the plug. All Mary needed was an electrical fire on top of the chaos raining down on her establishment like locusts.

It went downhill from there.

In the kitchen he found Blossom sitting Indian-style on a counter, penned in by jumbo canisters of ice cream. Twin tracks of red and brown made a highway down her tee shirt. The sugary stream dripping from her tennis shoes was sure to draw ants before she finished drowning herself in dairy.

Aw, man.

Striding past Finney, he approached his kid. "Blossom, what the hell are you doing?"

"Thoo thouldn't thwear," she garbled, her tongue evidently frozen.

He swung around to regard Finney, dashing between the oven and the grill. "How much did she eat?" he asked.

"No idea. She's your kid, your problem." Finney pulled a bubbling casserole from the oven. "Hey, Anthony—you're a mechanic."

"Thanks for noticing." He spotted her ill-mannered son leaning against the wall. Patches of chocolate streaked his cheeks. "How much ice cream did yours eat?"

"This isn't a contest. They're both eating dairy. Leave it at that."

"You don't approve of this, do you?"

"It's not heroin." She placed two plates on the ledge of the pass-through window before giving him the once-over. "You fixed the walk-in cooler. How 'bout you look at the stove? Something's wrong."

He watched her twirl the stove's knobs for three seconds. "Stop! You'll blow us up!"

Finney straightened. "You sound like Mary."

"Where is she?"

"Hiding in the hallway." The cook waved a paring knife due south.

"Stay away from the stove. I need to check the gas line." He frowned. "Why is Mary hiding?"

"I think she's crying."

He hurried to check on her. Sure enough, she was trembling by the door leading out the back of the building.

"Planning to bolt?" He appraised her flushed, sorrowful face. "Hey, your lip is bleeding. Must've been the door that hit you."

She pinned him with a gaze rife with desperation. "All I can feel are my arches," she said. "They're on fire. And I'm fed up with having to defend my life just because the ice cream melted."

From his pocket he withdrew a rag. "I don't know about defending yourself but you *are* bleeding. Here. Let me help."

He dabbed at the crimson drop by her mouth. She stilled as he touched her, and he smiled. The wound was just a nick, really. By morning, it'd be history.

Pleased with his ability to forestall electrical fires and

staunch the flow of blood, he began pulling back. As he did, his gaze slid to hers.

Connecting with her mossy green eyes made them open wide. There were golden flecks inside, a whole sunburst of color on top of the darker green. On an intake of breath, Anthony watched her lips part, her lower lip appearing slightly swollen and bruised—

The skin on his scalp tightened. Heat poured through his body. Sucking in air, he battled vertigo.

The reaction wasn't his fault. During adulthood he'd enjoyed sex so infrequently, he'd entered the priesthood without taking vows. Did his attraction have to knock him over like this?

The suggestive tempo of his breathing affected her too, putting a nice sheen on her forehead. She sent her tongue across her lips on a languid journey that sent his heartbeat into a crazy dance. Come to think of it, she was also breathing fast, her breasts straining against her pretty blouse—

He swiped the Rain Forest dampness from his forehead. "Bleeding's stopped," he mumbled. At this rate, he'd need to wring his shirt out in Finney's sink.

Mary regarded him with smoldering eyes. "Thank you," she murmured.

He tried to clamp his attention on anything but her. No dice.

Succumbing to the urge, he looked closer. Mary wasn't pretty in the classical sense. Her eyes were slightly close-set. Her nose—like his—was a tad too large. But her lips were full and pink, and her skin glowed. The combination made her beautiful.

"I'll get Blossom, take her home." He paused, confused. *Why* couldn't he stop looking at Mary?

She had a nice shape. Small waist, good curves. Breasts that would fill his hands just right.

Wrong thought.

A second wave of heat pummeled him. He was sweating like a gorilla. If this was his big debut as Mary's suitor, he'd blown the opening act.

"I'll get Blossom out of your hair," he said. "Need to pour some Pepto down her throat before she hits the sack."

"Oh. The ice cream." Mary stepped closer, effectively raising the temperature on his furnace. "It's my fault," she added.

"I doubt it. She's nuts for the stuff."

"I should have stopped her, Anthony."

Anthony. Nice how she murmured his name. She had nice hair too. A reddish hue subtly layered the strands of brown. He'd never seen her stand directly in the sun. When she did, she probably transformed into a redhead.

Even better, the light had shifted in her eyes the moment she'd mentioned Blossom. Mary liked his kid, maybe more than she realized. "If she's up at three A.M. with a sick belly you'll be my first call," he joked. "Seeing that you're guilty and all."

"Deal."

"I'm kidding."

She bobbed her head. "I know."

"I would never call you in the middle of the night."

"I didn't think you would."

"What is your phone number?" He erased the distance between them, cornering her against the wall. "Just rattle it off—I have a good memory. No need to write it down."

She did, in a quick, breathless voice.

Then she tipped her head to the side and tattooed his senses with a smile rife with enough mystery and spark to put him in danger. She finished the job by flitting her fingers down his rib cage.

Anthony froze.

But only for a second. Pressing her against the wall, he gave her a kiss she'd never forget. She gasped as he crushed his mouth against hers, sending them both into the stratosphere with the fuel of his desire. Something pure and sweet poured through him as they clung together like a couple that had been to the moon and back on more than one occasion. All his worries about his clumsy attempts at romance dissolved beneath her eager lips, and the hungry way she returned his every caress.

In the kitchen a pot clattered to the floor, the sound dousing them both with reality.

They leapt apart. Mary's eyesight whirled as gravity slowly returned. What was she doing? Anthony's pupils were dilated, his breath coming in stuttering gasps. The warmth flooding her blood scattered the thoughts from her head. With a start, she realized she was panting.

Anthony raked his hand through his hair. "I'll be going."

The formal remark started her neurons firing. "Thank you for stopping by." She leaned into the wall to avoid sinking to the floor. She was damp in unspeakable places. "Nice seeing you."

With a drunk's finesse, he swerved toward the kitchen. She followed in a state of shock nicely accented by the warmth tickling her skin. She stood speechless as Anthony steered Finney from the stove, all the while casting blistering glances as hot as the midday sun. The cook, missing the interchange, produced tools from a drawer. He used them to disconnect the gas lines.

When he'd finished, he took Blossom by the hand and helped her off the counter. Finney stood at the pass-through window shouting to Delia. She didn't notice Anthony and Blossom heading out the back door.

Dizzy and dumbstruck, Mary slumped against the sink.

What *had* just happened?

Chapter 9

Daylight filtered through the apartment. Weary from lack of sleep, Mary dragged the coffee table nearer to the couch and sorted the heap of mail she'd left growing like fungus. Her feet were on fire after running for her life last night at The Second Chance. She'd barely slept at all.

Yet her flaming arches and the restaurant's problems weren't the source of her exhaustion.

She'd relived the moments in Anthony's embrace a thousand times. In the slice of a second the courtly mechanic had become a sexually demanding lover, backing her to the wall in a hot tango of roving lust and outlaw caresses. The heat of his hands ranging over her body, the taste of his lips as he drove her passions higher—he'd given her a devastatingly pleasurable kiss.

The moment had brimmed with promise and the possibility of embarking on a satisfying relationship. It mattered little that, a few paces away, Finney clattered in the kitchen and Blossom lounged on the counter blitzing out in a sugar-fest. One kiss had given rise to a host of fanciful dreams.

Savoring the memory, Mary sorted the mail. Catalogs landed in a pile. Editions of a medical journal rustled to the floor. A manila envelope stuck out of the pile. She suffered misgiving as she scanned the familiar return address. Tearing open the flap, she spilled photographs across the coffee table.

The first photo displayed a whitewashed condo wrapped in climbing roses with rich, green vines and dewy, apricot blossoms. On the back, Abe had written, *The condo Jillian likes. Beautiful, yes?*

The condo was stunning. The foundation nestled in boxwood and lemony yellow bedding roses. A paved sidewalk led to the arched entryway. How many rooms inside? Efficient Abe provided the answer in the next three photographs, of the living room and a kitchen done with granite countertops. The back yard featured the azure waters of a private pool and lush palm trees.

Her thoughts turned to Abe's daughter, Sadie. If she'd lived, she would've enjoyed watching her parents enter a well-deserved retirement. If not for the drunk driver and Sadie's untimely death, how different would the circumstances be? Dr. Mary Chance and Dr. Sadie Goldstein—they would've begun work at the free clinic, eventually taken over the management, and allowed Abe to retire free of worry. Mary wouldn't have taken a sabbatical from medicine or accepted ownership of The Second Chance Grill. She never would've met an endearing girl with corkscrew curls and a dairy obsession. She never would've met Anthony, or reveled in his kiss.

Outside, the morning light intensified. Her throat tightening, she returned the photographs to the envelope.

Blossom pinched her nose in frustration. Across the shadowy office her best friend, Snoops, typed madly on her cell phone.

Immediately Blossom's cell vibrated. The text from Snoops read *Not cut out for life of crime. Going home.*

Behind purple-framed glasses, Snoops' black bean eyes were wide with fear. It was just like her to go chicken in the middle of a heist.

"You're staying," Blossom hissed.

"But I'm scared!"

Tyler paused midway across the room and glared. When they grew silent, he tiptoed to his cousin Judy's desk to begin a careful search. The office, located on the second floor of the county courthouse, smelled of paper and ink and some frilly floral perfume. Bookcases lined the walls. They didn't muffle the sounds of footsteps echoing down the corridor outside, probably a security guard on his rounds. At the opposite wall, Snoops whimpered.

In contrast, Tyler remained calm while rustling through papers. His thick bangs fell over his forehead, his mouth thinning with concentration. Blossom came close enough to grab his attention. His gaze stuck on her and she rode a wave of satisfaction as he gulped down air. Beneath her rib cage, her heart did the mambo.

Tyler was a year older, in seventh grade. Blossom loved him. She offered a pearly smile, which sent his brows leaping to his hairline.

She was pretty sure he loved her, too.

He stopped rifling through the desk to frown at Sweetcakes, obligingly sniffing his butt. "Blossom, did we need to bring your dog?" he whispered. "Stupid dog—sit!"

"Don't yell at her." To Sweetcakes, she said, "Sit like a good girl." After her pooch plunked down, she grabbed Tyler by the wrist. "That was cool how you picked the lock. Where'd you learn breaking and entering? Is there an online class?"

"Shut up! Mayor Ryan's office is down the hall. What if her secretary hasn't left?"

"Can we break in there if she's gone? It'd be bitchin' to see what the mayor keeps under lock and key."

Snoops shoved between them. "I'm not breaking into the mayor's office! What if there's an alarm or booby traps?"

Amusement bubbled up Blossom's throat. "There's a net that drops from the ceiling. Snatches you right up, Snoops. It's scary."

"Oh!"

Tyler rolled his eyes. "Freaking her out is a *big* help. Try calming her down, okay?"

Eager to please him, Blossom pulled Snoops close. "Listen amigo, I'll protect you. Our horses are outside at the hitching post. If trouble comes, we'll hightail it to Mexico."

Snoops pushed her away. "You watch too much TV."

True, Blossom *had* dozed through an old Western last night after her dad dragged her home from The Second Chance. He'd been flushed like a beet and went directly to bed, leaving her camped in front of the tube. He left her with a bottle of Pepto Bismol and a belly that looked like a blowfish after she'd pigged out on the restaurant's melting ice cream.

This morning her dad was even weirder, bumping into counters while brewing coffee and staring into space with his mouth hung open. Over her bowl of cereal, she'd shot random comments for a take on his mental health. He replied, *Uh-huh* to every one. So she asked to have her allowance doubled. When he'd agreed, the bald truth became obvious. He was hobbling down the road to senility.

While she ruminated about old age homes and spooning oatmeal into her dad's mouth, Tyler eased his lanky frame into the leather chair behind the desk. His blue eyes narrowed with evil purpose. Blissfully she listened to the pitter-patter of her heart.

She asked, "Where d'you think your cousin stashed the tickets?"

He opened a drawer. "Not sure." When she hung over his shoulder, his eyes threw darts. "Get back. You'll trash something. If my cousin finds out we broke into her office, she'll kill me."

Unimpressed, Blossom yawned. Sweetcakes showed equal disinterest, rolling onto her back with a rumble of canine delight. The dog wiggled a front paw to lure Blossom into giving a belly rub. Which she did as Tyler opened and closed drawers with stealthy intent, and Snoops rustled from behind.

From her roomy sweatshirt, Snoops withdrew a sandwich. The scent of fried sausages and onions bloomed in the air. Sweetcakes scrambled into a sitting position, her furry hindquarters quivering with anticipation.

"Put that away," Blossom whispered. The sandwich looked delicious. "Scratch that. Give me a bite."

She wolfed some down and Tyler said, "Can't you guys wait? We're in the middle of a robbery."

"This doesn't qualify as a robbery," Blossom pointed out between chews. "We'd need ski masks and a really scared bank teller."

"Whatever." To Snoops, he said, "What else you got?"

Snoops dug around her pockets. "Candy, grapes...here, Sweetcakes." She gave the dog a biscuit. "Do you like yogurt?" she asked Tyler.

Blossom wrinkled her nose. "Who lugs yogurt to a burglary?"

"Food makes me feel safe," Snoops said. She handed a yogurt to Tyler.

"Thanks." He tore off the top then opened another drawer. "Found them!"

The tickets to the mayor's fundraiser were bright orange and as big as index cards. They were also sequentially numbered.

"Blossom, they'll know if we take one." Tyler leafed through the stack. "Look—they cost a hundred dollars each. If you give one to Mary, the mayor will know it's stolen."

Frustration welled in Blossom. Her Dad was taking Meade to the benefit Saturday night. He was a lightweight with booze— a crafty woman like Meade would get him liquored up. He'd start seeing double, and she'd convince him to elope. They'd get hitched, forcing Blossom to endure the peeing Melbourne and a judgmental blonde for the rest of her life.

The prospect made her shudder.

Dodging the nightmare, she snatched a ticket from the stack. "Mary has to show up at the benefit," she insisted. "If my dad sees her dressed up, he'll fall for her. Work with me, Tyler. This is the only play I've got."

He reached for the stolen loot. "Give it back!"

She swung the ticket around her back. Fumbling, Snoops grabbed it.

Blossom made the time-out sign. "Tyler, just help me find the ledger. Your cousin must track payments for the tickets. Let's write a name in and pretend someone else bought it."

He looked at her like she'd lost her mind. "Like someone bought the ticket for Mary? No way."

"It'll work. Trust me."

"The last time I trusted you, we were in detention for a week."

"This time is different."

"You say that *every* time."

Bringing out the big guns, she batted her lashes. "Tyler, *please.*"

He stared at her for too long, and she experienced glee.

"Whatever," he muttered, opening the center drawer and producing a leather-bound book. "Yeah, this is it. Whose name should I write in?"

She considered suggesting the evil Chemistry teacher at Liberty Junior High. From behind, an *oomph* sounded.

Beads of mustard dotted Snoops' chin. Sausage grease shimmered on her contorted lips. Gesturing wildly, she made a half-hearted swallowing sound.

"Are you choking?" Blossom grabbed her by the shoulders. "Snoops, are you okay?"

She got the food down and belched. "Too big a bite." She wiped her mouth with a napkin.

Only it wasn't a napkin. Blossom yelped.

"What's wrong?" Snoops looked down at her hand. "Oh. Oh, I got mustard all over the ticket!"

The ticket's sausage grease sent Sweetcakes into a frenzy. Eager to get her canines into the savory loot, she butted her snout against Blossom's hip. Blossom shoved past her dog.

Grease and bright smears of mustard covered the ticket. "Give it here," she demanded. She did her best to wipe off the mess. "Mary's ticket smells awful. Snoops, what's wrong with you?"

"I didn't mean to mess everything up."

Tyler launched a warning look. "Quiet! Someone will hear us."

Snoops trembled. "Can we leave now?"

Blossom pushed her toward the door. "We're going. If the security guard catches a whiff of sausage on our way out, you're to blame."

They hightailed it out of the office and down the corridor with Sweetcakes bringing up the rear. Policeman Ernesto, who should've been guarding the entrance, was still in the cafeteria microwaving his dinner. True to the plan, they'd performed the heist in twelve minutes flat, the average time Ernesto required to heat up his frozen entrée.

Safe in the center green, Blossom pulled Tyler to a halt. "What name *did* you write in the ledger?" she asked.

"Mary, you sure clean up nice." Finney stopped cooking long enough to appreciate the cocktail dress. "The men at the banquet will be in hot pursuit."

At the sink, Delia laughed. "Anthony won't give the other men a chance. He's got it bad for you, Mary."

"I'm not his date. Blossom says he's taking Meade."

"Pity he's not taking you."

"If not for the mayor's generosity, I couldn't afford this. She was kind to include me."

Mary was touched and more than a little guilt-ridden when Blossom's friend, Tyler, dropped by with the ticket. Everyone else in town was paying to attend the bash yet Mary was invited free of charge. She assumed the mayor's kindness was meant to make her feel at home in Liberty.

With nervous moments she adjusted the gown's spaghetti straps. She'd planned to wear the chaste doctor-at-a-cocktail-party number, a coral-colored knit with pearl beading on the sleeves. For reasons too dangerous to ponder, she'd chosen the black sequin number instead. The dress that shouted, 'Open-for-business' in hip-hugging silk.

"My outfit isn't too risqué, is it?" she asked no one in particular.

"Your dress is a risk, all right," Finney said, misunderstanding the word, *risqué*. "Anthony will be staring at your ass and pouring ice down his pants. I hope you're wearing nice underwear. One stiff wind and you'll show your wares to the whole town."

Delia smirked. "Forget the wind. Anthony's the one who'll be stiff."

"For the record, he's attending the benefit with Meade," Mary reminded them.

"This must be your lucky day," Finney said. "A free ticket, and guess what else? Anthony came in first thing this morning to start work on the stove. He's not done yet, but he cleaned the gas lines and installed a new fuel gauge."

Mary smiled as the cook turned the knobs to demonstrate. "They're working beautifully!"

"Didn't I say Anthony could fix anything?"

Mary brushed her fingers across the stove's steel top. "I

guess so."

He'd certainly put her in a fix, she mused. She'd like to begin seeing him, a foolish notion.

Even more foolish, she'd leave him to Meade if she didn't explore a relationship.

Chapter 10

The green hills of the Honeyside Golf Course shimmered in the fading daylight. Nervously driving in circles, Mary found a parking space in the crowded lot. Honeysuckle lingered in the air and leaves rustled, throwing a patchwork of grey across the entryway into the banquet hall.

Couples swarmed before her, vying to reach the interior of the hall. Big band music punctuated the air. Several feet inside the hall, Mayor Ryan collected tickets with the help of the tall woman by her side.

The crowd jostled forward. Where was Anthony? Excitement darted through Mary as she noticed him by a table in the center of the hall. Behind him, a banner on the wall proclaimed, *Liberty High School Athletics. Teamwork Builds Tomorrow's Leaders.* Mary looked from the banner and back to him. Her heart sank. Meade appeared beside him in eye-popping red velvet, her dog squirming beneath her arm.

The balding man in front of Mary followed her line of sight. "Meade believes Melbourne brings her luck," he confided.

His wife, a bubbly matron in mauve taffeta, readily agreed. "Meade believes her poodle is a lucky charm. She got him the same week she landed her first big account. She imports cosmetics from France for some of the finer stores in Ohio. She flies to Paris twice a year. Isn't that exciting?"

"Quite," Mary replied with false cheer. Given Meade's success, she probably assumed she'd earned Liberty's most handsome boy-toy. *Which is none of my business.*

Anthony guided Meade to a chair. She sat, placing her poodle in her lap. Melbourne's diamond collar glittered. Red velvet bows were ridiculously tacked behind his ears.

The crowd moved forward, and the matron grasped Mary by the elbow. "Oh, look at the food!" she said. "Our school colors are orange and green. The orange is for Barrington. The green is for our lovely Irish mayor."

Mary peered over the matron's shoulder. Platters, dishes and crystal bowls brimmed with deviled eggs, succulent roast and gelatin molds. Baskets of crusty rolls competed for space beside large bowls of salad. Chicken breasts and pork chops were neatly arranged on silver platters.

She fought off the impulse to gag. Every dish was dyed orange . . . or green.

"Is that a roast?" As far as she was concerned, beef had no business wearing a color better suited for asparagus.

The matron's double chin wobbled. "We dye everything to honor the Liberty High football team, the *Battling Beavers*. Isn't it delightful? Are you hungry?"

"Not at the moment."

"We give Barrington a place of honor, you know."

"Barrington?"

"Over there. Do you see him?" The woman motioned to the farthest table. "You can't miss him, dear."

A woman stopped at the entryway to chat with the mayor, and Mary craned her neck. "Is Barrington a tall man? Or short?"

The matron laughed shrilly. "He's the mascot for the football team. He's a *beaver*. Inside the cage, dear. Right over there."

Sure enough, a twitching rodent sat in a cage on the last table. Banquet-goers stopped to gawk. The poor beaver scampered in a frantic circle inside its prison. Mary winced. The combination of caged wildlife and dyed food had banished her appetite for all time.

She reached the head of the line. Fumbling with her purse, she retrieved her envelope.

"Mayor Ryan, good evening." She motioned at the snaking line of people behind her. "You have an impressive crowd tonight."

"The town always turns out *en masse* to support our high school athletics," Mayor Ryan agreed. "Our football team ranks twenty-fifth in Ohio. Two up from last year."

Twenty-fifth? Who celebrated such a dismal ranking? "You must be proud," Mary said.

The tall woman rooted beside the mayor nodded vigorously. "We'll raise over ten thousand dollars tonight. Mayor Ryan has earmarked the money for the high school baseball team. Someday they'll be as successful as our football team."

The mayor made a soft *tush, tush* sound. "Judy, dear, I can't tell the high school how to use the money. However, I do hope they'll consider my suggestions." She held out her hand. "Your ticket, please."

Mary tore open the envelope. "Thank you for the generous invitation."

The mayor frowned, which hardly registered. Across the hall, Anthony caught her eye. She flashed a smile.

The mayor cleared her throat. "Mary? You're holding up the line."

She produced the ticket. Hesitating, she wafted the thick cardstock beneath her nose. Why, the ticket smelled like . . . sausage. Grease speckled the cardstock and stripes of mustard streaked the edges.

From behind, a man shuffled with impatience. Further down the line, a dog barked.

Someone else had brought a dog? What was this, the Kennel Club of America?

Zeroing in on the barking proved difficult. A queue of women in sparkling gowns and men in formalwear clogged the corridor. Shrugging it the off, Mary handed over the oddly aromatic ticket.

Twittering with her aide, the mayor checked the registry. As the women spoke in hushed voices, a prickle of awareness tickled Mary's spine. She swung her attention back to Anthony.

He hadn't taken his eyes off her. A dizzy sort of delight swept through her.

On a grin, he gestured her forward. To join him at the table? Doing so wasn't good manners—he was on a date with Meade. Mary shook her head in the negative and Meade, catching the exchange, shot a dark look. Between her regal gown and yipping dog, she resembled a queen who stashed poisoned apples in her purse.

Mayor Ryan asked, "Is the registry correct? Did a Mr. Razz-Pop purchase your ticket?"

The question lifted Mary's brows. "A musician bought my ticket?" The rapper's latest release topped music charts on four continents. Blossom and her friends were fans.

More barking erupted down the line. Deaf to the ruckus, the mayor said, "Disgusting! This is filthy." She waved the ticket through the air, releasing the scent of sausage in a pungent cloud. Switching topics, she added, "Celebrities never visit our proud town. Mary, can you get Mr. Razz-Pop's autograph? For my kids?"

"I'm sorry. I'm not acquainted with the musician."

Clearly the wrong reply, and the mayor's good cheer morphed into disapproval. "If you aren't his guest, *why* do you have his ticket? The food poisoning on your restaurant's opening day was bad enough. You aren't in trouble again, are you?"

Her accusatory tone raised Mary's ire. "The ticket was sent over from your office," she sputtered. "Tyler dropped it off."

Another bark, this time closer.

"I didn't send a ticket," Mayor Ryan snapped. "Mr. Razz-Pop paid for this. For all I know he's wandering the parking lot in search of the ticket. You haven't resorted to theft, have you?"

"Of course not!"

Helplessly, Mary surveyed the hall for an exit. A small crowd of onlookers formed around her. The sound of metal scraping the floor, and Anthony pushed out of his chair.

He strode to the rescue with Meade and her fierce poodle on his tail. He didn't like the way the other guests were closing in on Mary, as if she'd done something wrong. Why couldn't the town give her a break? She'd suffered enough humiliation during the reopening of the restaurant. Now the mayor seemed prepared to throw her out of the banquet.

The thought of anyone hurting Mary quickened his stride. A real disappointment if she left. She looked pretty in her skimpy dress.

Reaching her, he asked, "What's the problem?"

"I'm not sure."

The mayor held up the grease-stained ticket. "*This* is the problem. Stolen property."

Mary folded her arms. "Now, wait a second. I'm not a thief."

The opportunity to hash out the disagreement never arrived. A murmur rippled up the line, drawing his attention. A shout followed. The supercharged air tipped from surprise to pandemonium. A voice that sounded suspiciously like his daughter's rose from the line.

For the love of—had Blossom sneaked into the banquet to spy on him?

Midway down the line, a skirmish broke out. Snoops tumbled from the crowd, her glasses askew. Tyler, backing away from a chubby woman in black velvet, wore a look of terror. She batted his shoulders with her fan.

His daughter was restraining the skittering, mad mountain of fur that was Sweetcakes. Anthony's temper flared.

"Blossom, I'm counting to ten," he bellowed. "Scram, or you're grounded!"

Mary stepped forward, bumping into his shoulder. "Blossom's here?" She joggled on her stiletto heels, her arms swinging wide.

He caught her around the waist. "Didn't I say my kid is trouble? She's not supposed to be here."

The material of Mary's dress shifted beneath his fingertips. He tried to clear his brain before he got a visual of whatever she had on underneath. A frothy confection of lace? He fled the thought before desire barreled to his groin.

Meade stalked forward. Melbourne, spotting Anthony, growled. The combo did its bit to lower his flame, not douse it.

"Tell your daughter to go home," Meade demanded. "The banquet is for adults."

Anthony pulled his roving gaze from Mary to Melbourne's bared teeth. "Meade, go back to the table," he said. "I'll handle this."

"I'm staying until you *do* handle it!"

The mayor shoved between them. "Can we clear up the confusion surrounding this stolen ticket? If Mr. Razz-Pop is outside, I'll send someone to fetch him."

Meade snatched the ticket. "Razz-Popp bought this? The

113

rapper?"

"I didn't steal anything." Mary's growl competed nicely with the poodle's hostility.

The mayor grabbed for the prize. Frustration hissed from her lips.

Meade held the ticket aloft. "Mayor, would you make an introduction? I'd love to meet him."

The mayor grabbed at air. "Give that back!"

The women tussled. Melbourne's snout was a metronome keeping time as it bobbed between them. Anthony leapt forward to pull them apart. Then the sound—the familiar and irrepressible sound of disaster—scuttled his pulse.

Sweetcakes' deep and zesty bark resounded through the hall.

The golden retriever shot through the crowd. The dog nicked the table nearest the entryway. In a horrible chain reaction, the table rocked as if hit by an earthquake. An uproar rang out, and a man fell forward. One by one, all the tables shuddered. At the end of the line, the cage imprisoning Barrington the Beaver sprang open.

Anthony suffered the sensation of watching a train wreck in slow motion. The beaver scurried down the table. Dishes flew skyward. A gelatin mold whirled left, splattering a woman in green silk. She careened into a man in a tuxedo. His toupee spun through the air, landing on a rib roast. Barrington scurried across a wicker horn bursting with rolls. A baguette bounced off Sweetcakes' head, spooking the pooch. Rearing, the carnivorous mutt wheeled in Anthony's direction.

On a groan, he watched Sweetcakes zero in on the meat-scented ticket. As did Melbourne with a *yip* of fury as he squirmed to escape Meade's clutches. The poodle was small, but he was male—and determined to sink his teeth into the ticket. If someone didn't intervene, two salivating dogs would take down the battling women.

Anthony lunged forward.

Too late. Golden fur streamed past. Sweetcakes was airborne.

His heart stopped for a shattering moment. Sweetcakes was an incoming missile with Mary in the way.

The dog clipped her left shoulder, spinning her like a haywire top. Stupidly he grabbed for her, increasing her momentum. The dangers of physics and women, and he got a nice lungful of her perfume as her dress whipped high, momentarily blinding him. Together they fell to the floor.

Meade screamed. Sweetcakes propelled into her, shooting Melbourne loose from her talons. The poodle cartwheeled through the air with a *yip, yip, yip* of fear. In a heap of fur and velvet, Meade and Sweetcakes went down. The din of crashing china and screaming guests punctuated their fall.

"Get this infernal dog off me!" Meade roared.

Flat on his back, Anthony dragged his eyes open. Blackness wavered before his eyesight. Sharp bolts of pain zinged through his hip. Meade's screams barely registered. What *did* register, past the mayhem and his various injuries, was Mary. She laid sprawled across his chest in a delicious mess of silky dress and soft woman. She smelled great.

He allowed his fingers to amble down her back. "Any injuries to report?" He made himself stop before reaching her ass.

"I'm okay." One of her earrings hung from her hair like an ornament set askew on a Christmas tree. "What happened?"

"Blossom, what else? Trouble is her middle name." He lolled his head to the side. Sweetcakes and Melbourne were scuffling over shreds of the ticket. In a real disappointment, the poodle was winning. "Where's Meade?"

"Hmm?"

Mary rested her hands on his neck, luring his attention back to her. Pleasure surged through him. Meade's shouts floated above the banquet hall's chaos.

Mary smiled, and he wondered at the propriety of stealing a kiss as pandemonium reigned.

From above, his daughter came into view.

Blossom tapped her chin. She took a gander at Mary's rumpled attire.

"Nice thong," she said.

౭౨

Ten minutes later, Mary accepted the mayor's apology for

the misunderstanding and escaped to the women's lounge. Canned music drifted from the speakers hidden in the floral wallpaper. A woman's scream filtered from outside. Barrington the Beaver was still loose in the hall.

Anthony was gone. He'd taken home a despondent Blossom and her overexcited dog. She'd come clean about the theft, promising to provide restitution from her weekly allowance. It was shocking to consider that an eleven year old had managed to break into the courthouse and steal a ticket in the first place. The reason for the theft was obvious.

Mary's heart moved into her throat. Blossom had stolen the ticket for *her*. Obviously she'd wanted Mary at the banquet in hopes sparks would fly with Anthony. A silly, adolescent version of a romantic set-up. Who wouldn't feel honored? Stealing the ticket was wrong. Yet Blossom's motives were as sweet as they were troubling.

Before the mirror, Mary surveyed the damage to her dress. One of the straps had broken free. Most of the sequins on the bodice hung loosely. She'd have to throw the dress away.

"There's a tailor on Elm Street who can repair it."

She whirled around. She hadn't heard Meade enter.

Gamely, she nodded. "My dress is beyond repair."

"I hope not. It's lovely."

Meade lowered Melbourne to the lounge's plush couch. The poodle's bows were awry and he was panting.

"Is he okay?" Mary asked.

"He's winded. You don't carry doggie Valium, do you?"

"I'm an MD, not a vet." She approached, hesitated. "May I pet him?"

"Be my guest." Meade went to the mirror to examine her tousled coiffure and smudged lipstick. "He doesn't bite."

"Do you?"

"Depends."

Mary sent a swift glance. Discussing this was folly. She liked Anthony. She liked him a lot.

Unfortunately, Meade did, too.

Under normal circumstances, two professional women living in the same town might have become friends. Jealousy festered between them because they wanted the same man.

Mary, ever the doctor, felt compelled to heal their relationship. Was it possible? She didn't deserve Anthony.

Wearily she sat on the couch beside the panting Melbourne. Unfortunately, her decision to resume her practice in Cincinnati next year hadn't dampened her attraction to Liberty's Mr. Fix-It.

Meade broke the uncomfortable silence. "I'm not in love with Anthony," she said, "but I am crazy about him."

Mary scratched the poodle's ears. "I'm crazy about him, too. Not that my feelings are logical. I can't stay in Liberty."

"Why not?" After she'd explained, Meade asked, "Have you told Anthony you're leaving next year?"

"The topic has never come up."

"He's falling in love with you. Shouldn't you tell him?"

The question battered Mary's heart. Anthony visited The Second Chance daily. Broaching the subject of the free clinic and her plans—*why* put off telling him? The truth clogged her throat with emotion. She was falling for him too, and didn't wish to drive him off.

Beneath her touch Melbourne relaxed. He rolled over to give access to his belly, his tiny legs bobbing with her strokes. She gave out a nervous laugh. "Your dog is adorable," she said, needing to change course.

"He's a scoundrel," Meade replied, with pleasure.

"When I was young, I had a cocker spaniel. Troubadour was my stalwart companion. Awful when he died."

"Somehow I knew you were a dog lover."

"Through and through."

"So is Delia. Her mother breeds dogs."

"I hadn't heard."

Meade gave a surprising glance of concern. "Is it true? You're having trouble finding health insurance for your employees?"

Were her problems common knowledge? "The plans are more expensive than I anticipated."

"Employee benefits are a high cost of doing business."

The sympathy in Meade's voice compelled Mary to say, "When I worked in the ER, I used to complain with the other doctors about some of the patients. Not all the time . . . but sometimes I did."

"Which patients?"

"The poor ones," she admitted. "The patients without insurance."

She'd been young and callous, too foolish to understand how hard people worked to stay afloat. She was short-tempered when patients clogged the ER with ailments treated easily by a private doctor. Now she knew Finney, who struggled to support two kids. And Delia, a young woman with a bubbly personality and a car so old it grew rust spots like cancer.

She knew Anthony and Blossom, and had visited their gorgeous shell of a house. The floors would probably never be carpeted because of the thousands of dollars spent to keep Blossom alive.

"I'll never forgive myself for complaining about people who work so hard but never get a fair shake," she said, sick with self-reproach. "If you don't have health insurance, where do you go? To the ER where a young doctor grudgingly cares for you."

"A young, *exhausted* doctor, I'd wager." Meade withdrew a business card from her purse. "I have a friend who'll find an affordable rate."

Mary took the card. "Thank you."

"Thank Anthony. He asked me to use the connection weeks ago."

Guilt stung Mary. Meade's attraction to Anthony was strong. Yet he'd gone to her on Mary's behalf.

Apparently Meade was a mind reader because she said, "Don't be too hard on him. It never dawned on Anthony that I might not want to help. He's too decent."

"I'm sorry," Mary whispered. *For what?* she wondered. For how much she cared for Anthony? For Meade's pride, which must've been trampled when he sought her out? "I don't feel right accepting your help. All things considered, why should you?"

Skirting the question, Meade said, "You know, Anthony didn't plan to become a mechanic. He turned down a full scholarship to college when Cheryl got pregnant."

"Finney mentioned he tried to do the right thing from the very beginning."

"Unusual for an eighteen year old boy." Meade opened a

compact of blush and placed strokes of color on her cheeks. "When Blossom was a toddler? He'd tour her through Liberty Square in her stroller, the proud Papa. The other young men his age were buying motorcycles or moving into dorm rooms for college. Anthony never complained about fatherhood, Cheryl leaving, or the lot he'd drawn in life. Not once."

"You admire him."

"Don't you? He's decent down to the marrow."

Mary silently agreed. He'd greeted Blossom's arrival with joy. He'd celebrated her life despite everything he'd lost in the bargain. Finney affectionately called him Mr. Fix-It. Would Anthony have become an engineer? An architect? What dreams were laid to rest to welcome Blossom into his world?

Cuddling Melbourne close, Mary found the courage to say, "Blossom thinks you'd like to marry him. Is it true?"

"As a matter of fact, it is." A self-deprecating laugh drifted from Meade's lips. "Or was."

She let the comment hover between them. Slowly she rimmed her mouth with color, her poise unshakeable. At last, she snapped her purse shut and caught Mary's eyes in the mirror.

"And you, Mary?" she asked, "What do you want?"

Chapter 11

Steeling herself for the pain, Blossom bit down on her tongue. *I want is a life without needles.*

On the examination table in the Children's Hospital of St. Barnabas Hospital, she held her breath. The nurse dabbed cotton on her forearm. The sharp scent of rubbing alcohol struck her nostrils like fire. Her dad, leaning against the wall, sent a desperate smile. His encouragement diminished the fear raising goose bumps on her skin.

On their drive to the hospital, he'd announced a reprieve. She was no longer grounded for last week's breaking and entering spree at the courthouse. He was still angry, but he'd looked worried on the drive to St. Barnabas. All it took was a case of sniffles and a low-grade fever, and he'd released her from house arrest.

Now he'd gone into protective mode.

He'd nearly forgiven her for stealing the ticket. Relieved, Blossom held onto the lifeline of his reassuring gaze. The nurse brought the needle close.

Nothing was worse than needles. The sight of one pricking her skin sent fear rolling through her. The nurse withdrew the blood quickly.

Blossom could handle puny needles, hundreds of them, as long as no one made her watch one pierce her skin until the blood came out.

Big needles were awful. Blackness threatened whenever a

nurse brought one near. The scariest of all were the ones used to remove the samples of bone marrow from her hip. Her oncologist, Dr. Lash, checked the marrow samples to make sure the cancer hadn't returned.

They'd lay her face down on a table and a nurse would hold her legs. Even with the anesthetic Dr. Lash rubbed on her hip, the burst of pain always made her cry out. An awful sensation followed, a feeling of something thick, like Jell-O, being sucked from her hip.

Blood tests, fatigue, hospital stays, pills—she could handle the basics of cancer treatment. She'd hold her father's hand or visualize something nice, and she'd muddle through. But the awful needles used to extract marrow were terrifying. Not even her father's love kept the fear away.

"All done." The nurse taped a bandage on the site. "You can go to lunch now. Please return at one-thirty to see Dr. Lash."

Blossom hopped down from the table. "I'm starving."

Her father led her into the busy corridor. Families sat in colorful chairs outside the row of examination rooms. "You're always starving," he said.

The lighthearted conversation, their first in weeks, boosted her spirits. "It's an Italian thing."

"You're only half Italian."

"The better half." She tugged on his sleeve. "What was my mom?"

"Irish and French, I think." Anthony lifted a brow. "I can't remember the last time you asked about your mother."

She hadn't thought about Cheryl in eons. Blossom had been a toddler when her mom hit the trail. It wasn't like she had any memories. She had photos of Cheryl stashed in a drawer and that's how she thought of her: *Cheryl*, a teenager with a toothy smile and punk rocker hair.

"I don't remember her." She pushed back the sadness before it pricked like a needle. "Not even one memory."

"She left a long time ago."

The elevators came in view. "Hey, it's no big deal," she said, hating the sorrow washing through his expression. "I've done okay with you."

"Don't hold back on the validation. Keep it coming."

"Yeah, yeah, yeah." He'd relaxed, and she saw an opening. "What else do you like, Dad?" She wiggled her brows.

"Don't start. I like Mary. She's a good friend. What happens between us—if anything—is none of your business."

"I'm good friends with Tyler," she said, in case he needed a road map to the highway of love. "We've been pals forever. I'm going to marry him. I'm pretty sure he knows. It's good when friends marry."

"Aren't boys supposed to chase girls?" Her dad flicked her nose. "Tyler should ask you to marry him . . . in twenty years. Or thirty."

"Is that how long you'll wait to ask Mary?"

He rocked back on his heels. "Listen, stupido, I'm not getting hitched. Not right now, anyway."

"Because of Meade?" She hadn't stopped by since the disaster at the fundraiser. Blossom's initial relief had quickly morphed into guilt. "Dad, I was only trying to help. Meade isn't right for you."

"Kiddo, it's not so simple."

"Why not? Mary likes you. Can't you tell?"

He cast a sidelong glance. "You're not up to anything, are you? Half of the people in Liberty aren't speaking to me because you trashed the fundraiser."

"I've given up a life of crime."

It was for the best. Barrington the Beaver now suffered from a nervous tic and fur loss. They were finding chunks of the stuff all over his cage. She felt bad—she'd always liked the school's mascot.

"Good to know," he said. "I've got enough to worry about with your health . . ."

His voice trailed off. Emotion rolled through his expression in black waves. When he thrust out his hand, she eagerly clasped his fingers.

At a fast clip, he led her to the elevator. Why upset him? They'd been on the outs for months. The easy way they used to talk, the way they'd hang out together—she'd messed up their relationship, big time.

At the elevator, a nurse stood beside a boy in a wheelchair. The boy was pale, his eyes glassy. Blossom guessed he was five or six years old. A pretty blonde darted up and she knew the lady was his mother, just like she knew the boy had ALL.

Acute Lymphoblastic Leukemia—it was what she had, too. The cancer meant the boy was taking chemo pills and getting shots that made his stomach hurt. Soon, his fine, tawny hair would fall out. As the elevator slid open, Blossom looked closely at his scalp. Yep, it was already happening. She'd bet his mom was brushing his hair toward the back to hide the first bald patch on top of his scalp.

The ruse wouldn't work much longer. During her chemo treatments Blossom had favored silky scarves. The boy might choose a baseball cap to hide the humiliation of cancer. He'd miss school for months or maybe a year. She hadn't wanted to repeat, so she'd studied constantly during the summer before sixth grade.

People herded into the elevator. On instinct, she leaned against her father. He looped his arm around her shoulders, encouraging her to snuggle close. Even though she'd always been an oddity, he made her feel safe. The kid with cancer, she'd never been normal. Some of the kids at school actually thought they'd catch it from her like the flu. If not for Snoops, she'd eat lunch alone in the cafeteria.

But today was different. She enjoyed lunch with her dad in a café down the street from the hospital. They returned to St. Barnabas right on time for Dr. Lash.

He was a skinny doctor not much older than her dad with Coke bottle-thick glasses and a limp when he walked. Blossom adored him. Dr. Lash did Cat's Cradle faster than any kid she knew.

"Blossom has a summer cold," he said, completing the examination. "Other than that, she's fine."

Her dad jingled the keys in his pocket. "What about her white blood count?"

Dr. Lash checked his notes. "Looks good. Within acceptable range."

"She's running a fever."

"I'll wager she's worn out from her adventures," Dr. Lash quipped, referring to her antics at the fundraiser. He winked at her. "I won't be visiting you in the county lockup, will I?"

"Not in this lifetime," she said.

Anthony tousled her curls. "If she pulls another stunt, the lockup will be her bedroom for the rest of the summer."

"Then I suggest you toe the line, young lady." Dr. Lash made a note on the chart. "Get some rest. We're almost at twenty-three months. Your remission is holding beautifully."

She beamed at the oncologist. *Twenty-three months.* Once she made it to the two year mark, she was home free. ALL hardly ever came back if you were clean of cancer for two years.

Of course, her knees had ached this morning. Yesterday she'd felt so tired she'd dragged her feet during Sweetcakes' afternoon walk. She didn't mention it to Dr. Lash.

There wasn't any reason. She was finally healthy.

True to the offer she'd made at the fundraiser, Meade solved Mary's healthcare dilemma.

Hanging up the phone, Mary stared with relief at the rates she'd jotted down. Meade's friend, an insurance agent in Beachwood, had done her best to find affordable rates.

At the other end of the counter, Delia waited with ill-concealed excitement. "Well? Don't keep me in suspense." The waitress slid a soda before a woman at the counter. "Did you get coverage for me and Finney? You don't have to worry about Ethel Lynn. She's on Medicare."

"All done." Mary rechecked the quote. She felt odd, accepting Meade's help, even though she was delighted for Delia and Finney. "The policy goes into effect next week."

She tossed the notepad beside the stack of mail. Her emotions sank as she skimmed the envelope on top. Another correspondence from Abe. More photographs inside, with a gentle reminder that she still hadn't scheduled a visit? His staff wanted to meet her, even though she hadn't set a firm date on when she'd take over. Soon, she'd have to take a day off and drive down to Cincinnati. She couldn't stall forever.

No wonder she felt guilty about Meade. Liberty's Queen of Cosmetics was a lifelong resident. Liberty was her home.

Downcast, she returned to the kitchen. The air was hazy with smoke from the grill. A pot of mouth-watering barbecue sauce, for the rib special on tonight's menu, simmered on the stove. Finney placed a sprig of parsley on a plate of meatloaf and garlic potatoes.

Mary wiped her hands on a towel. "The lunch rush is winding down." She told Finney about the insurance.

"About time." Catching herself, the cook backpedaled. "Thank you."

"Will you be all right if I'm gone for a few minutes?"

Finney deposited the plate on the pass-through window. "Where are you going?"

"Across the street to the Gas & Go."

"Something wrong with your car?"

"No, it's nothing like that." She reached for shaved beef and thick slices of cheese. "Will you make a hot roast beef with double cheddar? I promised Anthony I'd bring dinner over. Actually, we're feeding him next week, too. A 'thank you' for working on the stove."

Finney nodded approvingly. "He came back on Tuesday bright and early. When I got here, he was under the stove with a thousand tools on the floor."

"I gave him a key."

This got the cook's full attention. "You did, now?" Finney chuckled. "Handing out keys—sounds cozy to me."

The insinuation raised Mary's defenses. "He's finishing work on the stove before our morning shift," she tossed back.

"What about the free meals? A woman offers a man food, it means something."

"I'm merely repaying a man who gallantly repaired my stove and refused my cash." Mary filled the sink with soapy water and reached for a greasy pot. "He needed the key because he wasn't sure how early he'd stop by. By the way, he told me to pitch the ice cream cooler. The new one arrives tomorrow."

"Praise the Lord." The cook ducked into the cooler and grabbed a generous serving of fries. "You sure nothing's going on between you two?"

"He's a good friend, that's all." Mary dunked the pot and scrubbed vigorously. "In a perfect world, I suspect he'd ask me out. I'd go willingly if—" Cutting off, she steeled herself. Finally she added, "Finney, I can't stay in Liberty. Not permanently."

The explanation stamped displeasure on the cook's face. "You're leaving?"

"In a matter of months."

After she explained about Abe's clinic, Finney asked, "Who'll run The Second Chance after you're gone?"

"Would you like to?" She'd been meaning to ask.

The cook dashed her hopes, saying, "What I'd like is for you to change your mind. We need you, Mary. I sure don't want to see you go."

"There isn't a choice. I have to take over Abe's clinic."

Finney tossed fries into a metal basket. "What about Anthony? He's got it bad for you." The cook lowered the basket into hot oil. "Mind you, I can see why a man with an ill child thinks twice before starting a romance. He's been alone for a long time."

"What about Meade?" She'd assumed they shared a history. A few dates, at least.

"Oh, she tries to get under his skin. She's wasting her time. I can't recall Anthony dating anyone. If you'd seen Blossom a few years ago, you'd understand. No one with a child on death's door has time for romance."

Mary's heart stilled. "Is it true . . . Blossom nearly died?"

"A miracle she didn't." Finney leaned heavily on the counter, the weight of the memory pressing down on her. "In fifth grade, she looked like a skeleton. We didn't think she'd make it."

"Thank goodness she's better now." She loved Blossom and couldn't bear to consider everything she'd endured.

"This is the first time in years Anthony's had time to think about a woman. He *is* smitten with you, Mary."

"Nonsense." But it wasn't, she knew.

"Can't you tell?"

Confusion swamped her as she weighed her growing attraction against her responsibility to the patients at Abe's clinic.

I can tell we're equally smitten.

Mary paused in the shade of the Gas & Go's service island. Even though it was late afternoon, the temperature remained in the eighties. Swabbing the perspiration from her brow, she came to a difficult decision. One way or another, she must tell Anthony that dating was out of the question. Leaving the loaded topic unexplored seemed cruel. She owed him nothing less than honesty.

Inside the garage, he worked beneath a black hatchback. On the bench Blossom, Tyler and Snoops sat in a row. Beneath them, Blossom's glossy-gold retriever dozed in the summer heat. The kids were sipping root beer floats and swinging their legs in tandem. Mary paused to enjoy the sight—three kids halfway through puberty, happily slurping ice cream drinks on a warm summer day.

Spotting her, Blossom leapt from the bench. "Mary, I told Snoops that you're taking me to the mall next week. Can she go with us?"

"She's more than welcome to come." Mary peered beneath the black hatchback. Anthony's legs twitched as he turned some type of wrench. "Did you mention our shopping expedition to your father?"

Blossom kicked at her father's oil-spattered shoes. "Dad, can I go?"

"You bet." Anthony slid out from beneath the car and got to his feet. "I hate shopping. I'd gladly buy all your clothes online." He opened one of the bags Mary held, took a sniff. "Is this dinner? Smells great."

Blossom squeezed between them. "Is there something for me?"

Anthony swatted her away. "Finish your ice cream, kiddo, then check out the chess tournament in the center green. I'm not sharing my dinner." He grabbed his daughter and pulled her under his arm. "Comprendo?"

She giggled. "Cheapskate."

He rubbed his knuckles across her scalp. "Now, scram."

The kids strolled out of the garage with Sweetcakes trotting behind. Mary and Anthony followed, watching as they crossed to the center green.

After they'd disappeared, Mary asked, "Why don't you put Blossom in a summer program? She can help at the restaurant whenever she likes, but she'll become bored soon enough."

"She *was* signed up for several programs."

"What happened?"

He steered her back inside. "*You* happened."

With dismay, she realized his hand remained pressed to the small of her back. "I never meant for Blossom to spend every minute at the restaurant," she said, acutely conscious of the pleasure of his touch. "Not at the expense of her summer activities."

"She thought her activities would intrude on her work schedule. She thinks working for you is a serious responsibility, right up there with keeping a four-point grade average. When she dropped her activities, Tyler and Snoops did too."

"I feel awful." Which was a lie. She felt uncommonly good with his hand melting into her back. His fingers moved in warming circles, sending ripples of sensation down her spine. "Blossom shouldn't alter her schedule. She can hang around the restaurant and still have time for fun."

"She prefers you. If she thought I'd let her, she'd bunk with you at night."

"I was only trying to help."

"You *are* helping." Chuckling, he clasped her shoulders and swiveled her to face him. "Don't get bent out of shape over this."

She looked up at him, astonished to discover she'd altered his daughter's schedule and he wasn't upset. "Scrubbing potatoes and handing out parade flags shouldn't be the highlights of her summer."

He fixed her with a sober, searching gaze. "You're pretty when you're upset." His attention worked slowly across her face, freezing the air in her lungs. "Do you always take everything so seriously?"

She told herself to breathe. "No. Not really." He'd pinned her with an earthy look both suggestive and tantalizing. "Well, sometimes."

"Sometimes?"

The intensity of his expression turned her legs rubbery. "Yes. Okay? I take things seriously." She needed to disconnect from his touch, roving in hot circles across her shoulders. "I care about your daughter. Eleven is an impressionable age."

"Afraid you'll make the wrong impression?" Grinning, he let

her go. "Mary, you're a nice woman. A little high strung, but I'm not worried you'll lead my daughter astray."

She licked her parched lips. "I never would."

"Why are you so high strung?"

Tell him about Abe's practice. "Lots of reasons," she prevaricated.

"Relax. Too much worry will make you sick. Learn to pace it out."

She thought of the debt she now owed Meade, who'd graciously located affordable health insurance. Next she reflected on her growing and increasingly complicated feelings for him, and the prospect of returning to medicine to take over Abe's clinic. How would he take the news?

"It's hard *not* to worry," she admitted.

"Give it your best shot. Learn to enjoy yourself more." Licking his lips, he opened one of the bags she'd brought. "I enjoy you."

"You do?"

He regarded her with a devilish grin. "You enjoy me, too."

She blinked, mesmerized. "Yeah?" He had a sexy voice. It worked well with his dark looks. The faded jeans molding to his thighs and the body-sculpting tee shirt were no great hardship, either. "You're okay, I guess," she added.

"Just okay?" The pleasure on his face increased. "Sure that's all I am?"

"Pretty sure."

"You don't think I'm hot stuff?"

The question bubbled out, hurried and unbidden. "Well, hot stuff—why haven't you called me?"

She'd meant to give him a red light. *No dating allowed.* His banter said *green,* and she'd sped right through.

Slow down.

She shrugged, feeling edgy beneath his tight appraisal. "What an awful thing to say. Why would you call me? I'd never expect you to call."

"I wanted to."

The softly issued pronouncement pulled her heart into her throat. Anthony stepped closer. His eyes were dark with a host of emotions she couldn't decipher. Their gazes dueled. When he reached up and rubbed his thumb across her lower lip, she nearly swayed into his arms.

"I think about calling you all the time," he said in a voice of torn velvet. "With Meade coming around . . . the situation's awkward. But I think about you constantly."

"Don't."

"Are you nervous about dating me?"

"It's not a good idea." They weren't discussing a few dates. Given the depth of their attraction, it could lead to so much more. "I need to be honest with you. I can't stay in Liberty."

He listened stone-faced as she laid out her plans. Sadness flickered through his expression.

"I thought you took over the restaurant because you wanted a change," he said, in an admirably calm tone.

"I wish it were that simple." She swallowed against the lump in her throat. "I love being a doctor."

"Why not set up shop here in Liberty?"

"It's not feasible."

"Why not?"

He appeared ready to add something more. Instead he bent slightly to brush his lips across hers. A feather-light warmth, a mere hint of a kiss. Pleasure rippled through her.

Quickly, he drew away. He looked briefly at Blossom and her friends walking toward the chess match in the center green. "Blossom is doing great. It's time for me to have my own life, and back off to give her space."

The sensually drugged sensation in her blood dissolved beneath a pebble of fear. "How *is* her remission?"

"Going well. We're nearing the two-year mark without a hitch."

What was it like to count the days when the life in the balance was your child's? Did you wake every morning praying for your daughter to remain healthy one more day?

On impulse, she grazed her fingers across his cheek. The dark, five o'clock shadow gave this very honorable man a disturbingly rakish quality.

"You're very brave," she said. "And I don't want to hurt you. I wish I could promise to stay. It would be a lie."

His gaze slid to hers. "I'm not asking for promises." He laid his hand over hers, pressing her fingers deep into the firm muscle of his cheek. Agony rimmed the corners of his mouth. "Let's go out, see where it leads."

"Why start something we'll have to end?" Did he think he'd talk her out of leaving? She wondered if she wanted him to try. Wavering, she added, "Be realistic."

"Pass."

"Anthony—"

He let out a low, startling curse. Then he surprised her by grazing his lips across hers. He moved slowly, thoroughly. Mary's heart reeled. She opened her mouth beneath his as he cradled her face in his palms. Deepening the kiss, he molded her against him, telegraphing his need through the hot press of flesh.

When he let her go, his strong features were flushed with arousal. "I can't wait any longer." On a jagged breath he added, "You can't either."

Chapter 12

"It's just a dent, Anthony. Can you fix it quick?"

Forcing himself to focus on the task at hand, Anthony ran his palm across the nicked hood of Theodora's Cadillac. This morning he'd skipped breakfast at the restaurant. Blossom was spending a few hours there, something about helping to organize the storage room.

Yesterday's conversation with Mary still rattled him. He should've known she'd leave.

Before the year was out, in fact.

Her former career in medicine wasn't a secret. She'd cleared Delia's ear infection and patched up Theodora's knee. In a town that hadn't boasted a doctor for decades, her medical expertise was a lively topic of conversation. What Anthony *hadn't* understood was her intention to return to southern Ohio.

Theodora stomped her foot. "What's wrong with you? Snap out of it!"

He flinched at the shrill command. "Okay, okay. Give me the day to work on the Cadillac."

"Finish by tonight." Theodora paused, considering. "Might spend the day hunting. Not sure if I should, though. Mary told me to stay put."

"You're following her instructions?" Usually Theodora was a law unto herself—one packing a Saturday Night Special loaded with rock salt.

"She's doing a fine job healing my leg."

"Have you thanked her?"

"What am I? Miss Congeniality?" She lowered her voice to a conspiratorial whisper. "The ointment Mary prescribed for the bruising on my knee? Keeps the pain at bay."

An unexpected jolt of guilt nicked him. What right did he have to woo her? She deserved patients and a successful medical practice. She deserved more than he could give her in small town USA.

Still, he wanted her.

Pulling a box close, Mary rummaged through the mound of tissue.

The diversion was welcome since she'd thought of little but Anthony since daybreak. Any resolve she'd harbored about avoiding a relationship dissolved the moment he'd kissed her at the Gas & Go. She was in deep, whether she was ready or not. Telling Anthony of her plans to leave town hadn't deterred him at all.

Her, either.

The storage room brimmed with treasure and antiques from the restaurant's illustrious past. Boxes once stacked against the walls and on shelves were brought down and opened. The seating arrangement, which served as Mary's makeshift clinic when she'd treated Delia and Theodora, was scooted apart to make way for the task of sorting china and whatever else they discovered. Ethel Lynn sat working in the comfy Queen Anne chair. Mary commandeered a smaller chair.

Working slowly, Mary let her thoughts drift. She recalled the feel of Anthony's arms around her waist and the warmth of his lips. She could easily fall in love with him. He was decent and true, the sort of man who'd care for a woman with tenderness and devotion. Falling in love was risk enough. The real crux of the problem?

Blossom.

She cared deeply for the girl. How would Blossom react when she learned of Mary's plans to return to Cincinnati? Disappointing a child who'd endured so many struggles was an unbearable prospect.

Blossom appeared in the doorway. "You started without me?"

"There's still lots to do." Mary lifted a pewter platter from the carton.

Blossom craned her neck to take in the rows of shelves and the miles of boxes. "Wow. This place is huge. Like a museum."

Ethel Lynn unwrapped a china plate. "Child, The Second Chance *is* a museum, in a manner of speaking. Every owner back to the 1800s left oodles of whatnots behind. All those treasures have passed down to Mary."

Mary pulled a set of candlesticks from the box. "I'm curious to know what we'll find. We've been so busy I've hardly had a chance to investigate." She wagged one of the candlesticks before Ethel Lynn's nose. "Every time I look around I find more decorations for the restaurant."

"Curiosity killed the cat," Ethel Lynn sniffed. "Your Aunt Meg and I rarely set foot in here. She's allergic to dust, and I live in mortal fear of spiders."

In the last half hour, the topic of spiders had come up repeatedly. "I haven't seen any." In truth, she'd seen several. "If I do, I'll take care of them."

"Heavens—I've seen leaping spiders too," Ethel Lynn said, ignoring the reassuring comment. "Jump ten feet, they do."

Blossom froze. "You've seen spiders that jump? Mary, do you have leaping spiders in here?"

Amusement tickled the corners of Mary's lips. "Of course not."

"You're sure?" Blossom dug her fingers into her curls. "Check my neck, will you? I feel something itchy."

Ethel Lynn snatched her hands from the box of china. "Heavens to Betsy!"

Blossom twitched. "Really. Someone look." She grabbed at her shirt collar and yanked herself in a circle. "Oh. Oh, no. Is something crawling down my back?"

Ethel Lynn clenched her fists to the sagging indentations of her breasts. "One's got the child!" she screamed as Blossom gyrated wildly.

Laughter popped from Mary's mouth. "Would you both calm down?" The unexpected amusement was a balm for her torn emotions. "Insects prefer damp places. This room is as dry as a bone. Try visiting Louisiana or Florida. The cockroaches are big enough to masquerade as house pets. Believe me—you're perfectly safe here."

"Bugs as big as pets?" Blossom shivered. "What if their smaller cousins are camped out here?" She hurried over to Mary. "Check out my neck, will you? To make sure."

She stuck her hand down the back of the girl's shirt. "Oooh—spiders!"

Giggling, Blossom jerked free. "Stop!"

Mary tousled her dark, curly hair. What would it be like to watch Blossom enter high school? Or send her from the house on her first date?

To become a part of her life forever?

Blossom said, "Last time I trust you." Her eyes full of merriment, she self-consciously rolled her shoulders then straightened her shirt.

There was something fetching about a girl's eleventh year. The changeable quality of her face and personality—Blossom appeared childlike one moment, a woman the next. Now, she eyed Mary with a hint of worldly sophistication, one woman to another. They shared a private moment that ferried volumes between them. Mary winked.

"You're bad, Mary. What if there *had* been a spider in my shirt?" The girl crossed her arms with mock sobriety. "Would you have let it crawl all the way to my butt?"

"I'd never let a spider near your butt."

Ethel Lynn produced a handkerchief and patted her brow. "The world is going to hell in a hand-basket when a young woman calls her fanny a 'butt'." She rose. "I've had enough excitement for one afternoon. It's time to dawdle on home for a nap."

Mary dragged another box close. "Finney made lunch if you're hungry."

"No, but thank you," Ethel Lynn said. "I need rest."

After she left, Blossom ducked in and out of the rows of boxes like a hound sniffing quarry. Evidently her fear of spiders had abated. She opened a poorly sealed box and withdrew a crystal goblet carved in an intricate diamond pattern.

"Are you sticking around all day?" Mary asked. She hoped so.

"I can only stay a few hours." The girl picked up a menu from the 1920s and fanned herself like the Queen of Sheba. "Snoops and Tyler miss me. They asked for some face-time." Blossom eyed her with concern. "You're okay without me?"

"I'll muddle through."

"I'll be back tomorrow."

"Sweetie, take tomorrow off. It's summer vacation. Go to the pool with your friends or to the movies." Even though Meade had assisted with the insurance, the threat about hiring a minor weighed heavily on Mary. Limiting Blossom's visits *was* a good idea. "We'll go to the mall soon for our shopping spree. Until then, cut loose with your friends."

Blossom lifted a section of broadcloth from a heap of forgotten treasure. Dust wafted skyward. "What's under here?"

"Furniture. Don't move it around. Something might fall on your head."

"Whatever you say, muchacha." Blossom shifted from foot to foot. "Can I ask you something?"

"Of course." Mary gave her full attention.

"Right." Blossom clasped her hands at her waist. "Tell the truth, okay?"

"Sure."

"You won't hurt my feelings if you give the wrong answer. Just be honest."

Mary crossed her heart. "The whole truth and nothing but the truth."

The earnest response lent Blossom courage. "I need a favor," she said in a rush. "If anything happens to me, will you look after my dad?"

Chapter 13

Of all the questions Blossom might have posed, this was the query Mary hadn't anticipated.

"Did something happen during your checkup to frighten you?" she asked. A doctor's instinct to find clues rose past her worry. "If Dr. Lash said anything that made you nervous, let's discuss it. Lots of people get cancer and survive. They go on to lead long, healthy lives. The more you understand, the less frightened you'll be."

The conversation, long overdue, was inevitable. She'd befriended a girl with a serious illness. Her medical training supplied the means to answer questions about leukemia and its aftermath with poise and reassurance.

"I have lots of books on leukemia," Blossom said. "My Dad's been buying them since I was a kid."

"Anything in particular you'd like to discuss?"

"I'm in remission. Everything's great."

The hurried reply sent fear darting through her. Suppressing it, she settled on the stickier dilemma—Anthony.

She selected her words with care. "If something ever happened to you—and honey, I'm sure nothing will—I'd help your father in any way possible. Friends help each other."

The explanation didn't satisfy. "Don't you like him?" Hope and hesitation knotted on Blossom's face. "The way I like Tyler? Boy-girl like?"

Mary became uncomfortably aware of the warmth seeping

up her neck. The memory of Anthony's kiss sent longing through her blood.

"How adults feel about each other is hard for kids to understand." Blossom wrinkled her nose at the evasion, prompting her to add, "You may think you understand, but attraction works differently for adults. When you're young, everything seems black and white. Adults see more, well, grey. It's complicated."

"My dad says stuff like that."

"You should listen to him."

Blossom puffed up her cheeks. Slowly she blew out a stream of air. "*Why* can't grownups keep it simple?"

Luckily she was spared from answering. Delia popped her head into the storage room.

"Oh, heck. Mary, I thought you were out running errands." The waitress held up a slip of paper. "Mayor Ryan called an hour ago. She asked to see you."

Blossom started toward the door but Mary snagged her wrist. "Hold on." She glimpsed the unsettled emotion in the girl's eyes, the hint of disappointment. Needing to quell it, she asked, "Can I have a hug before you go?"

Grudgingly, Blossom allowed Mary to draw her near. They shared a slow, rocking embrace.

"I'll see you tomorrow." On tiptoes, the girl landed a peck on Mary's cheek.

They'd never before shared a kiss. Moved by the affection, Mary lifted her hand to her cheek. Delight lit Blossom's face. Then she dashed from the room.

Delia leaned against the doorjamb. "The kid sure loves you."

"I'm fond of her, too." She took the slip of paper. "Why did the mayor call? Please tell me she isn't seeking reparations because the fundraiser was trashed."

"No one blames you for Blossom's antics."

She thought of Meade. "Not everyone in town approves of my friendship with Blossom."

Delia smirked. "And everyone knows Blossom cooks up the craziest schemes. You should've been around last winter when she pulled her computer caper with Snoops."

The story wasn't familiar. "What happened?"

Delia's mouth curved wryly. "They hacked into the junior high inter-office mail and sent fake love letters to Mrs. Wright, the English teacher. The letters were from a new teacher, just hired. Poor guy had a crush on Wright . . . she thought he was a stalker."

Mary tried not to laugh. "What is it with Blossom? Does she have romance on the brain?"

"She has Tyler Reevak on the brain. A real adolescent crush. But, yeah—the kid's middle name is trouble." Delia patted Mary's back. "So don't worry about the mayor. She won't make you leave town because Blossom trashed the fundraiser."

The assurance didn't banish the niggling worry. Returning to the kitchen, Mary felt certain the mayor's call didn't bode well.

"What's going on?" Finney asked.

Mary held the note up. "Mayor Ryan asked me to stop by this afternoon."

Finney read the note for herself. "Asking you over to the courthouse at four o'clock sure sounds like a summons. I don't like this."

"Me either."

"This is trouble," Finney said, confirming Mary's worst suspicions. "I like Mayor Ryan. She works hard but she's close to Meade. The way Anthony acts around you, not to mention Blossom's affection . . . you're rubbing salt in Meade's wounds."

Yet Meade had come to Mary's aid. She'd found the means to provide Delia and Finney with health insurance. She'd used her connections to secure an affordable rate. Why hold out a carrot with one hand and a stick with the other?

Reading her thoughts, the cook sighed. "For a doctor, you sure are dumb. Meade helped with the insurance to please Anthony. Doesn't mean she won't cut you deep when he's not looking."

The courthouse's marble corridor provided a cooling respite from the afternoon sun. Lightheaded from anxiety, Mary hurried to the mayor's office.

The officer seated outside was a customer at the restaurant. Ben or Bill—she couldn't recall his name. He nodded in greeting.

"The mayor's waiting for you," he said, waving Mary inside.

Long windows provided a stunning view of the center green, below. Mayor Ryan paced back and forth before them in deep concentration.

Midway across the office Mary paused. She drew a deep, steadying breath.

Mayor Ryan looked up. "Mary. Hello." She sat behind a desk covered with neat stacks of paper and leather volumes that looked like court dockets. "Sit down, please. It's about Blossom. I've received a complaint."

Mary sank into a chair. *Meade.* "What sort of complaint?"

"Is the child employed at your restaurant?"

"Blossom visits while her father works. With school out, she has time on her hands."

"Are you running a daycare?"

Mary blinked. "What?"

The smile melted from the mayor's lips. "Or . . . a clinic?" When Mary floundered, she added, "Of course not. You have an operating license to run a restaurant. The license is right here." She produced the paperwork. "You plan to continue operations?"

The barrage of questions left her queasy. Was Meade so vindictive she wanted The Second Chance closed? No doubt she'd complained that Mary was taking advantage of a child *and* running a medical practice in a building designated for restaurant use. If Meade were out for blood, she might contact the County Health Board. Lodging a complaint put Mary's future medical career in peril.

Fear poured into her gut. *I'll lose my medical license.*

The mayor's expression softened. "Mary, I like you. Granted, you had a bumpy start when you reopened the restaurant. Naturally, if the situation presented itself I'd gladly issue a license for you to set up a medical practice in the building housing your restaurant. There's ample space on the second floor, and the town would benefit from the services of a local MD."

"I'm not setting up a practice in Liberty."

"I understand your desire to return to Cincinnati once The Second Chance Grill becomes solvent. It's also my understanding that your relationship with Blossom may have encouraged her to steal the ticket to the fundraiser." When Mary began to object, the mayor raised a hand to silence her. "I don't believe you encouraged her to steal the ticket. But she *is* focused on you. Reconsider your relationship with the child."

"You're saying I shouldn't have a relationship with Blossom?"

"That isn't my call. You're an adult. Weigh the decision carefully." Her expression dour, the mayor added, "There's no question your restaurant provides a valuable service to the community. In time, you'll hire more employees. You'll prosper. Your success will become Liberty's success."

Locating a shred of pluck, she asked, "Do you mind revealing who lodged the complaint?"

The mayor surprised her with candor. "Be careful, dear. Meade isn't a bad person. She's done a lot of good for the town. Frankly, I suspect she admires you. Not many doctors would care about saving a restaurant in small-town America."

"What you aren't saying? I'm in her way."

"Are you? I thought we'd agreed that your plans to leave my town are firm." She nodded at Mary's purse, which gave out a barely discernable hum. "Go on, take the call. We're done here."

Mary withdrew her phone and darted into the corridor.

"Mary?" It was Abe.

"Abe. Hi. Listen, this isn't a good time." She cringed at her rude tone.

"Busy day feeding the masses?"

"Something like that. Would you mind if I called you tomorrow? Rough day."

The uneasy silence wound out. Finally Abe said, "This can't wait."

The fragile tone of his voice put her on alert. Glaring sunlight beat down on her as she trotted down the courthouse steps. At the bottom, she dropped onto the granite step. She was still trembling from the conversation with Mayor Ryan.

In a gentle voice, she asked, "What's going on?"

"I've been ordered to rest. Can you imagine? The doctor forced to follow another doctor's orders? Long story short, my cardiologist is concerned. My wife is frantic."

Her fingers icy, she gripped the cell. "What's going on?"

"I didn't want to tell you." He paused long enough for her emotions to hollow out. "Mary, I'm in early stage heart failure."

Chapter 14

In the eight hours since Anthony commenced work on Theodora's car, she'd checked back eight times. Not that he relished the interruptions. He was still trying to digest the news that Mary planned to leave Liberty. Convincing her to stay seemed an insurmountable problem.

Just thinking about the way he'd kissed her yesterday started his motor humming. He was falling for her throaty laugh, her compassion—and the sweet way she treated his kid. Finding a woman like Mary only to lose her made him cranky. Or Theodora was souring his mood.

She was glaring at him, even now.

Anthony moved a rag across the grill of her Cadillac. Squinting through the approaching dusk he glimpsed her in the center green, her fancy dress fluttering as she hopped to her feet. Unbelievably, she dragged a park bench to the curb, directly across the street from the Gas & Go. Grunts and choice words accompanied the effort. How a woman her age managed to haul a wrought iron bench, he couldn't fathom. She sat back down to throw black looks.

Hurling down the rag, he cupped his hands to his mouth. "I'm done, all right? You've got the patience of a three year old! You hear me, Theodora?"

Her silk-encrusted shoulders rippled with anger. Then she flipped him the bird.

Anthony spun on his heel. *Women.* They made no sense.

Theodora, begging him to work on her car then badgering him. Blossom, stealing tickets and destroying the banquet. Mary, luring him in then announcing she was packing her bags. He'd had it with the lot of them.

Muttering a curse, he flung Theodora's car keys on the Cadillac's driver seat and stalked into the Gas & Go.

No wonder he couldn't concentrate. Women needled a man's emotions until he couldn't think. Already today he'd misplaced his favorite socket wrench, forgotten an oil change and growled at Blossom and Snoops when they'd foolishly appeared at the garage to say hello.

He'd slapped a ten-note on the workbench, glad when they'd grabbed the cash and slunk away. They were at Tyler's house, avoiding him for the rest of the day.

Smart kids.

On the workbench, the phone rang. Picking up, he jotted down an appointment for a brake job with testy impatience. Outside tires squealed. The acrid scent of burnt rubber hit his nostrils. Theodora's Cadillac roared into the street.

The smoke cleared, and he rolled his eyes with disgust. Finney barreled through the waning daylight in a direct path for the gas station. Just his luck.

If ancient Theodora flipping him the bird wasn't weird enough, Finney had her beat. Brown sauce covered her apron. Something—spinach?—stuck in a messy glop on her chin. In her fist, a wooden spoon bobbed as she marched forward. All she was missing was her intimidating skillet.

"Do something to fix this," she said by way of greeting. "I'm not up to babysitting a grown woman."

A second phone call, and he gritted his teeth. He yanked up the receiver then slammed it down. "Go away," he said with the last of his patience. "I'm having a bad day."

Finney paused by the double doors. "What's your problem?"

"Problems, as in plural. They're none of your business."

"Don't get sassy with me. Why, you look like you could bite someone's head off."

"Don't tempt me."

The cook went silent. Ridiculously, she lifted her dukes. "You want a battle? Bring it on. I can go ten rounds, seeing that

Mary's already got me at wit's end."

"I don't fight women." He found his coffee mug on the workbench and drained the last cold gulp. "What do you want?"

Approaching, she planted her feet. She was a good eight inches shorter. Even so, he moved back. Given his recent batting average with women, he was taking no chances.

Finney smacked the wooden spoon against her thigh and he flinched. "Mary talked to the mayor this afternoon," she revealed.

Concerned, he ditched his irritation and found compassion. "And?"

"She wouldn't explain. So we argued. Who would've guessed Mary has a temper like a West Coast forest fire when you get her going? The tears were worse, though."

Tears? What had the mayor said to upset Mary? With effort, he squashed his concern. For once, he wouldn't play the role of Mr. Fix-it. "Finney, I know better than to get between two women if they're fighting. You and Mary have a problem? Fix it yourselves."

"You aren't listening." She whacked her thigh again and he jumped back. "Mary was so upset, she dropped a platter of my beautiful trout on the floor. My trout! Ten minutes later, she ran clean into Delia. Knocked right into her like a Mack truck overturning on the highway. Now Delia's taking orders with a fat lip. You've got to get to the bottom of it!"

"I do?" *Like hell.*

"She's not herself. Dropping china, spilling coffee all over the counter. I was by the stove and she bumped me so hard, I hit the flames. Pulled back before I torched myself."

She thumped on her abundantly endowed chest. He spotted black singe marks over her breasts. *For the love of—*

"Mary's still upset?" The urge to protect her grew strong. "What am I supposed to do?"

"Talk to her."

"Pass."

"Talk to her or I'll kill you." The cook emphasized the threat by whacking him on the chest with her spoon. He yelped, and she added, "I've got orders to rustle up and she's not fit for polite company. I sent her to her room. Delia tiptoed up there and heard crying. Go talk to Mary. Make her feel better."

Finney sent Mary to her room? Mary's apartment, he recalled, was above the restaurant.

How did one woman order another to go upstairs, like a grounding he'd give to his kid? Tricky, that. Once he'd seen his brother Nick order his wife around. For an entire week Liza kept him in an icy hell.

Given her banishment, Mary was probably livid. No sane man went near a woman stewing in her own juices. Not if he planned to keep his most cherished body parts. *Oh, hell!*

Sure he was making a mistake, Anthony rolled his shoulders and put on his game face. "Lead the way," he growled. "No guarantees. All I can do is try to settle her down."

Finney thumped him again with the spoon. "You're a good man," she said. "Just make sure to stitch her back together."

The door to the apartment hung ajar. Moving boxes flooded the living room like the debris brought in by the tides. Most were taped shut, in as pristine a condition as they'd been upon arrival from Cincinnati. Only a few were open, the contents scavenged and balls of packing newspaper strewn before them.

Anthony squinted in the dim light. A blanket hung over the window's curtain rod. Dust spun through the air. He spotted the one immaculate spot in the room, a pretty end table in the corner. On the polished surface, gold-framed photographs encircled a neat arrangement of magazines.

The arrangement was a shrine in the shadowy room. Gently, he picked up a magazine—no, a medical journal. He hesitated. All the magazines were medical journals. Did the good doctor keep up on her reading after sixteen-hour shifts at the restaurant?

Considering her dedication brought a memory of the day he'd first met Blossom's oncologist and his staff. How Dr. Lash had made jokes to put Anthony at ease. The heavyset black nurse, Tessa, watched him closely as Lash revealed the diagnosis that sent Anthony's life on a frightening journey. *Mr. Perini, your daughter has cancer.* When Anthony's legs buckled, Tessa had swiftly come forward, grasping him around the waist and settling him into a chair.

So many people at St. Barnabas had carried him through the

most difficult years of his life. Blossom was too young to comprehend the horrors awaiting her but he'd approached her treatment with full knowledge. Once, when he wept in the corridor during her chemo session, Dr. Lash appeared with news of a win by the Cleveland Indians. Despite the duties that crammed his day, he hung around discussing pitching techniques and upcoming games to keep his patient's father occupied. A few weeks later, when the last of Blossom's hair fell out, Tessa bought his daughter a Hermes scarf. Other nurses, whose names were lost from memory, had comforted his child with gifts of board games and other toys.

Mary's one of them—a healer. No wonder he was drawn to her.

With exquisite care, Anthony brought the largest frame off the table and studied the handsome faces of a man and a woman. Mary's parents? Another picture showed the couple again, this time with a pubescent Mary standing between them. Fat-cheeked and solemn, she wore an elementary school graduation gown.

He began to return the photograph to the table. Instinct stopped him. He studied it again, running his fingers around a frame free of dust and glinting in the diminished light. Where was her high school graduation photo? Or the one from med school? In a room steeped in dust, this small treasure was the only photograph of its kind. He held it close, frowning. Worried now, he spotted the narrow hallway and went down it.

"Mary?"

The hallway was a tube of blackness. He paused to let his eyes adjust.

In the tiny bathroom, towels littered the floor. The shower lacked a curtain. The sink looked like it hadn't been cleaned in a decade.

He came out with the photograph still clutched in his hand. "Mary, where are you?"

"I'm here."

Following her voice, he found a bedroom dominated by a four-poster bed of dark walnut. Little else was in evidence, just the depressing clutter of moving boxes. Blankets covered the bed in a rumpled mess. Mary sat on the edge with her hands in her lap.

From below, Finney rattled around the restaurant's kitchen. Late afternoon light crept through the shuttered window, a knife-thin band of gold. The air was thick with the scent of roses—Mary's perfume, which he'd grown to love. The sorrow on her face brought him to a standstill.

He held up the photograph. "Your parents?"

She waved half-heartedly at the photograph. "Dad was a doctor, Mom a nurse."

"And Mary makes three."

She ran her fingers through the tangled mess of her hair. "They wanted more kids but there wasn't enough money. Small-town doctors struggle."

The barest facts of her life remained a mystery. He hungered to learn more.

"Where did you grow up?" he asked.

"Marion. Small town outside Columbus." Emotion whispered across her features. "I'm taking over Abe's practice sooner than expected."

"Abe runs the free clinic?"

"He's like a second father." She pressed her palms flat to her knees as if her sense of herself had become vaporous. "His daughter was my best friend—also a doctor."

Anthony nodded. "Finney told me about your friend." She looked raw with emotion but he couldn't resist asking, "You're leaving soon?"

"Abe's health isn't good."

"I'm sorry."

"The clinic is fine, short term. Several doctors at Cinci General are covering."

"You'll go back to run the place?"

"It's the largest free clinic in Southern Ohio. My pay won't be much, but at least it'll make a dent in my college loans. You wouldn't believe what I owe for medical school." Absently she brushed a tendril of hair from her forehead. "I need a manager for the restaurant. It might take time to find and train my replacement but I *am* leaving."

"I hate to see you go," he said in a conversational tone that belied the pain shifting through his chest. He thought of something else. "What about Finney? Can she run The Second

Chance?"

Swiping at her eyes, Mary looked up. "I don't think she's interested. Who can blame her? It's a big job."

"I'll bet she'd take over if you stuck around, for guidance." When she looked at him, impatient, he let it go. "She's worried about you. Will you be all right?"

Her smile bloomed with sorrow. "I should go back downstairs."

"Finney won't allow it."

"Guess that's why I'm still here."

"You need to get some of this off your chest," he said, shifting the photo from hand to hand. "Talk to me."

She did, in a light, rambling voice. He listened as she told of Abe mentoring her and his daughter Sadie through the grueling years of their residency. How he delighted in the prospect of handing over the clinic to his favorite women doctors as soon as they were ready for the responsibility. She talked of the horrible weeks after Sadie died, and the surprising gift of the restaurant. The part about Theodora greasing the transaction—well, he wasn't surprised. Theodora was forever complaining about how Liberty needed a doctor.

When she'd finished, he asked, "How bad is Abe's heart?"

"Tomorrow he goes in for more tests. He'll get the results quickly."

She's leaving soon. "The other doctors? They'll handle the patients until you arrive?"

"Everyone knows I can't move back immediately. They've heard I inherited a restaurant." She pinioned him with hollowed eyes and his sorrow became excruciating. "How will I tell Blossom? She'll be so disappointed. I thought I'd have more time with her. A year, maybe. I didn't think—"

She doubled over, sobbing. He pressed her to his side, stroking the curved bow of her back and whispering endearments like he'd done a million times with Blossom, whenever she was hurt or scared.

Afterward he handed over the rag in his back pocket. It smelled of engine grease but she didn't notice. She rubbed her eyes and blew her nose. While she pulled herself together he found her purse and shoes.

CHAPTER 14

"You're taking the rest of day off," he decided, steering her to her feet, "and coming home with me."

Chapter 15

Shadows cradled the houses on North Street. The breeze rustled the canopy of leaves spread like welcoming arms above the ribbon of sidewalk. From her vantage point on the wide front porch, Mary watched the sun sink beneath the treetops.

From inside the house, Blossom called, "Dinner's almost ready."

Mary had stopped short of agreeing to stay for the meal. She needed to call Finney, ask how they'd managed the dinner rush. She was still putting off the call.

On the other side of the screen door, Blossom appeared. "Are you hungry?" she asked.

"Actually, I am," Mary admitted.

"Dad's making something great. You'll see."

Unsure of how to let the girl down, she simply nodded. Blossom ducked out of sight.

Head bowed, Mary turned back to the approaching night. In the hours since Anthony had insisted she come home with him, both he and Blossom had given her ample space. He'd disappeared at dusk as she dozed on the living room couch, returning quickly with two bags of groceries. Blossom had produced a game board and checkers, and announced they'd play a few rounds.

They'd played checkers until half an hour ago. Mary assumed contact with Blossom would be an agony—both the mayor's warning and her imminent departure weighed heavily on her mind—but she'd been mistaken. She felt better now, as if the day's events had drained her of all hope and Blossom's laughter had replenished her soul.

With misgiving she returned to her appraisal of the street. She needed to tell Anthony about the upsetting conversation with Mayor Ryan. She dreaded embarking on the conversation. And Blossom? Learning she couldn't stay at the restaurant constantly seemed a cruel disappointment. Especially now— soon she'd learn Mary was leaving.

Angry, Mary leaned heavily against the porch railing. Well, anger was better than sorrow, wasn't it? She didn't want to leave Liberty, not yet. She'd only lived here a few months. A full year away from medicine with time enough to heal her heart . . . wasn't that what she'd expected? She hadn't factored Blossom into her plans or how much she'd grow to care for the girl.

She paused to consider a second peril: she was at risk of falling in love with Anthony. If there'd been more time, if their relationship had received the opportunity to grow, she could've easily fallen for him.

On a wave of apprehension, she entered the house.

Slipping off her tennis shoes, she placed them alongside Blossom and Anthony's sneakers, tucked together by the front door. Blossom strolled into the foyer.

"Smells good in here," Mary said. "What's your dad making?"

Sweetcakes trotted up and Blossom knelt to rub her nose against the dog's snout. "See for yourself."

"I should go home."

"Don't start that again, okay? Dad's stubborn. If he says you're staying for the night, you're staying."

Sweetcakes trotted behind Mary's back, grabbed something and dashed off. "Honestly, it's getting late—"

"Dad's right. You worry too much." Blossom splayed her hands, the gesture adding maturity to her face. "Can't you just *relax?*"

"Sometimes." Mary rubbed her palms down her jeans. Leaving was harder than anticipated. "How 'bout we play another round of checkers? Then I'll get out of the way so you and your dad can eat."

"You're not in the way, and you're staying for dinner. It's an

Italian thing. We never send friends into the world on an empty stomach."

"Let me think about it . . ."

"No. Promise you'll eat with us *and* spent the night."

"All right! I'll stay ... for now." She eyed Sweetcakes. The dog had returned with something familiar hanging from her mouth. "Hey, that's my tennis shoe." She lunged in an unrewarded effort to free the shoe from Sweetcake's teeth. "Give it back!"

Sweetcakes angled out of reach, her butt quivering with canine delight. Blossom's dog was darling *and* rotten to the core.

She glared at the dog, bobbing her shoe up and down as if tempting her to reach for the goods. "Of all the silly—"

"You'll have to say please." Blossom plopped down on the floor between Mary and the scoundrel with the shoe. "Sweetcakes will give it back if you do."

"You've got to be kidding."

"I'm serious."

"She's serious," Anthony confirmed, sauntering in. He wiped his hands on the dishtowel he carried.

"You're a human who's been trained to beg," she told Anthony. "A human, by the way, who's begging a dog instead of the other way around. Who in their right mind teaches a dog to respond to *please?*"

He stuffed the dishtowel in the back pocket of his jeans. "When Blossom thought up the 'please' thing it seemed funny. Now it's just humiliating."

Blossom got to her feet. "*I* think it's funny."

Anthony poked her in the ribs. "Sicko." He bent to the dog. "Sweetcakes, please."

The retriever came, sat, and lifted its snout. As soon as Anthony took hold of the tennis shoe, Sweetcakes bounded from the foyer.

"Here." He dropped the shoe into Mary's outstretched hand. "If you insist on running around in socks, I can't be held responsible. And you're not leaving. You're staying for dinner and sleeping here tonight."

Stay the night? Anthony wasn't inoculated against falling in love. She wasn't either. Spending excessive time together put them both in contact with the pesky pathogen. Far better to run for the hills.

"Look, I appreciate your hospitality," she said. "Now I have to go. Finney probably needs Valium by now."

Anthony pinched the sides of his nose. "Like we've told you—Finney's on top of it. Ethel Lynn came in to help her."

"I can't imagine."

"Me, either. There'll be blood on the walls." He gave her shoulder a squeeze and fixed her with a look so tender, she felt her resolve melting. "It's best if you stay. You've had enough surprises for one day. Watching Finney and Ethel Lynn tear each other apart won't bolster your mood."

She was about to reply when Sweetcakes bounded back into the foyer. "Hey! That's my other shoe!"

A grin tugged at Anthony's lips. "Sweetcakes, please."

"Thanks." She took the offered shoe, her face flushing beneath his roving gaze. She really did need a vaccination. The way he eyed her would make *any* woman feverish. "I should get back to work."

His smile faded. "You're staying. I've already made up your room."

"Which is where, exactly?"

"Upstairs next to the master."

Next to the master bedroom? She swallowed hard.

Her sense of control eroding, she chose to focus on the savory aromas of roasted garlic and sweet basil drifting into the foyer. Relenting, she trailed Anthony and Blossom to the kitchen.

She paused to appreciate the well-designed space. Lots of work still needed to be done but there was a gorgeous butcher-block center island, miles of oak cupboards and a peach-hued stone on the floor that looked like it had been quarried in the heart of Italy.

She could live in this room. Pitch a tent and stay for the rest of her life. All that was missing were houseplants and an herb garden in front of the majestic windows framing the sink.

She seated herself at the table. "What's cooking?"

At the oven, Anthony yanked foil off a casserole. "Veggie lasagna, a Perini favorite. It's loaded with zucchini."

"We both love zucchini," Blossom chimed in, sliding onto a chair with her dog following close behind.

"Hey!" Mary grabbed for Sweetcakes and just missed a shuddering hank of fur. "Is that the hairbrush from my purse? I don't believe this!"

"You'll have to say please," Blossom and Anthony said as one voice.

She'd had enough. Her shoes. Her hairbrush.

She trained her eyes on the quivering, devilish dog—

And leapt toward the beast.

Anthony patted the lump on Mary's brow with the bag of ice he'd made. "We should've warned you—Sweetcakes is greased lightning," he said.

They were seated on the back steps as the three-acre yard turned inky beneath the stars. Inside, Blossom continued to wolf down the lasagna while he gladly remained outside with one fiery and amusing damsel in distress.

Mary grimaced as he moved the ice across her forehead. "It's not my fault," she said. "I didn't mean to run into the wall. I had no idea your dog could turn on a dime."

"Naturally," he said. "It's like the door in your restaurant. You know—the one that leapt out and bit you the night chaos reigned at The Second Chance."

She jerked back. "Don't press so hard." She glared at the bag of ice then him.

"It's ice, not Chinese water torture. It'll help."

"Stupid dog."

"We explained the code regarding Sweetcakes in some detail. We'd have let you in on our secret handshake too, if you'd asked." Anthony grabbed her arm, stilled her, and planted the ice on her forehead. "But no. Did you listen, muchacha?"

A squeak of pain popped from her lips. "Why do you and Blossom do that?"

"Do what?"

"The inane Spanish."

"What's the big deal?"

"It's a romance language. Show some respect for the beauty of the language."

Wow. Was there a woman prettier than Mary Chance when

she got on her soapbox? Her eyes sparked fire he'd damn well like to play in.

Instead he focused on the reality of his kid nearby, plowing through a jumbo-sized lasagna.

High romance this wasn't.

"I'm not sure why we're hooked on Spanish." The words were barely out when the memory jogged his mind. He marched right into it. "Wait. It was the cartoon with the Mexican gunslinger. Blossom watched the show all the time when she was bedridden. The chemo really knocked her out."

Affection warmed Mary's eyes. "You bastardized Spanish to amuse her? To take her mind off the pain?"

Anthony's brows lifted. That *had* been his rationale. "Hard enough being a kid," he said, needing to share the memory. "Imagine you're in elementary school. The biggest problem? Your shoes don't fit because you're in a growth spurt. Then you get knocked over the head with leukemia . . . which, by the way, Blossom confused with bulimia."

"You're kidding." Mary attempted to match his conversational tone despite the moisture gathering in her eyes.

"An older girl at school had bulimia. Blossom knew all about it. We'd head down to St. Barnabas for another session of chemo and she'd be desperately serious. 'Dad, I swear I never throw up food. I love your cooking. Take me home and I'll eat anything you want.' Took her a long time to come to terms with her prognosis." His mouth twisted. "Me, too."

"Oh, Anthony." She bumped her shoulder in a show of support.

Dismissing the memory before it tore through him, he asked, "Does it bother you? The goofy Spanish?"

"Of course not. It's darling."

He liked the way sincerity pursed her lips, her mouth becoming fuller, more kissable. "Different is okay," he said, scooting closer. She'd relaxed beneath the bag of ice and his gentle ministrations. "Variety being the spice of life and all."

"Sure."

He appraised her closely. "What was it like having a doctor and a nurse for parents?" he asked.

"Nice ... most of the time." She shrugged. "My father's

patients always came before our home life. Of course, my mother went along. I learned how to help around the office, answering calls from patients and refilling the supplies in the exam room. That sort of thing."

"How old were you?"

"When I started helping? Oh, I'm not sure. Eight or nine."

"Sounds like a lonely childhood."

Her gaze skittered away so quickly, his heart squeezed. "I didn't have many friends, not with all the time I spent working. But it was all right. Well, until my parents died."

"You've lost them both?"

"A long time ago." The bag leaked a rivulet of water down Mary's temple unnoticed. "They died within weeks of each other. I was in high school. Sadie's parents took me in."

"What happened?"

"For years Dad struggled with high blood pressure. Sudden coronary. Living without him wasn't on Mom's agenda. Seventeen days after his funeral, she died in her sleep. The autopsy found a congenital valve defect. I knew better. She died of a broken heart."

"I'm sorry."

Mary took the bag from his grasp and tossed it on the grass. "No need to apologize." She offered a brave smile that didn't reach her eyes. "They had one of those rare marriages, love and devotion 24/7. As much as I grieved, I was glad they'd scheduled the trip to heaven together."

Needing to provide comfort, he rubbed her back. Instinct stopped him from enfolding her into his arms. Intuition suggested there was more to the story.

Prodding her on, he said, "Nice sentiment, although losing your parents must've been rugged. How did you manage?"

"Sadie and her parents were angels." She hugged her knees and began rocking. "Abe scheduled a family vacation after my mother's funeral. He took all of us to the Bahamas. Sadie and I walked the beach for hours. I never would've survived without something—someone—to hang onto."

The sweetest wish lodged in his brain. *Hang onto me.* "They sound like good people."

"The best. When Sadie died, I felt like I'd switched places

with Abe and Jillian."

"They clung to you to get through the loss."

"They lost one daughter. I'm all they have left."

"So you'll continue the clinic for Abe. His life's work." Moved by the disclosure, he rested his palm on her shoulder. "You *are* a good daughter."

"I hope so."

"You deserve gold stars all around," he added, worried by the tearful notes in her voice. If he didn't lighten the mood, she'd fall apart. Watching her suffer was unbearable. She strived to lead an honorable life. "Come to think of it, Blossom has art crap all over her bedroom. We'll make an award for most devoted daughter."

Sniffling, she bumped his shoulder again. "You and Blossom are the best."

"Yeah, but you think we're weird. The way we screw up foreign languages and all." He studied her, suddenly serious. "*Do you think we're weird?*" He'd spent years chumming around with his kid and her buddies. Suave, he wasn't. "If you find it offensive, we won't corrupt foreign languages in your presence."

"I love everything about you and Blossom, including the humor you share. When I leave, I'll miss you both."

"Then don't go. Stay."

"I can't disappoint Abe."

"Then we'll have a long-distance romance. Couples do all the time."

More sniffles but she flashed a grin. "We can't commute from one end of Ohio to the other. There won't be any time to *see* each other."

So that was it? They'd give up? "All right," he replied, his throat tight. He *did* see her logic. "We have are a few weeks, maybe a few months. Let's build a lifetime's worth of memories until you find someone to manage The Second Chance."

She trailed her fingers down his cheek, scuttling his heartbeat. "I'd like that," she replied.

Mary's heart wheeled as he cupped her face and gently steered her lips to his. *Make it count.* She let the heartache die beneath the desire increasing her pulse. *So little time.* He kissed her fully and she arched against him. She needed the comfort of his embrace, the press of his body to hers. They didn't have much time. She'd cherish every moment.

Inside the house, Sweetcakes barked.

The possibility of canine intrusion and a curious adolescent nudged Anthony to his feet. "C'mon." He helped her up. "Let's walk. You've never seen the backyard. More than three acres back there."

Shadows formed a patchwork on the grass. The trees dotting the property were dark watchmen on the sloping hills. The cloudless sky revealed a scattering of stars.

She tripped over a tree root bulging from the earth. "Slow down. We'll get lost in the dark." He steadied her and she added, "I can't see where I'm going."

"You're safe. I won't let go."

His bat-like vision provided comfort, as did his fingers twined through hers. His grip tightened, the gesture territorial and protective. Her pulse leapt into a gallop.

When they paused beneath a maple tree far into the yard, she gratefully leaned against the trunk. The bark felt cool against her fevered skin. The inky night enveloped Anthony's shoulders, but she glimpsed heat in his expression.

"I'd like to make love to you," he murmured, trailing fingers down her neck in a pleasurable quest.

"Is that an invitation to sneak into your room tonight?" After Blossom went to bed they'd have time to themselves.

"My daughter will be out for the count by eleven o'clock." He nipped her earlobe. "I need to run to the drugstore. Keep her entertained while I'm gone."

"You don't have condoms in the house?"

He chuckled. "Mary, I haven't been seeing anyone. Certainly not Meade, if that's what you're asking."

"I don't mean to pry."

So Finney was correct. Anthony hadn't dated in a long time. Which meant he hadn't enjoyed sex in a long time. Desire spiked through her brain. *I haven't either.*

They'd never sleep tonight.

He regarded the loopy amusement on her face. "What's so

funny?" He closed in, backing her against the tree. The way he crowded her was very male, increasing her desire.

She flattened her palm to his chest. "I'm not on the pill. You *will* need to make a trip to the drugstore."

"I'll take care of it." He nibbled on the tender skin above her collarbone. "I'm happy to take care of it."

She angled her neck to give him room to explore. The rough bristle of his chin grazed her skin and she gasped. On a moan, he crushed her against the tree. The sound of his urgency threatened to dissolve her knees. He folded her tightly into his embrace.

Far across the yard, the back door swung open. Spotlights blinked on, flinging away the darkness. Like criminals caught in a prison break, they froze.

A second later they leapt apart.

Blossom raced down the steps. "Hey, I've got a great idea!" Spotting them, she sprinted across the yard. A long cardboard box joggled beneath her arm. "Dad, you'll never guess what I found. The *Risk* game."

Incredibly, Anthony located a casual tone. "I thought we'd lost it."

"Me, too."

For a heart-stopping moment, he planted his molten gaze on Mary. Then he pivoted away.

There was something admirable about a man capable of moving from sexual desire to cool sanity in a flash. Wryly, Mary wondered why she wasn't as poised. Her heart continued to flutter and her legs felt like jelly. If not for Blossom running toward them, she would've sunk to the grass in a desire-infused stupor.

The more responsible Anthony met his daughter at the lawn's midway point.

"I thought you and Snoops lost the *Risk* board," he said in a conversational voice that belied the lust swimming in his blood.

Blossom held up the box. "Found it under the couch. Must've kicked it underneath when we were playing *Nerf* basketball. Tyler loves *Nerf*."

"You're not allowed to play basketball in the living room, *Nerf* or otherwise." He tousled her curls. "How many times have we discussed this?"

She skirted past. "Do you like *Risk*?" she asked Mary. "I promise to give you a fighting chance before demolishing your armies."

"Sure." Mary tried to slow her pulse, and failed. She was still hot enough to bake a potato on her forehead. "Whatever you want."

"Great! After that, Dad'll stop bugging us. He never stays awake past eleven. He'll go to bed and we can paint our toenails."

Mary plastered on fake joy. "Girl pedicures—wonderful!" She imagined Anthony in bed waiting for her. Waiting to nibble on her toes, or . . .

"Yeah, we'll do a salon night. I have some really cool stuff I got for Christmas last year."

Despite Mary's best efforts, lusty thoughts intruded. *Christmas*. She'd unwrap him like a present. Crawl into his bed and . . .

Guilt squashed the fantasy. How could she think about intimacy when the mischievous preteen would soon learn of her departure to Cincinnati?

Shame on me.

She slung her arm across the kid's shoulders. "I can't wait to see all your salon stuff."

"I'll paint your toes and you'll do mine."

"Sounds cool," she replied, aping Blossom's enthusiasm. Peering over the girl's head, she regarded Anthony.

And bit back a laugh.

So much for faking a relaxed demeanor in front of your child. That was pure and unadulterated pain on his face.

Chapter 16

At daybreak, Mary wrote the Perinis a thank you note then tiptoed out.

Although a night of lovemaking never came to pass, they'd shared a wonderful evening playing the board game *Risk* until a chortling Blossom destroyed their armies and took over the world.

Throughout the game, Anthony and Blossom wore WWI pith helmets they'd found in an antique shop. Blossom dashed down to Tyler's house, returning with his childhood cowboy hat, vest, holster and guns. Mary eagerly donned the costume. Later, she remained in cowboy garb as Blossom munched Pop Tarts and they painted each other's toenails in the girl's bedroom.

The evening would've been perfect if Mary hadn't been riddled with nerves. In a brief moment alone, Anthony made clear he didn't want to ruin his daughter's summer vacation by telling her about the free clinic awaiting Mary in Cincinnati. Worse still, an opportunity to tell him about the conversation with Mayor Ryan never arrived. She resolved to stop by the Gas & Go today to fill him in.

Light crested over the buildings of Liberty Square. Parking in back of the building, Mary wondered if Anthony would limit his daughter's visits once he learned of the mayor's warning. No matter his decision, she'd soften the blow—starting with the shopping trip to the mall. For Blossom's sake, she'd make every day they shared a happy one.

Mary went inside and began organizing the day's menu. She gave the dining room a quick cleaning. By the time the others appeared for work, the place was spotless. Afterward she was too busy to worry.

On this beautiful Saturday in June, the restaurant was mobbed.

The balmy weather brought people out in droves. A line of waiting customers wove out the door. An hour after the day's produce arrived, Finney called in a second order. Two hundred Grade A Extra Large eggs were delivered in the second shipment.

Mary lost count of the number of omelets they whipped up. The cash register never stopped ringing

And to think, the lunch rush lay ahead. She wiped her brow as Finney finished a call on her cell.

"Who was it?" she asked, refilling the dishwasher.

"My daughter, Marla. She's rounding up friends to help Delia and Ethel Lynn wait tables." The cook filled a glass with water and guzzled it down.

"Thanks for calling them in."

"Marla and her friends are happy to work. They'll stay until closing." Finney walked to the pass-through window with another order. "Whenever we *do* close." She glanced over her shoulder, at Mary. "Guess who just came in?"

Mary peered through the window, her emotions plummeting. Blossom and Anthony elbowed their way through the crowd. Clearly the discussion she'd avoided would take place sooner than expected. "What's she doing here? She's supposed to be at the water park with Snoops and Tyler."

Finney gave a look of puzzlement. "Aren't you glad to see her?"

She explained about the mayor's threat. Summing up, she added, "Meade lodged the complaint. I'll happily string her up for making trouble."

"I'd help." Finney gave her a push. "Go. Bring the child down gently. Tell her you feel awful, but she can't spend every free minute here."

"Oh, Finney. I don't want to hurt Blossom."

The cook scowled. "Get out there. Say *something* to the child."

≈

Dancing through the aisles between tables, Blossom handed out flags by the dozen.

Mary grabbed the coffee pot and refilled cups all the way down the counter. She was stalling, she knew. Anthony came behind the counter, moving with the slow, sexy gait that heated her blood even though her heart ached.

He gave her a peck on the forehead. "Where do you want me? Behind the counter or out on the floor?"

"You're helping?" They *were* desperately short staffed.

"For an hour or so." He nodded toward the center green. "My brother, Nick, is manning the phone at the Gas & Go while I pitch in. He's grousing about a golf game with his pals. Personally, I think your business is more important than eighteen holes."

There wasn't time to thank him. Delia seated Mayor Ryan and several members of the town council at a table directly in front of the counter. The mayor appraised Blossom, dashing from table to table with an armload of flags. She gave Mary a pointed look.

Anthony caught the interchange. "Mind telling me what's going on?"

She gave a brief summary of the conversation in the mayor's office. By the time she'd finished, his features had turned to stone.

"I've had it with Meade." He yanked his cell from his jeans.

Mary clasped his wrist, stopping him. "The damage is already done."

"Are you kidding? She caused the damage!"

"Please don't call Meade. She's throwing her weight around because she has the power to do so. Don't make this worse than it is."

His resolve slipping, he slid the phone into his pocket. Together, they regarded Blossom.

"Let's get this over with," he said grimly. "I'll tell her."

"No, I should. She'll be furious with me for buckling under the mayor's threats."

Anthony hooked a lock of her hair behind her ear. "She'll be upset, but this isn't your fault." He brushed her lips with a reassuring kiss. "She's my daughter. I'll take care of it."

Without a glance he strode past the mayor. Air locked painfully in Mary's lungs as he tapped Blossom on the shoulder. He led her to a corner of the noisy dining room. Blossom's expression cartwheeled through a series of emotions: curiosity, surprise—

Anger.

Anthony placed his hand on her shoulder. She shrugged him off. Despair swamped Mary as Blossom spun around. Their gazes locked.

Severing the connection, Blossom threw down the flags and walked out.

Chapter 17

In the two weeks since Blossom had stormed out of the restaurant, Mary only caught fleeting glimpses of her strolling through the center green with Tyler and Snoops.

Whenever Anthony stopped in, he'd assure Mary that his daughter would calm down. Never did he ask if she'd begun the search for the restaurant's new manager. Nor did he allude to their fleeting moment of passion on the night of the *Risk* game. In an unspoken agreement, they suppressed their attraction.

The Fourth of July came and went. Customers packed The Second Chance from morning to night. When Mary took a break from waiting tables or helping Finney in the kitchen, she phoned Abe. He was doing reasonably well on the medications his cardiologist had prescribed. Several doctors from the hospital would continue pitching in at the free clinic until she found a manager for the restaurant.

A hundred convenient excuses allowed her to put off the search for her replacement at The Second Chance, and the thought of leaving without mending her relationship with Blossom was difficult to bear. Not that she could stall forever on either count.

One balmy morning in late July, Anthony said, "Find a way to thaw her out tomorrow."

She flipped the OPEN sign. His appearance at first light was heartening.

She went to the coffee station. "What's going on tomorrow?"

She placed a cup before him.

"A barbecue at my house. Family and friends."

"A big party?"

"My parents, brother and sisters. Spouses and the kids, of course. Relatives, mostly." He hesitated. "A few of my neighbors will stop by. Hopefully my friend will too."

"I'm the friend?" When his eyes twinkled, she murmured, "I don't know, Anthony."

Since her falling out with Blossom, she hadn't seen him for more than a few minutes each day. His absence had filled her with longing. She wanted to feel his arms around her again and share a few private moments. Silly, true, since they both knew she was leaving. Besides, it was increasingly difficult to remain sensible given his sweet change of tactics.

Anthony had begun to romance her.

She'd received a variety of gifts: a dozen red roses, a lavish vase of lilies, and a box of chocolates. Godiva chocolates.

Now he was suggesting she 'meet the parents'.

"I shouldn't attend a family gathering." Doing so meant they were taking their relationship up a notch, a foolish choice. Instead of mentioning how their time together would soon end, she voiced her other concern. "Blossom isn't finished giving me the cold shoulder. I haven't patched things up with your sidekick."

Reaching across the counter, he tilted up her chin. "I hate it when you're upset." He sat down, satisfied when her attention remained fixed on him. "Anyway, it's not just you. Blossom hasn't been herself for days. She's sleeping a lot. Some days she drags around the house and hardly talks. Probably a virus."

A twinge of worry darted through her. "You're sure?"

"She always catches a bug in the middle of summer. Snoops, too. They've been living on potato chips and late-night slumber parties."

"Should you bring her in to see Dr. Lash?"

"No worries. She has a check-up in ten days." Anthony brushed his knuckles across her wrist, and tingling pleasure coasted up her arm. "Come to the barbecue. I promise Blossom will be cordial. If she isn't, I'll cut off her social life, which I *should* do until she catches up on rest."

"Anthony—"

"You'll like my sister-in-law, Liza. She's an attorney. Smartest woman I know." Reconsidering, he grinned. "Second smartest woman."

"Thanks."

"Liza's married to Nick. Watch out for my older brother. We call him 'the mauler'."

The amusement on his features proved contagious. She laughed. "Why do you call him 'the mauler'?"

"He's affectionate in the extreme." Anthony leaned over the counter and nipped at her ear, sending desire through her blood. "Come to the barbecue."

She darted out of reach. "Your daughter is right. You *are* stubborn."

Steering the car onto River Street, Anthony went over his mental list of items purchased for the barbecue. He'd raced through the grocery store, filling a cart with ribs, chicken and all the trimmings. After dropping the supplies at home, he'd checked on Blossom—over at Tyler's for the afternoon. There was time for one more errand before returning to the Gas & Go.

Midway down the street, he flipped on the radio. For twenty seconds he sang at the top of his lungs. At the corner of River and Third he turned off the jazzy tune and zoomed into the drugstore's lot.

Inside, he roamed the aisles in search of inspiration. Convincing himself to be satisfied with a few months of romance wasn't easy, but he was trying. Buying gifts for a woman gave an unexpected thrill, something he'd never before experienced. The florist, Wanda, the UPS man, even Delia and Finney seemed eager to deposit his presents in The Second Chance before the pretty owner arrived for work. Deep down, he wondered if he was intent on using every trick in his arsenal to convince Mary to stay in Liberty.

Courting her was now an obsession. He resolved to do it right.

He'd buy a card, something sweet but not too serious. Drugstore chocolates were out. After the excursion into pricy

Legacy Village, he couldn't follow up Godiva chocolates with some caramel crap.

An iTunes gift card? Too adolescent. Cosmetics? Insulting. In Aisle Four, he loped past Theodora. She stood comparing a monstrous jar of glycerin suppositories with a discreet box of laxative pills.

The pills, appearing less life threatening, would've received his vote.

Shuddering, he strode past. Another mile and a half of aimless wandering brought him to the center of the drugstore. Card racks stood on both sides of the aisle. He selected one with a goofy drawing of a cartoon couple in mid-smack. Lord, he wanted to kiss Mary again. Their fleeting moments alone in his backyard sure hadn't kept him sated.

Racing from the thought of down and dirty necking, he walked to the back of the store. Near the drug counter with its line of hostile children and impatient adults, he spotted a music box in a discounted seasonal display. Desperate, he went to investigate.

Cheesy music box. Gray lacquer, with weird cherries stamped on top. The cherries looked like bombs set to explode. *With all my love—kaboom!* He returned it to the shelf.

Intrigued by the alluring scents, he moseyed up the aisle containing women's bath stuff. He picked up a bottle filled with a thick purple liquid. It looked like a champagne bottle. He'd promised himself not to buy anything too suggestive. The treacherous label read *Luxurious Bubble Bath.*

Luxurious.

Damn it.

He got the visual with no effort at all, an erotic image of Mary relaxing in one of those antique bathtubs, the kind of tub with claw feet. She had bubbles on her shoulders, a few on her breasts and absolutely no bubbles on her nipples. Which would be pink, no—they'd be red because he'd have been sucking on them, since he would've climbed into the tub with her.

Anthony shook off the vision like a man battling a grizzly bear. He hurled the bottle back onto the shelf, clattering glass in a humiliating crescendo of sound. Fleeing the seductive scent, he scrambled to the back of the store.

And nearly crashed into the macho display. His vision clearing, he gulped down air.

Aw, man.

The display rack brimmed with boxes of condoms.

When had he last *needed* condoms?

He didn't dare figure it out. The math was too painful.

Did it matter? He wasn't here to shop for rubbers. Mary had agreed to the barbecue, not a romp in his bed. He'd buy a card and another gift capable of holding its own in a fistfight with roses, Italian chocolates, and one damn fine vase of lilies.

But curiosity was a dangerous companion, and he reached into the rack. Black box, extra ribbed. The guy on the front stared over the woman's shoulder with smug superiority.

Bastard.

He picked up a second brand. Extra thin. Black box, green trim. He couldn't bring himself to analyze the guy's expression, envy being a deadly sin and all.

Third box. Nice royal blue. Fourth box? Rubbers in a whole bunch of bright colors. *For the love of—*

He and Mary could celebrate Mardi Gras in the privacy of his bedroom.

Anthony couldn't thwart the euphoria from messing with his grey matter. He picked up the box.

Grinning like the devil, he dodged Theodora and her horse-sized suppositories and shot to the cash register.

Chapter 18

Music thundered across the porch. Knocking harder, Mary allowed the thought crystallize.

This is a mistake.

Why show up at a family gathering? What was she thinking? Giving Anthony's family the impression she'd embarked on a romance with Mr. Fix-It would make her departure from Liberty more difficult.

She spun around, miserable with second thoughts.

The door hurtled open with a *crack!* Wood met plaster, and she nearly jumped out of her shoes. A stocky man not quite as tall as Anthony gave her the once-over. Appearing satisfied, he latched onto her wrist and hauled her inside.

"Liza," he shouted over the heads of the children streaming through the foyer, "Anthony's babe is here! She's damn attractive. Not as hot as you but a real find for our ugly boy."

"You must be Nick," Mary squeaked.

He wrenched her close, nearly toppling the cheesecake in her hands. "Who squealed? Listen babe, I never give my name to strangers."

A tot in red plaid scudded to a halt and gaped at her.

"I'm no one's 'babe'." The boy ran off, and she added, "Anthony and I are just friends."

"Sure you are. Explains why he's in the kitchen making barbecue sauce with an idiotic grin on his face."

Skirting the comment, she eased out of his clutches. "I can

see why your brother calls you the mauler."

"It's a lie."

"Oh, yeah?"

He grabbed the girl hovering by his hip and thrust her forward. "Tell her, Angela. Do I maul?" Before the child located her voice, he added, "She's one of my sister Anna's kids." Wisely the child dashed off, avoiding further manhandling. "Hey, come back! Say 'hi' to Uncle Anthony's babe!"

Mary tried to follow.

Yanking her close, Nick asked, "Are you Catholic?"

"Lapsed." Her cheeks warmed. "Well, not exactly. I joined the Liberty parish but don't often get to Mass."

"Shame on you." He brightened. "Training?"

"Jesuit."

"You're in." He screwed up his face, aping contemplative thought. "Okay. I'll give you an easy one. What year did the Roman Empire fall?"

"Can't recall." The hold on her shoulders tightened as she screwed on her thinking cap. "Name the Founding Father who edited Jefferson's draft of the Declaration of Independence."

"What kind of question is that? If you want to play, ask a real history question."

"That *is* a real history question."

He feigned insult. "You're killing me. The Declaration of Independence doesn't have anything to do with Italian history. Play fair."

A slender African American woman strolled in from the foyer. She wore a short linen dress of periwinkle blue that showed off model-perfect legs. "You're a sick man, Nick." She whacked him on the back. "Get off our guest."

The cheesecake wobbling, Mary stumbled from his clutches.

The woman offered a welcoming smile. "I'm Liza. How are you?"

"Better now. I couldn't breathe." Mary introduced herself then added, "I should pay you for getting the madman off me."

Liza rested her hands on her slender hips. "Honey, I'd never take your money. Anthony would forbid it."

On a mock growl, Nick grabbed his wife around the waist. "Anthony won't take her money, either. Perini men don't take advantage of their women." He nibbled on his wife's neck until, giggling, she threw him off. "We take other stuff, instead." He wiggled his brows at Mary. "Wanna meet our kids?"

Liza elbowed him into silence. "She'll meet Jordan, not the twins. Why frighten her? Let her meet your parents first. Lianna and Mario lend the rest of you a modicum of respectability."

From the kitchen, Anthony shouted, "I'll take her to meet Mom and Dad in a sec."

The crash of china followed. Had he dropped a platter on the floor?

Her pulse jumpy, Mary asked, "How many people did Anthony invite?" He'd described a small party. *Get out of here.*

The query stamped mirth in Nick's gaze. "Oh, Liza—she doesn't get it."

He faked a swoon against his chuckling wife. "Now you've done it," Liza said, her eyes sparkling with mirth. "He's going to give us the Italian routine."

"Italian routine?"

"How they love the world. Feed the world. Must be surrounded by dozens of people at every family function."

"Meaning Anthony invited a large crowd?"

"Everyone brings potluck but you don't want to get Nick or Anthony started about their big Italian hearts. It'll begin nice enough. By the end, they'll be doing Marlon Brando impressions from *The Godfather.*"

Anthony came into the foyer. "Telling our dark secrets?" He tugged Mary close. Despite her determination to remain aloof she melted into his arms. "Hey, there," he murmured, leaning in for a kiss.

Nick squeezed in between them. "Can I have a kiss, Mary?" He chortled when she batted him back. "C'mon, you two—no necking. There are children present."

Liza grinned. "Nick, you're the only child present." She regarded Anthony. "Let's go to the veranda to chat. We'll get acquainted then you can take Mary to meet the horde."

Relieved by the suggestion, Mary held out the cheesecake. "Where should I put this?"

Liza rushed forward. "I'll take it. Nick, go away. On second thought, run and fetch plates and forks."

"Yes, ma'am." He started toward the kitchen.

She grabbed him by the collar. "Tell the kids to turn the music down."

He bowed. "Sure, baby doll."

"Steer clear of Blossom. We'll never get rid of her if she finds out what Mary brought." Liza motioned Mary near, lowered her voice. "Cheesecake is in the dairy family. You know how Blossom loves dairy. For the best if we hide."

Mary's heart lurched. "We're safe," she replied glumly. "If Blossom knows I'm on the veranda, it's the last place she'll go."

While Mary cut generous slices of cheesecake, Anthony caught up on family gossip with Liza.

Watching the interchange, Mary's heart warmed. The subject of Blossom's leukemia came up, and Liza made a light-hearted joke about the thousands they'd all spent ensuring her remission—the entire family had pitched in. Mary's background gave her a good idea of just how expensive the fight had been. Insurance covered only so much. Catastrophic illness, like childhood cancer, took a heavy toll on the family wallet.

And not just Anthony's wallet. Liza and Nick had helped, too. So had his parents and his three sisters. The Perinis' combined effort to keep Blossom healthy sent something good through Mary's chest. *This is how people show love and devotion.*

Her gaze lingered on Anthony's profile as he chatted with his sister-in-law. She hadn't been prepared to meet a man like him. He was beautiful and strong. What would he look like at age forty? And older? Would his gorgeous crown of curls turn white, or soft grey?

Leaving the world she'd stumbled into seemed a hardship. The July sun caught his profile and she was grateful to savor the moment. Wasn't life all about timing? Sometimes everything clicked and you confidently put it all together. Other times? You took the puzzle and worked it out one piece at a time.

If only there were a way to work it out . . .

A teenager appeared in the doorway. He was more man than boy, with the unmistakable Perini nose and Liza's soulful brown eyes. Liza smiled.

"Hey, Jordan." She took his hand then regarded Mary. "My oldest."

Mary returned his bashful smile with a look of pleasure. She was about to introduce herself when he handed Anthony a slip of paper.

"Don't ask me what's wrong with Blossom," he remarked as Anthony unfolded the note. "She's upstairs with one of her friends. She's on the rag or something. She looks like shit."

Liza's brows shot up. "Jordan!"

The teenager rubbed his face. "Sorry." He motioned toward the note. "I don't know why she wrote it. Anyway, she doesn't look right."

A niggling sensation crept up Mary's spine. "What do you mean?"

"She looks sick."

Her worried gaze found Liza's. Together they turned to Anthony. He was scanning the note with disapproval.

"How *is* she doing?" Liza asked.

"Dr. Lash says she's doing great, but she's in deep water." Switching topics, he squeezed Mary's knee. "Let me apologize for my obnoxious kid and girls everywhere who become pubescent monsters in their eleventh year of life."

He handed over the note. Taking a deep breath, she read:

Father,

Please notify me when your friend has vacated the premises. Since she's staying for the barbecue, my supremo cousin Jordan has agreed to bring dinner to Tyler and me in my bedroom. We both want a side of ribs and Ty wants three ears of corn.

Since your friend is sticking around for the evening, I'm spending the night with Snoops.

Your favorite daughter,

Blossom

Mary handed back the note. "Blossom has nice penmanship." She tried to hide the hurt behind a chipper tone.

A muscle twitched in Anthony's jaw. "I'm going up there and grounding her. No friends, no movies, no sleepovers."

Liza snatched the note from his lap. She read quickly. "I'm going up," she announced. "This is rude in the extreme. Mary, for all of us, I apologize."

179

"Mom, wait." From his pocket, Jordan produced a second note. "Give the brat credit. She's smart enough to go to law school someday."

"I don't believe this." Liza thrust the note toward Anthony. "Jordan's right. After you punish your daughter, consider sending her to law school. She has a mind like a steel trap."

From over his shoulder, Mary scanned the second note. She had to laugh despite the hurt bounding into her chest:

Dearest, Most Loving Aunt Liza,

Don't come upstairs and bug me. I know you want to.

Your favorite niece,

Blossom

"Vote?" Mary held up her hand. "Forget Blossom and enjoy ourselves?"

Anthony and Liza raised their hands.

"The ayes have it," she said.

Who cared if a precocious preteen remained upstairs fomenting a one-kid rebellion? Maybe it was for the best. Mary knew she'd leave Liberty soon. Wasn't a clean break easier?

She frowned. Were breaks *ever* clean?

Chapter 19

Anthony launched up the stairs. If there were ever a time a gift came in handy, this was it.

Liza had escorted Mary to the backyard. Hopefully Mary was taking his kid's rejection well. Now he was glad for the opportunity to make it up to her.

At the landing on the second floor, he stalked past Blossom's bedroom. He quelled the urge to step inside and reprimand her for the obnoxious notes sent downstairs with Jordan. A suitable punishment would have to wait. Out of respect for Mary's wishes, he kept moving.

At the far end of the hallway, the master bedroom rested in shadow. French doors led out to a small, two-story deck trimmed with the same type of frilly woodwork adorning the front of the house. Looking out, he surveyed the crowd milling below. His sister Rennie manned the grill. His mother placed a bowl of green beans on one of the picnic tables. Between his family and folks from the neighborhood, he was entertaining a large crowd.

Returning to the task at hand, he retreated into the bedroom's cool spaces. First, the card. If Nick kept to the plan, he'd politely remove Mary's purse from her arm and offer to stow it. Later Anthony would slip the card inside.

Satisfied with phase one of the plan, he knelt before the bed. He slid out the hatbox he'd asked Liza to purchase yesterday.

A design of swirls and hearts covered the cream fabric. The juxtaposition of a modern design on such an old-fashioned, feminine item was attractive.

Count on Liza to make a statement.

He owed her one. He'd have to baby-sit her rotten twins or take them to the zoo. Hell, he owed her even more. She'd helped pick out the jewelry too.

Working off the hatbox's lid, he peered inside. The gift was supposed to be amusing—a large box with something small inside. Anthony lifted out the earrings. They were pinned to a tiny, satin pillow of the palest pink.

Tiny jewels dangled from chains so delicate they must have been woven by angels. The earrings were gold, 18 karat. Like Mary's heart.

Was proffering an expensive gift reckless in the extreme? They'd embarked on a romance with no real future. Did he actually believe a hurried courtship would change the outcome? He put the earrings back in the box and closed the lid. The risk he took with his heart filled him with trepidation. *I'll never forgive myself if I don't try.*

On the nightstand sat the bag from the drugstore.

Despite the urge to return downstairs and slip the hatbox into Mary's car, he opened the bag. He sat on the bed. On impulse, he dumped the contents onto the quilt.

Would the opportunity to make love to Mary ever arise? If he did, and he fell completely for her, how to survive the heartache when she did leave?

He needed to believe she'd stay, that his love possessed the power to alter the course of her life.

Waiting for intimacy was difficult. They'd missed the opportunity on the night of the *Risk* game. If Blossom hadn't interrupted, if his kid had chosen to bunk at Snoops' house, he would've made love to Mary beneath the star-studded sky.

With a rueful smile, he shoved the condoms back into the bag. He tossed the bag onto the bed. Picking up the hatbox, he walked out. Sweetcakes bounded near to nose his hip. He batted her away and she ran off.

Drawing from his musings, he muttered a curse. *Mary.* He'd gone upstairs to fetch her gift without introducing her to his parents first.

Faster, he sped down the hallway.

"Ty, stop it! That doesn't tickle—it hurts!"

Blossom's singsong-y voice drifted from her room. Oddly, the door was shut. Usually it hung ajar with junk trailing into the hallway.

He threw open the door. "What's going on in here?"

Shock lanced through him. He ground to a halt.

On the bed, Tyler clung to Blossom's waist. They were on their knees facing each other. Blossom wore a new outfit he didn't recall buying, skin-tight blue jeans with silver cord running up the sides. The shirt, nearly see-through gauze, bore a design of butterflies. Beneath the fabric her breasts strained as Tyler squeezed her ribs.

His hands. Her ribs. Her breasts.

Breasts.

Anthony's breath stuttered. *Blossom has breasts.*

A few ridiculous and maudlin tears burned his eyes. Without warning, she'd leapt into another stage of development.

He wasn't prepared for the change. A child raced ahead so quickly, how was a parent to keep up? Now she'd rushed ahead once again, with Tyler, who was tickling her on her bed with his hair thrown across his forehead and the shadowy evidence of a beard sprouting on his chin—

Tyler. With peach fuzz on his chin.

The maudlin tears gave way to a stronger emotion.

"Get off the bed!" He shoved the hatbox onto the dresser and stalked to the foot of the bed. "What do you think you're doing?"

His daughter scurried across the comforter then stumbled to her feet. Tyler was faster. He shot to the center of the room.

Blossom needed all of three seconds to regain her cocksure attitude. "We're goofing off," she said. "What's the big deal?"

Anthony cornered her. "Why don't you goof off downstairs?"

"Why are you acting weird?" She squared off before him. "We always come upstairs. Why do you care?"

"New rules, kiddo. No boys in your bedroom. If Tyler stops over, he stays in the living room. Comprendo?"

"Ty isn't a *boy*. He's my buddy. Right, Ty?"

Anthony swung around. Tyler blanched.

He was a year older than Blossom and it showed. Something masculine crackled in the exchange—Anthony felt it. With sudden clarity he understood Tyler felt it, too.

"Sir, I'm sorry," Tyler said. "I wasn't aware of the rule. I'll follow it."

Sir. A kid I held as a baby just called me Sir. Anthony's world shifted. The map he'd understood with some confidence was redrawn in the space of a heartbeat.

Ungrounded, he held Tyler in his sights. "Then we understand each other?"

"I won't forget, sir. You have my word."

"Good."

Blossom flapped her arms. "Will someone tell me what's going on?"

"No!" they shouted as one voice.

She angled her neck. "Wow. Did you guys practice? Freaky. Do it again."

Tyler dashed out. Footsteps thundered down the stairwell.

Anthony grabbed the hatbox and his daughter. "Get moving. I'm not too young for a heart attack, muchacha."

She swiveled to face him and they collided with a smack. The hatbox flew into the air. He lunged, catching Mary's gift before it hit the ground.

He shot a look of pure frustration. "Watch it," he growled.

Blossom thrust out her chin. "What's in the box? A gift for *her?*"

Bile rose in his throat. Hadn't his rotten kid spent months playing matchmaker? Why was she angered by the evidence of her success?

"Yes, this is for Mary," he said with all the dignity he could muster. "I thought you wanted us to . . ."

He clamped his mouth shut. 'Get along' didn't cut it. He sure as hell wasn't going to say, 'fall in love'. What happened from this point forward was private. Blossom didn't need specifics.

At last, he said, "Damn it, I thought you wanted us to be friendly."

She planted her feet. "You shouldn't swear."

"You shouldn't make me."

"I've had it." She shoved past and stormed back into her bedroom. "I'm sitting in the unemployment line and you don't care. Whose side are you on anyway?"

Anthony clawed his scalp. "I'm on your side," he replied, "and Mary's. This isn't a world war, and you aren't occupied France. I don't have to take sides. By the way, you didn't lose your job. You didn't *have* a job."

Obviously the wrong thing to say. Snatching up her sleeping bag, Blossom gave out a snarl.

"You're really something, Dad." She flung open her closet and grabbed her suitcase. "I *did* have a job. I was good at it. Think I don't know what's going on? You want me out of the way. I messed up your love life the last time. Now you and Mary are hot to trot and you're afraid I'll mess everything up again. *That's* why I lost my job."

"You aren't making sense." Her rising anger compelled him to tamp down his own. The argument was making her unbearably pale. Worried, he added, "Honey, I don't know what you mean by 'last time' and 'this time.'"

She tossed the suitcase onto her bed, hurled clothes and a few CDs inside. "You know exactly what I'm talking about."

"I don't."

"Cheryl." She snapped the suitcase shut. "I messed up your marriage to my mom. Isn't that why she ran off? Now you think I'll mess up your chance with Mary so you begged her to fire me. You want me out of the way."

Speechless, he gaped at her. In his wildest nightmares he never suspected she doubted his love. How could she think she was in the way? Her eyes swam in tears as he searched in vain for reassuring words. When he neared to wrap her in his arms, the fire in her gaze warned him off.

He said, "You're not in the way. Blossom, you're the best part of my life."

"Yeah. Right." She swept past. "I'm hanging with Snoops until tomorrow. Have fun at the picnic with your girlfriend."

Girlfriend Anthony thought, torn between anger and worry. *My kid thinks I have a girlfriend.*

He grimaced. *A girlfriend who's packing her bags within weeks.* Muttering a curse, he strode down the driveway.

Well, Mary was his for now, if he hadn't blown it by pushing too hard.

Stowing the hatbox in the back seat of her car, he hurried into the backyard. He glanced at the white Colonial house next door, where Snoops lived. Separating the diverse emotions bounding through him seemed impossible.

He wanted to go next door and give Blossom a bear hug to reassure her that Cheryl had left him, not her. He wanted to banish any doubts she harbored about his love. Then again, he needed to find Mary.

He'd try to do both.

At a quickening pace, he jogged across the lawn. Nick's older son had one of the neighbor boys in a headlock. On the grass nearby, Anna's youngest boy played egg toss with a rather somber-looking Tyler. Anna's kid was outgunned. Enough egg covered his tee shirt to make an omelet.

Anthony's parents had cornered Mary by the grill. He was about to perform a rescue operation when his older sister blocked his path.

Anna clamped down on his arm. "I was in the foyer getting the door when you and Blossom went at it upstairs. Lucky for you no one else heard the fireworks."

"I'd be lying if I didn't admit I'm rattled. She argued with me like an adult."

"She's upset about Cheryl."

"I got that."

Anna snapped her fingers, pulling his attention off Mary. "It's okay for you to fall in love," she told him. "Give Blossom time to cool off. It isn't healthy to focus completely on your child."

"My health's fine," he snapped.

"This isn't healthy for Blossom either." Wisdom showed in his sister's honey-colored eyes. "Kids grow up, little brother. They need to learn they aren't the center of your universe. When they do, they discover it's okay to leave the nest, to find someone to love and share their life with."

Did she also mean it was okay for him to love Mary first—to love her best? "You're losing me here," he said, too upset to decipher her meaning. "I'd lay my life down for Blossom."

"No one's doubting your devotion."

"I can't love someone more than that."

The words were barely out when an unnerving image of Cheryl accosted him.

He recalled the day she'd slipped into his bedroom while his parents were at work. They'd dated on and off since ninth grade, had a few steamy necking sessions. During those last months of his senior year she never crossed his mind. All he cared about was enrolling in college and the freedom sure to come.

They hadn't seen each other in months. It was a shock finding her in his bedroom on a bright spring day, naked on his bed. He'd just aced an Economics test and was flying high.

Finding her reclining and willing, he dropped his books on the floor.

Wordlessly he climbed on top of her. Undressing was too much of a hassle—he merely unzipped and wrenched his jeans down. When he sunk himself inside her, Cheryl laughed. Then they were both laughing, unaware how a few thoughtless minutes of pleasure would alter the trajectory of their lives.

His sister rested her palm against his cheek, and he heard himself admit, "I've never been in love."

"When would you have found the time? You've been a father since you were a kid."

Pain knotted in his chest. "How is this supposed to work? I had Blossom before I became a man. Now Mary shows up in my life. She's the one, the *only* woman for me, and she's leaving." He gave Anna the rundown on the medical practice waiting for Mary in Cincinnati.

A slow smile crept across his sister's mouth. "She's here now, isn't she? Use your time well."

"How can I court her when Blossom has all these crazy ideas? She's angry, and I'm bouncing between happiness and heartache."

"Think about Mary today—and yourself. Let Blossom pout with her friend next door. She won't call tomorrow. Don't go and fetch her. She needs time to work through this."

"All right," Anthony said, his spirits rebounding.

"When Blossom *does* return home, sit her down and discuss Cheryl. Everything, little brother. Whatever questions she has, answer them. Put her worries to rest and give her a hug. If she doesn't pull her out of her funk, ground her for a week. A real grounding, buster."

"Make it real. Check."

"None of your backpedaling. You spoil her something awful."

Anthony bounced on the balls of his feet. "May I go now?"

She gave him a push. "Go. None of us will stay much longer, promise. You and Mary need time alone."

At least his family had the sense to hit the trail early. The neighbors, seeing his family take off, would follow.

Babe, I'm coming to the rescue! He'd almost reached her when his brother leapt into his path.

"Not so fast, ugly boy." Nick, the pig, held him in a lock. "Your woman is ours. Mom is prying into her private life. Think I'll help."

Anthony caught his parents' attention. "Isn't she great?" he called over Nick's shoulder. "Bet you never thought you'd meet a doctor who runs a restaurant, did you?"

Nick dragged them both forward. "Hey, Ma! Ask if she's been to Mass."

Incensed, Anthony tried struggling free. "Leave my girl alone. Damn it, Nick—leave *me* alone."

"Weakling."

He broke loose from the hold. "Get away from me, lunatic."

To Mary, his mother confided, "Nick was always my strange child. Forever sticking things up his nose—like that marble at age five."

"Ma, you're embarrassing me."

Rennie, manning the grill, said, "Ignore him, Mary. He's a pain. I don't know how Liza stands—hey!"

Sweetcakes nicked Rennie then trotted past. The white bag hanging from the dog's mouth was instantly recognizable. Anthony's stomach did a nasty roll.

Oh, dear God. No!

Nick snapped his fingers. "Sweetcakes, please."

He wasn't fast enough reaching for the bag taken from the master bedroom. Sweetcakes dropped the bag, spilling condoms across the grass. Nosing through the pile, the mutt picked up a rainbow-colored packet and obediently placed it at Anthony's feet.

His mother covered her mouth. Pop regarded him with ill-concealed mirth. Nick guffawed at the top of his lungs, drawing curious stares from too many of the neighbors.

Mary looked faint.

"Look, Mary, don't get the wrong idea," Anthony croaked. When her gaze turned icy, he dived for the grass and threw the loot into the bag. By the time he'd struggled to his feet, his brother, the bastard, was making an awkward situation worse.

Nick gave the horrified Mary a playful nudge. "My ugly boy must have a hundred of 'em," he said. "What are you two—rabbits?"

She swayed on her sensible loafers, got her bearings.

Stiffly, she faced Anthony's parents. "Mr. and Mrs. Perini, please allow me to assure you that I'm not engaging in sexual activity with your son. I would never, uh, we never—well, we haven't—"

Nick snorted. "Save it for the confessional." Rennie swung a spatula at his head and he ducked without a moment to spare. "Hey! Don't touch the hairdo!"

Anthony shoved him aside. Murder could wait. *Later.*

He took Mary by the hand. "Excuse us," he said, pulling her behind him like a toy train.

In search of privacy he led her into the house. The kitchen, smelling of barbecue and jammed with people, wasn't the best place to fall to his knees and grovel. Portly Mr. Zimski appeared drunk and had broken into song. The living room proved as crowded. In the foyer, Justin was cornering one of Nick's evil twins, who'd snatched an electronic game from a whimpering Timmy Zimski.

The only quiet place in the house? Upstairs.

He led Mary up the stairwell. Anna's kids were parked on the steps like three blind mice in their matching black eyeglasses. They scrambled out of the way. Someone in the bathroom was running the water full blast and bumping against the door. Probably several kids were inside, but he didn't give a damn. Neighbor kids were playing hide and seek in the unfinished rooms between Blossom's bedroom and the bathroom, and he shielded Mary when a girl in braids raced past.

Oh, hell.

CHAPTER 19

Miles away from the chaos, the only place left was . . . his bedroom.

Chapter 20

Stunned beyond speech, Mary allowed Anthony to tug her into the master bedroom. He kicked the door shut, locked it, and let her go.

She wavered in the center of the room while he stalked to the nightstand and tossed the bag of condoms on top. He muttered something under his breath, an entire string of unintelligible phrases. While he verbally flogged himself she canvassed the room, noting the family photos on the walls and the heavy oak dresser. The enticing scent of men's cologne hung in the air.

Beneath her feet, the grass green carpeting muffled the sounds of revelry in the rest of the house. Thick drapes, in a subdued grey and green stripe, were partially drawn across French doors that were flung open to lend a nice view of the second-story deck. Anthony stood rubbing his forearms, evidently searching for a proper apology.

After long minutes, he said, "Look, I'm sorry about what happened."

The contrition on his face helped shore up her composure. "I'm sure there's a logical explanation."

"Blame Theodora's horse tranquilizers."

"Tranquilizers?"

"Well, actually, they were suppositories."

Where is this headed? "Theodora owns a horse?"

"No, no. We were in the drugstore." Frustration welled on

Anthony's face. "I was trying to dodge her. I ran into the rack of condoms. I wanted to buy you a sweet gift but I knocked into the rack—"

She nicked him with a narrowed glance. "The next time you want to add condoms to a sweet gift, choose a more opportune moment. Like when your parents aren't around. For the record, I don't think rubbers fall into the 'sweet gift' category."

"It was a crazy, impulse purchase—"

"Keep your impulses to yourself!"

He took a step closer then halted beneath her warning glance. "I didn't mean to embarrass you," he said. "It's not like I thought we'd have sex today—"

"Got that right."

What *had* he been thinking—they'd get down to the good stuff in the middle of a picnic? Granted, their attraction had reached a fever pitch. Even if they were foolish enough to broach intimacy, where would it lead? She couldn't let him into her heart, not with the move back to Cincinnati looming on the horizon.

Instead of listing her objections, Mary said, "We shouldn't have this discussion in your bedroom. We're both at the end of our rope."

"Are you talking about our attraction?"

"We aren't kids, Anthony. It's safe to acknowledge if we don't leave your bedroom, we *will* end up making love."

Her sudden candor squashed the distress on his face. Grinning, he threw his hands over his heart. "Making love—you didn't refer to it in a cold, clinical way as 'having sex'." He went into a fake swoon. "We use the same love language. We *are* meant for each other."

She laughed, easing the tension between them. "You're crazy. You know that?"

"For you alone."

"We aren't embarrassing ourselves with a quick roll in the sack while your parents eat barbecue out back." She paused, unnerved by the rising excitement stirring her blood. Anthony was to blame. The way his lusty gaze roamed her face, it was difficult to have *any* restraint.

"No worries," he said, advancing. "My parents aren't virgins.

There's nothing we can dream up they haven't tried."

"Stay where you are."

"I can't."

He appeared intent on cornering her. Grinning, she backed toward the wall between the nightstand and the French doors. She hung on his gaze, the arousal he telegraphed heightening her senses as he erased the ground between them.

"I care about you," he said, crowding her.

"Let's go downstairs." She gulped, her resolve slipping. "The look on your face is unnerving. It's so . . . focused."

"Yeah?"

"It's way too yummy. Get back."

"You're breaking my heart."

"I'm not trying to," she said in a breathless voice. "I'm not sure who I distrust more—you or me."

Her confession altered his expression so quickly, her heart thudded. A very male sort of determination glinted in his eyes. But his gaze skittered as he rubbed his hands down his thighs, his thoughts tumbling one over the next. The air between them stilled with the promise of beginnings.

He stepped back, as though coming to a decision. "Look, Mary," he said, suddenly serious. Licking his lips, he stalled for time. Then he plunged forward quickly. "You're the best thing that's ever happened to me."

The best thing? When was the last time a man had said that to her?

Never.

"I'm the luckiest man in the world," he added, moving back in to trace hesitant fingertips beneath her lips. He urged her into a loose embrace, his expression softly vulnerable. "I never expected someone like you to come into my life. But you're here . . . and I'm grateful."

"I am too," she whispered. "I never thought—"

That she'd find a man like him, sweet and devoted, with a sexy gaze she'd gladly lose herself in for decades?

A frown whispered across his lips as he caressed her cheek. "I was a cynic before I met you," he admitted. "Cheryl left when Blossom was just a toddler. Since then, I've never been willing to trust a woman."

"Trust isn't easy." His eyes were beautiful, dusky and deep. She couldn't halt her fingertips from straying to the edges of his lashes. "People don't understand what it's like to be left behind. It doesn't matter if you're a kid in high school who loses her parents or your spouse walks off. It hurts."

"I'd never hurt you."

"I wouldn't hurt you, either." She read the hesitancy in his eyes, the hint of painful memories. "Not intentionally."

He feathered kisses across her brow. "I've never felt this way before. Looking at you is like staring at the sun. I get dizzy."

Dizzy. She was more than that.

Spinning.

"I don't want to lose you," he added. "I lost the last time around. Maybe it was me, and I did something wrong. I don't want the same outcome this time."

"I don't want to lose you, either. It's scary to feel this way, like I'm in free-fall without a parachute."

"I'll catch you."

He brushed his lips across hers with such gentle devotion her heart tumbled. Time beat down like a hummingbird's wings, slowing until there was only this moment, the catch of a fevered breath, a faltering touch, a gentle exploration. One moment, and they were suspended within it.

A needy whimper escaped her throat, increasing the tempo of his mouth upon hers. She let her eyes drift shut as he deepened the kiss, his fingers trailing across her cheeks, her neck, awakening her senses. She couldn't stop her hands from traversing the roping muscles of his torso then up to his neck, and higher, to brush the coarse stubble on his chin.

Breaking off the kiss, he said, "I'm sick with the need for you." He pinioned her with a troubled gaze. "I'm trying to do this right."

His sincerity was deeply moving. "You're very proper, aren't you?"

"I don't want to scare you away."

"I'm not frightened," she said, stunned to realize the truth.

A sudden agony creased his features. Losing the private battle he waged, he hauled her against his hips. The urgency in his expression, the erotic movement of their bodies as he molded her close, sent fire cascading through her veins.

She flung her arms over his shoulders as he steered her to the bed, the agony on his face suffusing with pleasure. The barrier of clothing was a torment and she tugged her dress over her head. The raspy breaths issuing from his lips as he hungrily watched her unclasp her bra and shimmy out of her panties, the anguish in his eyes as he captured her gaze—everything about him was so male, so predatory, it was nearly animalistic.

A new, wilder heat swirled like a tempest. She scooted up the bed to make room for him. Anthony planted his knees between her thighs, shoved his jeans and his briefs midway down his thighs. She held him in a fevered gaze as he steered himself to her and sank deep, sank to the hilt.

They stilled for a moment. He squeezed his eyes shut. Digging her nails into his shoulders, she did the same, needing to concentrate on the intense pleasure of their mating.

He arched away slightly. "Come undone with me—" He splayed his hands on either side of her head. "I love you, Mary, I—"

"Anthony, I love you too." She dragged his mouth near and let the emotion twining between them become part and parcel of every cell in her body.

Afterward, they lay tangled together for long minutes. Racket from the lower regions of the house vibrated along the bedroom's walls. Yet the partygoers outside were oddly quiet.

Eyes shut, Anthony said, "I think we broke the world record for speed."

His voice nudged past her lethargy. "Hmm?" She sat up.

An amusing sight, he was flat on his back with arms and legs splayed. "We made love in record time," he elaborated.

"Really? I thought we took our time."

"Thanks."

She searched the floor for her clothes. A feeling of completeness wove through her blood. The hasty declaration they'd shared—was it real? Immediately she found the answer. Yes, they *did* love each other. Despite her worry, she smiled.

"Truth is, we haven't been up here for more than twenty minutes," he was saying. "Next time, I won't rush."

"Great." Common sense gave a persistent nudge. They

needed to return downstairs before anyone noticed they'd disappeared. She reached for her bra, a twisted mess on the carpeting. Putting it on, she glanced toward the French doors. "Sure we haven't been gone long?"

"Positive."

Leaving the guests milling around the macaroni salad while they engaged in wild jungle sex was an unforgivable breach of etiquette. "Anthony, you have to get up." The drug-like euphoria receding, she shrugged into her dress and searched for her shoes. "I prefer not to leave the impression with your family that I'm improper."

He dragged his eyes open. "Not likely. They think we ran off to squabble. Our first fight."

"That's all they'll think?"

He pulled on his jeans. "No one makes love in the middle of a picnic. They think you're up here slapping me silly."

"I *am* upset about the condoms."

"That's not how it looks from the cheap seats."

Playfully she shoved him. "What if they think something else?" she asked, craving reassurance.

He gave a suggestive glance. "If they do, what the hell. We'll stay up here all night. One thing's for certain. We won't run out of rubbers."

"Don't come near me."

"You're a cruel woman, Mary."

The summer breeze wafting through the French doors beckoned her near. "If your family knew the truth, I'd never be able to face them." She'd leave the country, move to Europe to ensure she never ran into them again. "I can't imagine anything more humiliating."

"Stop worrying." He planted a kiss on her forehead. "And by the way, feel free to jump my bones any time you're in the mood."

She darted back before the suggestion stole into her blood. If they didn't tone down the sex talk, they *would* spend the rest of the afternoon in bed. Throwing off the delicious thought, she padded out the French doors for a quick peek at the crowd. Logic suggested Anthony was correct. No one had noticed the absence.

She was mistaken. Beneath her feet, the earth wobbled. As did her composure.

Directly below, the Perini clan stood in a gawking row. Mortified, she dashed out of view. But not before Nick cupped his hands over his mouth.

"Hey, noisy lady! Next time, close the French doors before you hit pay dirt!"

Biting out a curse, Anthony leapt onto the patio. "Nick, watch your mouth. You're talking about my girl, you bastard!" Silence, then, "Oh, Ma—hi. Sorry about the language. I didn't see you there."

Which was enough to send Mary hurtling for the door.

Chapter 21

Mary flung herself against the door. *Escape!*

If she'd been stripped down to her skivvies and paraded before Anthony's family, she couldn't have been more humiliated. Grabbing the doorknob, she rattled the door against the frame in an unrewarded effort to gain her freedom.

"Mary, hold up." Anthony leaned over the balcony's railing. "You've got to see this. Liza's beating Nick over the head with a plastic plate. He's going down fast."

The amusement in Anthony's voice barely registered. Too mortified for words, she wrenched open the door.

Thankfully the hallway was free of screaming kids. None in sight on the stairwell or in the foyer, either. Reaching the living room, she spun in a frantic circle. Where was her purse?

"Hey!" Anthony's voice echoed down the stairwell. "Baby, it's okay. Don't leave."

The veranda. Hadn't Nick left her purse on the veranda while she'd pigged out on cheesecake? Bolting past a tyke spooning food into his mouth, she nicked his shoulder. The plate of franks and beans flipped to the floor. He let out a wail. She was too frantic to stop and comfort him.

My purse! Snatching it from the couch, she raced outside and down the driveway. She'd reached her car before Anthony caught up with her.

"See you later." She lunged for the driver side door. "Please give your parents my regards. Tell them I don't normally have sex at picnics."

"Baby, calm down." He steered her into his arms. "So they know. It's embarrassing, sure. Want me to go and scope out the situation? Everyone will act like nothing happened, I swear it."

She buried her face against his chest. "What about Nick?"

"I'll beat him to a quivering pulp. It'll only take a minute. Then come back."

"No."

"Please?"

"No."

He held her at arm's length, his eyes shimmering with glee. "Okay. I understand." He placed a chaste peck on her cheek. "Run on back to work. I'll stop by at closing time."

The suggestion warmed her. "What about Blossom?"

"She'll never know we're on a midnight date. She's spending the night with Snoops."

Mary opened the driver side door. "All right. I'll see you tonight—"

The words evaporated on her lips. Unbidden, a wave of anxiety swept through her. Cold, intense, the anxiety started a buzzing in her ears.

The emotion was distressingly familiar. During her residency at Cinci General, the other doctors had joked about her unerring sixth sense. But it hadn't been a joke. She'd unnerved the lot of them every time she arrived in the ER seconds before an ambulance pulled up.

Now the same fearful knowing coiled in her gut. Perspiration sprouted on her brow.

Anthony palmed her hair. "What's wrong?"

She trained her eyes on the white Colonial next door. "Blossom." She gripped his wrist. "Check on her. Go now."

His jaw twitched at the command. "Will do." He held open the car door. "I'll go right over, see if she's okay."

She slid behind the wheel then froze with indecision.

Taking the key from her fingers, Anthony brought the engine to life. "Don't worry. I'm on it."

She was about to suggest accompanying him. The notion barely cleared her brain when the Colonial's front door flew open. Snoops raced down the steps.

"Mr. Perini!" She wagged her arms at the house. "Come quick! Something is wrong with Blossom."

Which was enough incentive to propel Mary from the car. Together they ran to the house.

They entered the foyer. Gently Anthony moved the trembling Snoops out of their path. "Honey, where's Blossom?" he asked her.

She pointed skyward. "In my room. Mr. Perini, she's real sick. She didn't want me to tell you."

He bolted up the stairwell. Remaining calm was difficult but Mary didn't want to frighten Snoops. "It's okay," she said, steering the girl into the living room. "Wait for us here."

Upstairs, she sprinted across the landing in time to glimpse Anthony striding into a bedroom at the opposite end.

"Dad?"

"Blossom, what's going on?"

"Not sure. I'm cold."

On the rug in Snoops' bedroom, Blossom rocked back and forth with her teeth chattering. Bluish veins throbbed beneath the translucent skin of her neck. Approaching, Mary wondered if the girl's blood pressure was stable. A CD player sat on the floor beside her. Scissors, construction paper and bottles of glue lay in heaps on the bed.

Mary crouched to check Blossom's pulse. It was thready and weak. Fear slicked through her. She fought it off as she pressed her palm to Blossom's forehead.

"She's running a fever," she told Anthony. She wished fervently for her medical bag, which would allow for a more thorough examination. "This isn't good—she's burning up."

"I'm freezing," Blossom whispered. "I'm a popsicle."

'You feel more like Finney's hot stove." She nodded toward the hallway. "Anthony, find a blanket. And check the bathroom for Tylenol."

After he dashed out, she began rubbing Blossom's arms. She savored a moment's relief when their eyes connected and Blossom seemed happy to see her.

She pressed her palm to Blossom's neck. "We're taking you to St. Barnabas."

"Do we have to? I hate the hospital."

"Sweetie, you're running a high temperature. We're going to the hospital. No discussion." She slipped her hand inside the girl's grey sweatshirt. "You're shivering. Are you too weak to stand? Your father can carry you if—My God!"

Shock throttled her heart. Mary pulled the sweatshirt back to expose more skin. Blossom's bluish lips tipped into a frown.

A ghastly series of bruises scattered across the skin of her collarbone. Brownish-black in color, they were spreading.

Rising to her knees, Mary shouted for Anthony to call 911.

Chapter 22

Numb with shock, Anthony listened to oncologist explain the course of chemotherapy required to fight Blossom's leukemia.

He carried enough fear in his gut to pass out in the exam room, enough fear to stop his heart cold as he struggled to maintain his composure beneath the calm, killing words Dr. Lash used.

Aggressively recurrent disease. Unexpectedly high lymphocyte count.

His daughter, shivering on the examination table, leaned against Mary. The nurse produced another needle. *Further tests. A more aggressive course of treatment.* Mary remained preternaturally calm, her medical training coming to the fore as she battered Lash with questions. Anthony caught mere snatches of conversation, his world collapsing. *More invasive course of chemotherapy drugs.* He remained silent although the horror had him screaming inside his head.

When they'd finished, he asked Lash, "How long must Blossom stay in the hospital?"

"I can't give you a timeline until we run more tests," Lash said. "At this early date, I'd rather not hazard a guess."

Mary asked, "When will you have the results?"

"Tomorrow." The doctor fiddled with his glasses. "I'm optimistic more aggressive drugs will bring about the results we'd like."

Anthony thrust his fists deep in his pockets. Lash didn't sound optimistic. He appeared frightened like the rest of them.

"Did you follow a marrow protocol during remission?" Mary asked the oncologist. Anthony gave a questioning look and she added, "It's a safeguard. The healthy marrow comes into play if chemo isn't successful."

Lash nodded in agreement. "We collected healthy marrow during Blossom's remission. We may need to discuss the option if we don't see improvement quickly."

A wave of nausea rolled through Anthony. "What option?" His mind, scarred by the sudden downturn of his daughter's health, refused to process the information.

Mary cleared her throat. "A bone marrow transplant."

Blossom, silent until now, peered into Mary's shuttered face. "I don't want a transplant." She looked to him with eyes full of dread. "Dad, tell them I don't need one."

A trapdoor opened on his fear and he plummeted through. A bone marrow transplant was a risky procedure used to insert healthy tissue after the body was rid of cancerous marrow. Imagining Blossom surviving the grueling operation was beyond him. She was already much sicker than he'd realized.

"I'm not sure my insurance covers the procedure," he said to no one in particular. Ashamed, he stared blankly at his feet.

Mary went to him. "Most plans cover the procedure."

Disagreeing made him feel like a failure, a man incapable of protecting his child. "I'll check, all right?"

Over the years he'd cobbled together a decent medical plan. The deductibles and co-pays, difficult to manage in the best of times, would multiply during this latest course of treatment. Where would the money come from? The rates had been rising for years, the coverage declining. He'd been fighting a losing battle since Blossom was a toddler.

Lash said, "We aren't at the phase yet to consider a bone marrow transplant. However, you should be aware we might need to discuss the option."

Dropping the subject, Lash resumed his explanation of the cocktail of drugs he planned to use. The nurse placed another bandage on Blossom's arm then collected up the supplies.

Lash's voice broke through his muddled thoughts. "Anthony,

let's talk outside."

He followed the doctor out. The gleaming corridor bloomed with noise—the whir of machines, the clack of a nurse's heels as she marched past. Lash, in a transparent attempt at stalling, ran his hand over his prematurely balding head. The gesture, revealing anxiety, threw chips of ice into Anthony's blood.

Lash said, "I don't want to be a pessimist, but I am concerned. We may find cancer cells outside the bone marrow. We'll know definitively with the next batch of test results."

The news nearly melted the strength in Anthony's legs. Never before had they found cancer outside his daughter's bones.

He forced air into his lungs, exhaled. "Why do you think the cancer is spreading?"

"Blossom's lymphocyte count is radically elevated. Keep in mind she was cancer-free one month ago. The disease has recurred quickly."

"You'll beat the disease like the last time."

Lash rocked on his heels, his expression dour. "Let's be clear. This isn't like the last time. The induction phase of treatment will be extremely aggressive."

Breathe. Lightheaded, Anthony leaned against the wall. "You'll pour higher doses of poison through her, more than you'd like. Am I catching all of this?"

"Unfortunately, yes."

Rage planted his feet. An unwarranted reaction, he wanted to punch the doctor who kept Sponge Bob stickers for Blossom and enough jokes to keep a stand-up comic working year round. He couldn't process Lash's kindness or his concern. He couldn't see anything but the memory of his daughter the last time. Blossom, losing her hair. Blossom, little more than a skeleton.

"The last time nearly killed her," he said, angry at Fate and cancer and the tears scalding his eyes. "She can't do this. Increase the dosage, and she won't survive your chemo drugs."

Lash was quiet for an excruciating moment.

"She'll have to," he said at last, "or she won't survive at all."

Mary held Blossom in a rocking embrace. The nurse, oblivious, continued to insist on the wheelchair for the ride upstairs to the children's wing of the hospital.

"I'm not sitting in another wheelchair." Blossom peered around Mary's shoulder. "Where'd Dad go?"

"He's talking to Dr. Lash." Mary's voice shook. She needed to stay detached, for Blossom's sake. *Your fear becomes the patient's fear.* A cardinal rule in med school, she tried to draw on its cool logic. "Sweetie, he'll be back in a sec."

"No wheelchair. Comprendo?"

The nurse, an attractive woman with silvering hair, sighed with exasperation.

"You've been in and out of wheelchairs for hours," Mary said, relieved when the woman left. She grappled to recall every lesson from med school about dealing with a frightened patient. *Your confidence becomes the patient's confidence.* "We're just taking a short ride upstairs. Why make a big deal out of it?"

"Because it *is* a big deal."

She stroked Blossom's hair. "They've got a room waiting for you, with a roommate and everything. I'll get you tucked in and there won't be any more wheelchairs today."

"If I go up to the kid's area, I'm done for." Blossom's eyes grew wide, as she glimpsed Death creeping into the room. "Please don't make me go. If I do, I'll die."

Emotion clouds the physician's ability to make sound judgments. "No, baby, it'll be okay."

"You're wrong. I almost died the last time. Dad got me out of St. Barnabas just in time. He saved me. If I go home everything will get better."

Distance yourself from your emotions. How to break through a child's teary rant? *Don't feel.* Her heart seized as her love for Blossom collided with the terrifying suspicion that the girl was correct.

Despite the finest advancements in medical care, children were struck down by cancer every day. Never again did they sit beneath a blue sky or ride a bicycle with their arms outstretched to catch the wind. They never left the four walls of a sterile room, never reached high school, never stepped into the ruffled confection of a prom dress or experienced their first kiss.

Not Blossom. No.

Finding an inner reservoir of strength, she took Blossom's

face in her hands. "Listen to me," she said. "I won't leave you. I'll stay all night. Nothing will happen to you."

"But you have to go to work." Blossom's eyes brimmed with tears. "Dad said Grandma is coming, and Aunt Liza. But I'm safer with you."

The child's implicit trust was daunting. Mary couldn't keep her safer—she couldn't keep her *safe*. Not from cancer, not from the vicious arithmetic of cells bent on multiplying until every tender organ inside the girl's body collapsed beneath the onslaught. Recurrent cancer possessed a savage intelligence. It sabotaged every chemical pathway in the human body. It was relentless.

Retreating from the grim facts, Mary put fire in her voice. "I won't leave." She'd call Finney to explain. If the staff couldn't manage, she'd suggest they close early. "When you wake up tomorrow, I'll be the first thing you see."

The nurse with the silvering hair reentered the examination room. She brought with her a burly man with bushy eyebrows and a tall black woman whose impatience tipped down the corners of her mouth.

To Mary, the nurse said, "Dr. Lash won't allow us to give her a sedative."

The announcement increased Blossom's agitation. "Please, Mary," she whispered, her gaze black with terror. "Don't let them put me in the wheelchair."

The man approached. Instinctively, Mary blocked him. "I have this under control," she said.

He unlocked the brake and rolled the wheelchair near. "I'm sure you do, ma'am." He sent a sidelong glance to the others.

"Just give me a moment. Let me calm her down."

"I'd like to wait, but . . ."

He didn't finish the lie. Arms outstretched, the trio came at her. Their movements sent fearsome electricity snapping through the air. A pitiful whimper rose from Blossom.

Mary shoved the man back. "Don't touch her!" The fear she'd kept at bay issued out with enough heat to stop all movement. "We're walking upstairs. She's not getting into the wheelchair."

The black nurse broke the spell. "Ma'am, be reasonable."

Recklessly, she stepped closer. "We must obey the rules. I'm sure you understand."

Mary wheeled on her. "WE'RE WALKING UPSTAIRS."

The fracas brought Anthony and Dr. Lash racing into the room. The doctor, so unprepossessing he'd vanish in a crowd, stunned Mary when he gave his staff a dressing down that snapped them to attention.

Afterward he held the door as Mary, Blossom and Anthony walked out.

With Blossom huddled beneath her arm, Mary continued a soothing babble. Anthony led them toward the elevators, his face bleached of emotion. He'd withdrawn to a dark place, and she left him alone in his misery.

There wasn't time to help him. She directed all her energy on keeping Blossom calm.

The elevator closed, and Anthony stood before them like a shield. They cowered against the wall. The carriage lifted into the gleaming, barren reaches of the hospital.

Once they'd reached the fifth floor, Blossom allowed Mary to steer her forward. They walked past the nurses' station and down the corridor. They entered the semi-private room. On the other side of the privacy curtain, machines beeped and whirred.

Anthony nodded at Blossom's suitcase, which someone had deposited by the bed. He smiled at his daughter then brushed his hand down Mary's arm. "Can you help her change into pajamas?" he asked.

Blossom peered up at her father. "Wait outside, Dad. We're okay."

He cupped her cheek. "Take your time." He turned to Mary. "Want coffee?"

She sighed. "That would be great."

After he'd gone, she hoisted the suitcase onto the bed. The privacy curtain fluttered open the barest inch.

In the other bed, a girl in a gypsy turban lay sleeping. Her face was a startling mask of white, as fragile as Medieval parchment. Skin seemed to collapse at the edges of her sunken eye sockets as if the weight of cancer had dissolved each delicate fiber. The sheet had slipped down to her waist. Beneath the flowered pajamas Mary saw the heartrending outline of a young woman's body. The girl's dawning maturity hinted at hopes dashed and dreams foregone, and the promise she'd never live long enough to fulfill.

Mary pulled Blossom close. She glimpsed a journey she didn't have the courage to make.

Chapter 23

The days ran together.

Inside the elevator, Mary punched the button for the hospital's fifth floor. She was thankful for the isolation to organize her thoughts.

This afternoon she'd argued again with Finney. The cook had taken over the operation of the restaurant with the finesse of a hostile general, rebuffing all attempts at intervention. To her way of thinking, Mary's only obligation was to remain at Blossom's bedside morning and night. Several teenagers in Liberty were now pitching in, including the cook's daughter Marla. They waited tables and helped in the kitchen in a scattershot approach that left piles of dishes for Delia, Ethel Lynn and Finney to tend to long after closing.

Today, when Mary had announced she'd stay for the evening rush, Finney blew sky high. She'd wrapped up the argument by forcing Mary into a chair and slapping a plate brimming with meat loaf and mashed potatoes beneath her nose.

After eating the first full meal in days, Mary *had* felt better.

The elevator slid open and she walked slowly past the nurse's station. A man stood at the counter with the balloons in his fist bobbing. *Get Well Soon* was written in pink lettering on the middle balloon. No doubt the balloons were a gift for a child hospitalized for something simple, like a tonsillectomy. Something that wasn't life threatening.

Anger sizzled through Mary. Why become upset because

another child would soon leave the hospital? Eventually Blossom would too. Mary needed to believe, needed the comforting thought, especially since she couldn't stay long today. A mountain of bookkeeping awaited her at The Second Chance.

And Finney—this morning she'd looked worn out. Expecting the cook to handle extra tasks for the restaurant's owner wasn't fair, especially now that diners filled the tables at all hours. The Second Chance was earning healthy profits. Mary had surprised Finney with a pay raise, but the increase didn't seem adequate.

How to explain adult responsibilities to a grievously ill child?

Once the worst of the chemotherapy was finished, Blossom would recuperate at home. Visiting the Perini's house for an hour or two would prove easier. In fact, all she and Anthony talked about these days were the long months of healing ahead. They never discussed Mary's imminent move to Cincinnati. The topic was an additional burden neither chose to carry.

They also hadn't discussed how they'd made love on the day of the picnic, or the devotion they'd professed. Blossom's health crisis precluded any discussion of their private feelings. Most days their conversations were infrequent and abrupt, a hurried interchange regarding errands to run and chores completed to ensure Blossom's comfort. Now, in the second week of treatment, they rarely saw each other for more than a few moments each day.

Pausing outside the hospital room, Mary smoothed down her cotton dress. *It'll all work out. After she's released, we'll manage better.* Holding onto her optimism was important—especially since the last few days had been incredibly difficult.

Inside, she found Nick on the bed. A *Risk* board sat between him and Blossom.

"I'm losing," he said in greeting. He handed Blossom the dice. "The kid here is taking over the world."

"I get a lot of practice," Blossom lifted her shoulders in a careless shrug. "I play with Tyler and Snoops at least once a week. I usually win."

"You win because you cheat," her uncle said.

Blossom sniggered. "Look who's talking."

Nick rose and grabbed Mary by the shoulders. "How are you?" He shook her gently. "Has anyone mentioned you look like shit?"

"Thanks. Just what I needed to hear."

"How 'bout this? You smell damn good. No wonder my ugly boy likes you." He let her go. "I'd better get back to marching through the kid's armies. She's already taken over Europe." He raised a fist. "Italia! I shall free you!"

Blossom rolled her eyes. "I'm keeping Italy and *all* the spaghetti. You'll stay cooped up in Sydney."

While they engaged in a playful squabble, Mary dragged a chair near. Blossom looked tired. She threw the dice, which shifted her nightgown to reveal a collarbone protruding out of garishly bruised skin. Her wrists seemed larger than usual, the bones overlarge beneath diminished muscle. Dr. Lash had warned about weight loss. The end result was harrowing. At the best of times, Blossom was a skinny kid. Now every pound lost was a pound too many.

"Where's Anthony?" Nick asked, drawing her from the troubling thoughts.

She crossed her legs, settled back. "He works until seven tonight."

"Shouldn't you be at work, too?"

"Finney has everything under control." She glanced apprehensively at Blossom. "I'll stay for a couple of hours."

The IV line hanging from Blossom's arm shuddered as she shifted to the edge of the bed. "You stayed last night." A hint of accusation layered the statement. She began chewing her thumbnail, a nervous habit she'd picked up recently.

"Honey, I need to do payroll and pay taxes. Finney doesn't know how."

"I'll be sick tonight—worse than last night. You should stay."

The nausea brought on by the chemotherapy represented the most difficult aspect of treatment. Nothing in Mary's medical training had prepared her for the experience of watching a child she loved suffer. This wasn't a patient she'd been assigned during a rotation at Cinci General. This was Blossom, growing weaker by the day beneath the unpredictable benefits of science.

"Your dad will be here tonight," Mary said, guilty when the

pronouncement brought tears to Blossom's eyes. "He'll take care of you. I'll return in the morning."

Nick nodded in agreement. "Your dad can handle it, kiddo. Grandma's coming, too."

"I want Mary."

"Ease up on her. The lady has a business to run." Nick wiggled his brows in a valiant attempt to lighten the mood. "I'm sure she'd like time alone with your dad . . . to make some noise."

Mary poked him with the toe of her tennis shoe. To Blossom, she said, "I'll return before you wake up tomorrow."

"Don't worry about it. If you have to go, who cares?"

"Don't be angry. Everything's okay."

"It's not okay. Look, Mary. Just look." Tears rolled down Blossom's cheeks. Tipping her head forward, she pointed at her crown. "My hair's falling out and I'm scared."

Sorrow gripped Mary. *She's losing her beautiful hair.*

She forced a smile on her lips. "Dr. Lash said this would happen. Remember?" With the lightest touch, she skimmed her palm over the crown of curls. Her stomach lurched when a couple of strands came free. "Your hair will grow back. You'll see. When you're better, you'll grow your hair all the way to your toes."

Throwing herself against the pillows, Blossom stared dejectedly at the ceiling. "My hair won't grow back. I'll lose it and I'll die. No one sneaks past leukemia twice. I'm in deep shit."

"You shouldn't swear," Nick said, his voice catching.

Tears streamed down Blossom's face. "What are you going to do? Ground me?"

"Naw. Seems like you've had enough punishment."

Rising, he strode quickly from the room. The sound of muffled tears drifted in from the corridor, and Mary's heart went out to him.

Taking the place on the bed he'd warmed, she said, "I won't go back to work tonight, okay? I'll stay all night."

Suspicion gathered in Blossom's eyes. "Really?"

"You bet, muchacha. But if I stay, we'll let your father leave at ten o'clock. He hasn't enjoyed a full night's sleep in weeks. Comprendo?"

Brightening, Blossom gulped down tears. "No problemo."

"We're not playing games until midnight. You'll sleep until you get sick."

"Sure."

"You aren't sucking me into hours of late night TV. If I'm forced to watch another cartoon, my brains will melt."

Nick returned and she asked him, "How long are you staying?"

His mouth curved wryly. "You tell me."

"Plan on two more hours." She rummaged through her purse for her cell phone. "I have to call Finney and walk her through Payroll 101. Why don't you set up the Risk board so all three of us can play?"

Chapter 24

Fingers of lightning burst across the Cincinnati skyline. Booming thunder followed.

Cutting the engine, Mary reached for the umbrella stashed in the glove compartment. The sky unleashed the summer storm.

She dashed for the clinic's entrance with her favorite Liberty preteen planted firmly in mind. Keeping Blossom entertained during her stay at St. Barnabas had become an obsession. Mary made a mental note to visit a toy store before wrapping up her visit in Cincinnati. Gifts would lift Blossom's spirits and were as good a way as any to dodge the emotional tumult of watching a child battle cancer. Several board games were on the list; Mary was still undecided about visiting The Apple Store for an iPad. Blossom desperately longed for one, but Mary hadn't discussed the purchase with Anthony.

Rain splattered underfoot. At the clinic's door, she donned a pleasant, professional expression. Perhaps she would stop by the Apple store after her visit with Abe and his staff.

Soon, they'd be *her* staff.

With summer winding down, she was trying to make the best of an agonizing situation. Blossom still didn't know about Mary's impending return to Cincinnati—given her health, Anthony refused to tell her—and it seemed counterproductive to brood over the injury the news would cause. Nor did it make sense to examine her own emotions regarding Blossom . . . or Anthony. She despised the prospect of leaving them.

When would she assume control of Abe's practice? She hadn't yet decided, and he was kind enough not to ask.

With mixed emotions, she strode into the low-slung building. Abe's wife Lillian never stopped lavishing her interior design expertise on the clinic. Tasteful Arts and Crafts style chairs formed an L in the waiting room. A gas-powered fireplace dominated one wall, and Mary imagined the welcoming fire during the winter months when Cincinnati's poorest citizens flocked to the facility for care.

"Mary!"

Despite the cane, Abe Goldstein came forward at a steady gait. Beneath the white goatee and trim mustache, his lips curved in welcome. She assessed him with a practiced eye. His skin was peaked and she caught the rasp of labored breathing. He'd begun a regimen of medications to manage his failing heart. Retirement wouldn't arrive too soon.

"Let's sit down and talk in your office," she said, wanting to get him off his feet.

His tawny eyes blazed. "My feet won't give way, young lady." Evidently his pride was unaffected by his failing heart. "The staff isn't here yet. There's time for a quick tour. Buzz Mickerson is doing the rotation today."

She recalled several of the doctors at Cinci General had taken over Abe's patient load pending her arrival. "I'll stay long enough to see a few patients with Buzz," she said.

"He'll expect that. Frankly, several patients are nervous about switching to a young doctor."

"Understandable." She followed him into the reception area. Someone had placed attractive pots of yellow chrysanthemums by the computer. "I'm assuming your elderly patients are the most nervous about the switch?"

"Good girl. You recall the coursework on elder care at Ohio State."

"Of course."

He opened the door to the first examination room and ushered her inside. "This is general practice, dear. Some of my patients have been with me for years."

I'm doing the right thing. "I can't wait to meet them all." An image of Blossom leapt before her eyesight, Blossom with her curls thinning beneath the onslaught of chemotherapy. *I'm a doctor with a duty to put my patients first. Blossom's family will provide all the love she needs.* "Are any of your elderly patients scheduled today? If we have a chance to get acquainted, they'll be less nervous when I become their primary caretaker."

"There's one couple in particular I'm concerned about. Both in their eighties. They're scared like the dickens about the change."

"I'll do my best to put them at ease."

"I know you will. He has mild hypertension. She's in early-stage Alzheimer's. Great folks."

A shuffling of feet sounded from the reception area. Abe gave a questioning look. She went to investigate.

A couple stood in the alcove of the reception area. Wisps of snowy hair drifted onto the man's brow. The woman, pencil-thin, held his arm with a palsied grip. Behind the lenses of her bifocals, her blue eyes were serene.

They were a heartwarming sight in their matching green jackets. She wore a skirt—plaid. The yellow barrettes in her silver hair seemed better suited for a child.

Abe stepped from the exam room. "Mildred, you're early!" He patted the man on the back. "How is she today, George?"

"She's fine, Dr. Goldstein. No wandering last night. Mildred stayed in bed, thank goodness."

Abe approached Mildred and her hand lifted from her husband's sleeve, to clasp his arm. "No midnight gardening, then?" he asked her. "Have you given it up, dear?"

"The rabbits eat my lettuce."

"Wait until the morning to fend them off. Gardening by starlight is dangerous, don't you think?"

Confusion passed through Mildred's gaze. Then her expression cleared like clouds shuttled off the ocean by a strong breeze. "Mind your own business, doctor," she said in a surprisingly firm voice. "Who has the green thumb—you, or me?"

"You, dear. One of the best gardeners in the city." Abe led her to Mary. "I have someone I'd like you to meet."

Mary offered her hand. As she did, a slide show of memories fell before her eyesight—the day Blossom introduced her to Anthony and he held her fingers too long, and her first moments in Anthony's arms. She recalled the quaver in Blossom's voice when they'd organized the storage room. *If something happens to me, will you take care of my dad?* She tasted the grit in the air when, last spring, the farmers in Liberty tilled the cornfields surrounding the town. She smelled Finney's special trout sizzling on the grill the day the cook revealed Anthony had it bad for Mary.

The memories settled in the seedbed of her soul. She stitched them up quickly with memories much older—the scent of antiseptic stinging her eyes as her father cared for patients. She imagined her mother, dressed neatly in a white nurse's uniform. She recalled the day her father discovered her before the bathroom mirror with his stethoscope hanging down her school uniform, all the way down to her waist. How he came up behind her and clasped her shoulders, his gaze misting over when it merged with hers in the mirror. He'd filled her with pride and expectation when he'd whispered that, one day, she'd make a fine doctor.

A physician's calling was a noble one. In a world of specialists, Mary had chosen a difficult track. A general practitioner worked grueling days and earned far less than a doctor who specialized.

She'd have it no other way.

To Mildred, she said, "It's a pleasure to meet you."

"How was the trip to Cincinnati?"

Needing distance, Anthony wandered onto the bedroom's second-story balcony. The storm buffeting Ohio was letting up, leaving the acres behind his house sweet smelling. Pearly globes of water hung from the leaves of the maple tree. They were a translucent display of violets and blues in the moonlight. He tried to appreciate the otherworldly beauty despite his mood.

How to pretend everything was fine? Flowers, chocolates, and weeks of romance—none of his attempts to win Mary had dented her resolve.

She leaned against the doorjamb separating the porch from the master bedroom. "I had a nice day catching up with Abe," she said, and he caught the tentative quality of her voice, the careful journey she took across his emotions. "I stopped by the Apple Store afterward. I hope you don't mind."

"You bought the iPad?"

"And a few board games at a toy store. Is it all right? I should've talked to you first."

He reached into the maple's thick crown of leaves. Raindrops rolled down his forearm, evading the moonlight. "It's fine." He cast a sideways glance before returning to his appraisal of the night. "She's dying. If an iPad makes her happy, what the hell."

"Don't talk like that," she said, and he was glad for her discomfort. It was pathetic and immature, but he wanted her to feel as badly as he did. "I was driving back to the restaurant when I saw your car in the driveway. Why aren't you at the hospital?"

"I was. I'll go back later."

"How is Blossom today?"

"The same." He gave his full attention. "What did you think of Abe's clinic?"

"I got reacquainted with two of the doctors from the hospital who are seeing his patients. I also met the nicest couple. The wife has early stage Alzheimer's." She noticed the navy blazer he wore. "Are you going out?"

Dodging the question, he returned to the bedroom. Mary seemed aware of his churning emotions—she'd clasped her hands at her waist in a white-knuckled grip. The urge to go to her was strong. Resisting, he went to the closet and selected a tie.

He was about to ask if she'd had dinner when she said, "We have to tell Blossom about the clinic. I know we agreed to wait until summer's over. We shouldn't."

"Let's decide later." He was meeting with Dr. Lash this evening, something he preferred not to discuss. Adding a discussion of Blossom was beyond his emotional reserves. "When *are* you leaving?"

"October, I think."

"You're stalling." He yanked the tie around his neck. "Are you interviewing managers for The Second Chance? Have you started looking for a replacement?"

She flinched beneath his sudden anger. "I don't want to leave. I want you and Blossom." He'd made a mess of his tie and she took over, knotting the fabric expertly at his throat. When she'd finished, she asked, "Why don't you sell the Gas & Go? Move with me to Cincinnati."

They'd discussed this countless times. "If the economy in Liberty were better, if there were any chance of finding a buyer for the gas station, I'd consider selling."

"So you have to stay. Your work is here, and I can't imagine Blossom growing up without all her cousins, your parents . . ." Cutting off, she slipped her hands beneath his shirt. An involuntary dart of pleasure tripped across his skin. "She'll live, Anthony. She'll grow into a beautiful young woman. She'll be grateful she grew up with so many loving relatives nearby."

Mary drew her hips close, an invitation he didn't have the strength to resist. Every time he made love to her, his despair snuffed out another dream. Mary, pregnant with his child. Blossom, growing into womanhood beneath a doting mother's attentions. And him, reveling in the sanctuary of marriage after years of lonely bachelorhood.

On impulse, he clasped her chin. She met his eyes with a look of sadness quickly fusing with desire. "Mary, you can't leave. Blossom needs you." His expression crumbled. "*I* need you."

Her lips trembled. "Don't you know how much I love you?" For proof, she rained kisses on his cheeks. "I'll visit twice a month. More often, if possible."

"Then what?" he asked, angry at her cool logic. "What happens when we get sick of dating and want to marry? Should we keep two houses, one at either end of the state?"

Her eyes dilated with an urgency that was part heat, part desperation. "Other people do. Why can't we?"

"It won't work."

"Maybe it will, for a few years. Then you and Blossom will move to Cincinnati. You'll find a new business." She dragged her hand across her damp eyes, smearing mascara to her temple. "Why are you determined to give up?"

Her teary rant melted his rage. He couldn't bear to see her in agony. Why thrust harsh realities at her when she couldn't accept them? He took her mouth in a hungry kiss, working fast to unbutton her blouse, backing her up to the bed until they were falling down onto the mattress.

Shadows crept across the carpet. From the street, a motorcycle sent a roar through the room. Anthony barely heard the racket as he stripped off her clothes then his own, and buried himself deep inside her.

For a moment, he let the warm surf of ecstasy wash over him. The sensation was meager consolation.

Chapter 25

At St. Barnabas Hospital, Mary woke to find Anthony and his father talking in hushed voices.

The clock read four thirty-seven A.M. Groggy, she sat up in the chair where she'd curled up with her tennis shoes kicked off.

In the bed Blossom was burrowed under the blankets with only a sliver of her mouth exposed. Shallow, labored breaths issued from her lips. They'd endured a rough night with more hair loss while Mary held Blossom as she bent over the toilet. The rich brown curls drifting to the floor gave indisputable proof of the chemotherapy drugs' raw power to kill healthy cells along with the cancer.

Retreating from the memory, Mary tugged on her shoes. "What are you doing here?" she whispered. Anthony helped her to her feet. "You should be home sleeping."

"Tried to," he said.

Rubbing the sleep from her eyes, Mary studied his attractive navy blue suit with the brass buttons on the sleeves, the same suit he'd worn yesterday. The unexpectedly formal attire, more than anything else, brought her to full wakefulness.

His father smoothed his palm down his slumbering granddaughter's spine. A large man with a wide forehead, and salt and pepper hair, he possessed eyes as beautiful as Anthony's. He smiled in greeting.

"Let's talk in the parents' room down the hall," he suggested.

At the end of the corridor, there was a suite for parents of critically ill children. The living room-dinette area was outfitted with faux leather couches and a well-stocked kitchenette.

Mary took a seat on one of the couches beside Mario. Anthony rummaged around the kitchenette, plugged in the coffee maker and filled the pot with water. Soon the aroma of brewing coffee scented the air.

He found a carton of milk in the refrigerator. "I met with Dr. Lash after I left Blossom last night," he told Mary.

She gripped the couch's armrest. "Has the cancer metastasized?"

"No, but the chemo isn't killing the leukemia. Lash wants to do the bone marrow transplant."

"That's great. Let's move forward." Relief flooded her veins. She recalled Lash mentioning he'd collected healthy marrow from Blossom during her remission. "How fast can we set up the procedure?"

"Blossom's weak," Anthony said. "She's not a good candidate for this."

"She *may* respond to healthy marrow. Reason enough to proceed."

A muscle worked in his jaw. He remained silent.

Mario leaned forward on the couch. Steadily, he watched his son. At length, he looked away. When his gaze sought out hers, she read the pity in his eyes. The regret.

Her stomach twisted. "Oh, God. What aren't you telling me?"

Mario squeezed her knee. With a start, she realized he was preparing her for an awful truth.

Anthony said, "I can't afford a bone marrow transplant. I'll do the rounds this morning to the banks, but my credit's shot. I'll never get a loan." The explanation filled the room with an impossible void. Finally, he added, "It's not just the procedure but everything else. We're talking six figures, more money than I can pull together."

Her skin icy, she managed to suppress her fear. "I don't understand," she said, resisting the hard facts he'd laid out.

"Mary, you're a doctor. You know we're talking about more than the transplant. Blossom will spend extra time in the hospital at thousands of dollars per day. Lash isn't sure how long she'd need to stay. Every day she's here, I accrue expenses outside the limits of my insurance."

"You've spoken to your insurer? They won't consider paying for the procedure?"

"It's an out-of-pocket expense."

Never before had the awful calculus of the disintegrating U.S. healthcare system seemed such a hardship. How often did catastrophic illness put hardworking folks in the poorhouse? Gridlocked legislation, an aging population, and the dizzying expenses of the latest medical technologies—only the wealthiest Americans enjoyed full coverage.

Still, she refused to surrender. "What about a second mortgage? Get an equity line."

He came across the room with two cups of coffee. "We did that the last time," he said in a voice so calm, her pulse tripped. "We all did."

"All .. ?"

She recalled Liza's comment during the picnic. The entire Perini family had provided money the last time Blossom became ill, in elementary school. They'd all pitched in.

"Even Rennie helped," he said with a dry laugh. "Hell, she's my kid sister. She'd only been in business for a few years when we got Blossom's diagnosis. She'd been making money hand over fist and she'd saved every penny."

He stopped, too choked up to continue.

Mary set her coffee aside. "Your sister gave you the money she'd saved." An awful stillness filled her as she reached for his hand. His fingers were cold. "There isn't any money left, is there?"

When the question went unanswered, Mario patted her knee. "My son cleaned us out. Not that we'd have it any other way." He paused to sip his coffee, and Mary caught the fleeting distress clouding his features. Quashing it, he asked his son, "Did you need to speak to us to get our opinion? About Blossom?"

The conversation had taken a dangerous turn. Mary was falling toward a dark truth.

She came to her feet. "What do you mean?"

Anthony trained his eyes on his father. "I can't make the decision alone."

"Son, we should include your mother."

"This is too much for her. We'll leave her out of it."

"You promised Blossom you'd take her home if the chemo didn't work."

"Pop, I don't want to keep that promise but the chemo isn't enough. Am I taking the right course, following Blossom's wishes?"

"She doesn't want to die here." Mario's brows lowered. "She'd rather be in her own room surrounded by the things that bring comfort. Your mother and I will move in with you until—"

Breaking off, he walked to the kitchenette. His back shuddered beneath the weight of silent tears. The urge to provide comfort swept through Mary. She couldn't move, couldn't wrap her mind around what they'd decided.

Life returned to her limbs on a wave of sizzling impatience. She pushed hard against Anthony's chest. He stumbled back a few paces.

"Stop it," she said, rushing back in. She grabbed the lapels of his suit and hung tight. "Do the bone marrow transplant. I'll cosign your loan. If that won't work, *I'll* get the loan."

Anthony stood immobile as her fingers curled into the fabric of his sports coat. "Mary, you can't go into hock for me. You won't have anything left to keep The Second Chance afloat. This is the end game."

"Bone marrow transplants save leukemia patients every day. There's time to save her. *I'll* save her."

The compassion seeped from his face. "I won't accept your help."

She pushed him back another foot. "If everyone in your family is tapped out, you have no choice."

He caught her wrists, stilled her. "My daughter has been through enough."

Why was he giving up? For a split second she hated him, hated how the ordeal had whittled away his ability to hope. "I'll sell everything. The Second Chance is filled with antiques. I'll hold an auction, make enough money to save Blossom."

"Mary—"

"I found a chair the other day in the storage room, Chippendale in the Philadelphia style. Not a side chair, an armchair with scrolled arms. It's old and rare and in mint condition. That chair alone will fetch thousands."

Mario's brows lifted. "Did you say thousands?" He approached. "What else is in the storage room?"

"Pop, she's not doing this!"

"If you won't help her, I will. Your mother, Nick, your sisters—we'll all help."

Anthony went bright with anger. "We're done here. I'm taking Blossom home."

Rushing past him, Mary latched onto his father's arm. "There's so much furniture," she assured Mario, glad when his eyes glinted with hope. "And silver. Gold, too. Tankards and punch bowls—I found the sweetest porringer last month. It's a shallow bowl with a design around the edges. Solid gold."

"We can put an auction together quickly," Mario said. "We'll all help distribute flyers. What about a notice in the *County Crier?*"

"We'll draw a huge crowd." She imagined Blossom growing healthy and strong. "Even if Blossom is hospitalized for another month, we'll have money enough to manage."

Anthony pushed between them. "Damn it, I can't let you lose everything. I'll make the rounds to the banks but that's it. After every loan officer in Northeast Ohio turns me down, I'm taking Blossom home where she belongs."

At that precise moment something altered in their relationship, a shifting of fault lines below the surface of the love they'd forged. Now they stood on opposite sides of a chasm neither had known existed. Mary sensed the rift with growing alarm.

Their gazes dueled. Gruffly Anthony said, "She's not your daughter."

The words struck with the power of a fist. She wasn't prepared for the perfect aim he took at her heart. Crushed, she searched for a rebuttal. None was forthcoming.

Anthony was immune to her pain. "Do you understand?" he demanded, his voice choking on a sob. He hauled her close. No love, no sympathy—he looked as if he despised her. "Blossom is dying. You think she's beating the cancer. She's not. She's been through enough pain for three lifetimes."

Miraculously, Mary found her voice. "I want her out of pain

too. I want her to live."

"You don't know her like I do. The minute she loses the rest of her hair, she'll collapse like the last time. Only now she's too weak to fight." He let her go. "I've spent years watching her suffer and I won't let you throw everything away because the truth is, *nothing will save her.*"

Anger welled so quickly she struggled against the urge to slap him. "How dare you. You *have* given up." He'd visit a few banks but it was a ruse. He'd let Blossom die. "I trust Dr. Lash. If he thinks there's any chance, we forge on. I don't care if it puts me in the poorhouse."

The grief she'd managed to suppress gripped her. But she refused to fall apart, not when there was so much to organize.

She marched to the door. "Tell Blossom I'll see her tonight."

Mario nodded. "I'll tell her."

Controlling the quaver in her voice proved impossible. "I love her, too," she told Anthony. "I'm not losing her."

During the lonely drive back to Liberty, thoughts of Blossom mingled with her reflection on the argument with Anthony. The dispute had broken their relationship.

Reaching the Square, Mary nursed her gloom. It wasn't yet dawn. A cold front had blown in from Lake Erie. In the glare of streetlamps, the center green's maple leaves wore the first patches of autumn gold.

Shifting the car into park, she appraised the storefronts slumbering in the waning night.

Odd how things worked out. With enough prayers and luck, an auction would give Blossom a second chance at life. Yet the same lucky events would destroy Mary's relationship with the girl's father. Anthony would never forgive her for going ahead without his consent. If she sold all the antiques and Blossom lived, he'd be overwhelmed by guilt. She'd found a way to save his daughter after he'd bailed out. If she sold everything and Blossom died? He'd suffer shame. She'd used her last dime in a failed attempt to save his child.

Heartache accompanied her into The Second Chance Grill. For weeks now, she'd worn her grief like a second skin. She didn't want to lose Anthony this way. Oh, she knew eventually she'd lose him once she returned to Cincinnati and the demands of a long-distance relationship became untenable. But she'd hoped for a bittersweet end to their relationship. Not this.

In the kitchen, Finney was at the table filling out checks. A stack of bank notes sat by her elbow awaiting Mary's signature. "What're you doing back so early?" the cook asked, glancing at her watch.

"Thought I'd help you open this morning." She frowned. "Finney, I have news." She explained about the auction they'd hold to pay for the bone marrow transplant.

"We're selling everything off and shutting down the restaurant?"

"There's no other way."

"Does the auction have Anthony's blessing?"

"He's vehemently opposed."

"Can't blame him. You didn't see Blossom during her last go-round with cancer. Doubt he likes the odds this time."

"Even if the transplant is a long shot, it's worth asking Blossom to endure more pain for the chance to live."

"Yes, you're right." Finney trailed her fingers across the table's edge, deep in thought. After a moment, she asked, "You're sure Anthony's father wants the auction? He thinks you're doing the right thing?"

"Mario promised the entire Perini clan would help."

Finney pulled out a chair. After Mary sat, she said, "I'll miss this place. I liked working here." Mary started to apologize but the cook waved her off. "Hush, now. I want to save Blossom as much as you do."

"We *will* save her." Mary rubbed her hands together. She felt cold, her emotions stilled by the intimidating amount of work ahead. Was Anthony correct? They'd hold the auction but Blossom was too weak to survive the transplant? "We need to believe everything will work out. *I* need to believe."

The cook snorted. "Believe what you will. Our Blossom suffering so, and you ready to enter the poorhouse. What about all those college loans you owe for medical school? Mind you, I understand you'll get decent pay at Abe's clinic. But without a nest egg from The Second Chance, how will you ever get out of debt?"

"I can't think about that right now."

"You're too young for burdens so great. As far as I'm concerned, this is the worst thing in the world."

"Not the worst thing, Finney." A ghastly image of Blossom lying in a coffin swept before Mary's eyesight. Shuddering, she dismissed the image. "Not even close."

"Well, I'm sorry about you and Anthony. Call me silly, but I thought you'd find a way to stay together. Guess I was hoping for a miracle."

A miracle. If only . . . "We're beyond that."

The cook laid gentle fingers on Mary's wrist. "How *is* Blossom?" she asked.

Mary's composure threatened to crumble. She shored up her emotions. "She's great. Last night was rough but everything will get better once she has the marrow transplant."

"You're sure, honey?"

"Absolutely."

"Then why are you crying? For someone spouting optimism, you're falling apart."

Mary laughed through her tears. She hadn't meant to cry. She really hadn't.

Sniffling, she switched topics. "Mind if we start cataloguing the antiques today? We'll find time between the lunch and dinner rushes."

"Rest assured, we'll get to it." The cook's gaze grew dewy but she set her jaw. "I'll find moving boxes. We might as well put a price tag on everything. Tables, chairs—everything. I'll bet we'll even sell the nice bunting you put in the window."

"Yes, we'll take it all down," Mary said. *Like my dreams.*

Chapter 26

True to his word, Mario enlisted the entire Perini clan in helping with the auction's preparations. "My daughters are having the flyers printed," he announced, slipping onto a barstool early one morning. "They'll drop them off later today."

"I can't wait to see them." Eyes downcast, Mary reached for the coffee pot. Unwittingly he'd chosen his son's favorite barstool.

She hadn't seen Anthony in days. His absence kept her in a state of perpetual gloom.

"My wife will bake goodies for the auction," Mario was saying. "Even Blossom's friends, Snoops and Tyler, are pitching in. At least they think they are."

Curious, she tipped her head to the side. "What are they doing?"

"I don't know about Tyler but Snoops is a whiz on a computer. She's building a website about Blossom. She's also 'blogging the news' about the auction. What is 'blogging' anyway?" After Mary explained, he said, "Seems like a silly idea but if it makes Snoops feel like she's helping, I'm all for it."

Naturally Blossom's friends wanted to show their support. "We're making progress with the antiques," Mary said. "Nearly half are now catalogued."

"Did you find an appraiser?"

"He came by yesterday to start giving estimates. With so many antiques, he's a bit overwhelmed."

Mario dumped sugar into his coffee, stirred. "How long until he's done?"

"Another day or two."

The answer pleased him. Murmuring farewell, he left with a bounce in his step. Like everyone else, he held out hope the bone marrow transplant would save Blossom.

He'd barely cleared the door when Theodora marched in. Liberty's elderly matriarch wore a green sateen dress, circa 1960, with a rhinestone belt cinching the waist. Despite her petite frame, a decidedly unpleasant frisson of energy followed her to the counter.

She looked like a shark scenting blood in the water as she plunked down on a barstool. "I want the gold porringer," she announced. "It belonged to my great grandfather, Lucas. He brought it clear from South Carolina after The Civil War. I love Blossom same as everyone else but if the porringer leaves The Second Chance, it leaves with me."

"It *is* gorgeous." The rare service piece was one of Mary's favorite antiques. "The porringer's worth a lot of money," she added, thinking of Blossom. "Would you like to make an offer?"

Ethel Lynn, clearly eavesdropping, flew across the dining room. "Mary, don't give her anything unless she pays," she said with surprising firmness. Never before had she stood up to Theodora. "She lost the restaurant and all its contents fair and square."

Theodora shimmied her shoulders. "Like hell I did."

Ethel Lynn batted the air with her handkerchief. "I'm not discussing this, Theodora." She flounced a step closer and struck a pose. "Stop blaming me for a poker game from decades ago. I've had it!"

Mary said, "The poker game?" She recalled the conversation with Theodora on the day she'd injured her knee.

On a huff, Ethel Lynn jabbed her thumb in Theodora's general direction. "Why am I to blame because her late husband liked whiskey? No one told him to gamble away this fine establishment. The restaurant had closed up. Meg thought she could revive the business."

"Just like my Aunt Meg to win this place in a hand of poker," Mary put in. Her aunt led an eccentric life of odd turns and rare luck.

Her comment disappeared into the simmering silence as Theodora held Ethel Lynn in a beady-eyed stare. "I also want the gravy boat," Theodora said. "The one with 'Gimlet' engraved on the side. Barnabas called Ethel Lynn's great-aunt, Mildred, his gimlet. He loved her nearly as much as a good bottle of gin."

"Who's Barnabas?" Mary asked, trying to keep up.

"My great-uncle," Theodora snapped.

Ethel Lynn cast a look of displeasure. "He drank as regularly as Theodora's late husband. I do believe the men of her clan are born with firewater in their veins." She returned the handkerchief to the pocket of her dress—a warm weather number with a design of cucumbers and tomatoes stamped on the ivory cloth. "Barnabas was an Ohio judge," she told Mary. "After his first wife died, he met my great-aunt, married her, and moved to Liberty. No one knows why so many of those wedding gifts were left here, at The Second Chance. But they were, a century ago. And they don't belong to Theodora. Not anymore."

"Lucas and Barnabas are my blood." Theodora raised a fist. "I won't see their possessions sold to strangers!"

Despite her low spirits, Mary stifled a giggle. There was something ridiculous about the elderly matriarch railing about her inheritance.

"Let me get this straight," she said. "One of your ancestors was a judge and the other came here after The Civil War?"

The petite firebrand leapt off the barstool and flew around the counter. "Love brought Lucas to Liberty if you must know." She batted Mary on the shoulder. "He *was* my kin and that's my porringer!"

Ethel Lynn rushed in. "Settle down. Hells bells, your senility has completely taken hold. Mary is holding the auction next weekend. Pay for any items you want *at the auction*."

Theodora glowered, the webbed plane of her forehead growing taut. "Don't sass me, girl."

Mary blocked her before she launched her eighty or so pounds at Ethel Lynn. From the looks of it, she'd be stitching up old woman flesh if she didn't ward off a battle.

"And Barnabas?" she asked, attempting to defuse the situation. "When did he court Mildred?"

"Around the same time Teddy Roosevelt carried a big stick," Theodora said. "Not that it makes any difference. What's mine is mine." She leaned around Mary's waist to stick her tongue out at Ethel Lynn. "He imbibed too much but he was in the throes of passion for Mildred. The man was senseless with desire."

"Well, I'm happy to sell all his love tokens," Mary said. "Seeing you don't own them now."

Ethel Lynn wagged a finger. "I hope Mary takes all your money at the auction. This is Blossom's life we're talking about, and you've got money enough to pad a hundred mattresses. Demanding luxury goods that aren't yours—shame! I mean, really. Will you serve squirrel gravy in the porringer? Disgusting!"

The insult was a match to dynamite. Theodora shot around Mary.

She took a wobbly swing at Ethel Lynn, missed. "I've had enough of your lip, girl!"

"I'm not a girl. I haven't menstruated since Clinton was in office."

Finney barreled in from the kitchen. "Will you old bats stop bickering? Mary's doing her best to save a child at death's door. I ought to string you both up by your varicose veins."

Theodora peered down her hawk nose. "I'll ask you to mind your own beeswax."

A growl rumbled from the cook. "Can't you fools see how you're upsetting Mary? Why, you've been arguing about that poker game for as long as I can remember. No, Ethel Lynn—don't open your mouth. I'll knock you out, I swear I will."

Theodora's mouth lifted in a parody of a grin. "I'll help."

Ethel Lynn dashed behind Mary. "Good heavens, the nerve!"

Finney stomped her foot. "Enough already. We have work to do." She turned to Delia, sensibly watching the fracas from ten paces away. "Run down to the hardware store and buy all the silver polish you can find. Get enough furniture soap to wash down half the wood in a forest. Don't forget the furniture polish and don't waste time flirting with the manager's son."

Delia rushed out.

The cook wound her arm around Mary's shoulders. "Why don't you start phoning the papers in nearby communities?"

"I'll ask for a display ad in the classified section." Mary said, grateful for the cook's take-charge attitude. "I still need to find an auctioneer."

"Consider it done," Ethel Lynn said in a suitably contrite tone. "Billy Bob's Auction House handles all the auctions in our farming community. I'll call him immediately." She hurried out of Theodora's fiery line of vision.

Finney steered Mary toward the kitchen. "Now, how 'bout we head in back and get started on those antiques?" the cook suggested.

Blossom's health continued to decline. During the next week her family took turns holding a bedside vigil, allowing Mary to split time between the hospital and the restaurant.

Preparations for the auction proceeded quickly. Flyers went up across town, and a daily ad appeared in the *County Crier*. The appraiser gave estimates on the price each antique should fetch, a dizzying tally well over six figures. Inside the storage room Mary and Finney sorted furniture, silver and decorative antiques in separate areas. Delia and Ethel Lynn scribbled a hurried description for each item. Then the item was dusted, or sent to the kitchen where Anthony's father and his daughters polished silver and washed crystal until their fingers wore red welts.

Now, with midnight approaching, Mary took a break from the endless chores. To the town's dismay, they'd stopped serving customers yesterday. Liberty's only restaurant boasted tall stacks of boxes in the dining room and a vacant area near the counter where the auctioneer would set up his podium on Saturday. Saddened by the sight, Mary reminded herself that everything she'd done gave Blossom a fighting chance to live.

Finished for the night, she climbed the stairwell to her apartment. Within minutes she fell into a dreamless sleep. Finney, on a promise, woke her at dawn.

"Drink this," the cook said. "Strongest coffee I've ever made."

Mary dragged herself upright then took a grateful sip. "Perfect. Have more downstairs?"

"Gallons."

"I'll need a second cup." She padded into the bathroom and splashed water on her face. "I hope you're planning to sleep in tomorrow. We both should to ensure we're fresh for Saturday."

"We'll manage. The Perinis will help at the auction."

"Delia and Ethel Lynn also promised to help."

"We'll get a big crowd for the auction, that's for sure." Finney noticed the white plastic bag Mary had left on the nightstand. "Mind telling me what this is?" The cook held it up. "I heard you asking Delia yesterday to go to the drugstore. I'm guessing whatever she bought is in here."

Mary picked up her toothbrush then opened the medicine cabinet. "Go ahead and look." She squeezed paste onto the toothbrush.

Finney peered inside the bag. "Scissors? Stickers?" She pulled out the sheet of sixties inspired stickers: peace symbols, smiley faces and flowers drawn in hot pink and neon green. "I do like these," she added, wagging them around. "Are you planning to make a scrapbook with Blossom today?"

"Not exactly," Mary said when she'd finished brushing her teeth.

"Then what *are* you doing?" Brows lowering, the cook pulled out a set of electric hair trimmers. "A salon day?"

"Um, no." She took the bag and deftly switched topics. "Did Ethel Lynn finish tagging the crystal?" They'd found several more boxes of goblets from the restaurant's glory days in the early 1900s.

"She's downstairs finishing now." The cook studied her hands for a moment. Finally she looked up. "Have you told Blossom?"

"About the auction? I'm not sure how to bring it up."

"She deserves to know what you're doing to save her."

"I'll get to it." Before she lost the nerve, Mary took the cook's hand. "Finney, we've spent all these months together. I can't thank you enough for your hard work."

"Don't be silly. You're the salt of the earth, Mary. Best kind of woman there is."

"No, *you're* the salt of the earth. I've learned so much from you."

"Nonsense!"

She gave out a gurgling laugh. Without thinking, she rubbed her nose on her sleeve like a child might if overcome by grief or brimming with gratitude.

Or both.

The cook's bosom shuddered but she stuck out her chin. She refused to let emotion get the best of her. "Are you leaving right after the auction?"

"I need to find a realtor to sell the building." The prospect was depressing but she shook off her gloom. "I'll stay in a hotel near St. Barnabas. I want to be with Blossom when she has the bone marrow transplant."

"Thank goodness. She won't survive without your encouragement."

The cook's eyes grew damp, and Mary sighed. "Finney, if you start crying, I'll never stop. Now, go downstairs. I have to get ready to see Blossom."

Though her skin wore a blue-white pallor, a hint of color seeped into Blossom's cheeks as Mary entered. The plastic bag swung at her side.

Furtively, Mary peered through the slit in the privacy curtain. Just as she'd suspected, the bed was sadly empty. Blossom's roommate had lost her battle with cancer late last night. Mary prayed Blossom wouldn't be too upset when she noticed the loss. Given her lethargy, the day might pass before she did.

"What's that, another game?" Blossom frowned as the bag landed in her lap. She dumped the contents on the blanket. "Geez, you really went to town. Why'd you buy all this stuff?"

"You'll see." Mary inched past the IV strung to Blossom's arm. "Where's your hand mirror? The one covered with Sponge Bob stickers?"

"Check the nightstand." Revulsion spread across the preteen's gaunt features. "Listen, I don't want to look at myself. Not today."

"Today's as good a day as any," she said, pleased when her no-nonsense approach put the faintest curiosity in the girl's eyes. "Ah, here it is. One Sponge Bob mirror coming up."

She risked a full appraisal of Blossom's scalp. The mottled skin appeared inflamed from abuse. The girl had been scratching her scalp, punishing every spot where lavish curls once flourished. The self-inflicted wounds provided yet another indication of her accelerating bouts of depression.

Seating herself, Mary scooted close. "Hold this." She handed over the mirror then pointed to the wall behind the IV stand. "See the electrical socket behind your bed? Plug this in." She tossed over the electric hair trimmers then glanced at the door. "Where is everyone?"

"Dad went to the lobby with Uncle Nick. They're meeting Grandma and Aunt Liza."

"Your father is here?" This wasn't his morning to sit with his daughter. "I wasn't aware he was coming down."

"Grandpa's here too. So are my aunts."

The appearance of so many family members was an ominous sign. "Everyone is visiting today?"

Blossom fanned herself with the mirror. "Grandma just left. Running errands or something. Everyone's being real secretive." She held the mirror still. "Dad was talking to Dr. Lash outside my room. What's going on?"

"I'm not sure."

Irritation glinted in the girl's eyes. She stared at the ceiling, searching for truths in an unknowable universe. The clear-eyed innocence of youth bled from her expression.

"I'm almost twelve years old. I can tell when grownups are hiding stuff." She swallowed, the words coming at a cost. Quickly, she added, "Am I dying?"

The question hung between them. Steadying herself, Mary brushed her fingers across Blossom's cheek.

"Do you want to die?" she made herself ask.

"No!"

"Then don't." The steel in her voice surprised them both. "You have to fight, more than you ever have before. I'll help. Your family will too. But in the final analysis, this is up to you."

The girl bit at her lips. "Okay." She returned to her appraisal of the ceiling. "Last night? I heard Dad and Uncle Nick arguing about what you're doing. Really arguing outside my room. Uncle Nick's on your side one hundred percent."

"What did you overhear?" She still wasn't sure it was wise to explain.

"You're having an auction to raise money for me." Blossom shrugged. "The auction sounds nice. But they said other stuff . . . about you leaving."

Her heart moved into her throat. "I am."

"Why?"

Calmly, she explained about her responsibility to take over the free clinic. The conversation lengthened, and Blossom's eyes grew large. There wasn't a simple way to explain adult obligations to a critically ill child. Wasn't this what she'd dreaded all along? Letting Blossom down?

Summing up, she said, "Sweetie, we'll still see each other. I'll drive up on weekends. When you're feeling better, I'm sure your dad will let you visit me in Cincinnati."

"Sounds cool." Fierce emotion swept through Blossom's expression, a defiance competing with her disappointment. "Then you can't marry my dad because you're moving?"

"No, sweetie. I can't."

"That's what Grandma said. She said you and Dad love each other but the timing is wrong."

"She's right."

"Is my dad going to stay mad at you?"

"I hope not."

"I won't stay mad because you're leaving. I guess I understand." Tentatively, Blossom traced her fingers in an affectionate path across Mary's wrist. "You're a good doctor. I hope you like your new patients."

The sadness overtaking her expression prodded Mary to lighten the mood. "It's nice your relatives came down today," she said, trying for a cheery note. "When we're finished with our handiwork, let's throw a party and invite them. We'll be the party girls."

"What *are* we doing?"

"Hold the mirror straight." Blossom did, and Mary added, "Put my hair in the bag. No sense messing up the floor. We'll do the same with yours."

"You're cutting off your hair? You've got to be shitting me."

"You shouldn't swear."

Blossom's eyes danced. "Right."

Mary reached for the scissors. "First I'll snip most of my hair. After that, it's stage two—electric trimmers. You, on the other hand, can go straight to the trimmers for a baldy look. The chemo is giving you one anyway."

Blossom grinned. "Whatever you say."

Entering the hospital room, Anthony halted so quickly that Nick crashed into him. On the bed, his daughter and Mary sat with a fluffy pile of mingled hair between them.

His mother gasped. So did his sisters. His father pulled out a handkerchief and hurried into the corner, ostensibly to blow his nose. Anna's husband Joe, and Liza stared in wide-eyed wonder. They understood if you married into the Perini clan, anything was possible.

His brother found the situation hilarious.

Striding to the bed, Nick gave each of the baldies a pat on the head. He complimented them on the neon-bright stickers they'd stuck on their noggins and asked if they had more. They did. Satisfied, he picked up the trimmers and buzzed right down the center of his thick, curly hair. Thus shorn, he leered maniacally at the rest of the Perini brood.

Then Nick made the announcement: they were about to become the Gutless and the Glory groups.

Liza took one look at her husband and fled into the ranks of the gutless. Full of apology, she explained no attorney worth her salt entered a courtroom with her locks shorn down to her glossy brown skin. A bald pate would send a confusing message to the judge and frighten jurors.

Frannie, a wild-hearted junior at Kent State, took one look at Blossom and Mary, and grabbed the trimmers. She shaved off her short, cropped hair in two minutes flat. No one would describe KSU as a conservative college, and she announced her new look might start a trend.

In a show of grandparent solidarity, both of Anthony's parents shaved. They did so after Frannie. In a bow to his Italian roots, Nick grabbed the trimmers and sang *O Solo Mio* while he finished doing a number on his head.

Joe shaved. His wife ran from the room with Liza on her heels.

Anthony was sure his sister, Rennie, intended to join the glory bunch. She marched into the bathroom. She fluffed up her long, wavy tresses. With a flourish she picked up the scissors and stared hard at her reflection in the mirror.

The scissors never found their target. She tossed them down and bolted. Anthony knew she'd forever diminished herself in Nick's eyes by joining Anna and Liza in the gutless group.

Anthony was last. By the time he'd wrestled the trimmers from his cackling brother—who the nurses threatened to evict if he didn't quiet down—tufts of hair covered the linoleum floor like tumbleweeds drifting across the prairie. He tried to catch Mary's eye as he shaved down to his scalp. To his disappointment, she seemed intent on serenely covering Blossom's forehead with stickers while his family surrounded the bed.

In the center of it all, his daughter sat like a princess holding court in a roomful of admirers.

Lost amidst the revelry, Anthony stood silent at the foot of the bed. He wanted to take Mary's hand and beg her forgiveness. He wanted to nestle his daughter in his lap and shield her from the future she'd been meted out by Fate. He wanted so many things, but what he saw on his daughter's face left him too stunned for sadness or self-pity.

Throughout the arduous weeks in the hospital, Blossom had cartwheeled through a gamut of emotions. Some days she was stoic or quiet. At times she chatted about school or spent the hours drifting on an ocean of tears. She was optimistic one minute; a child trapped in sorrow the next.

It was all to be expected. Anthony was old enough to have seen death up close. He'd lost his grandparents, an uncle, two friends. The human body wasn't built on forevers; the heart clogged and slowed, and muscles grew frail and weak. Age happened to us all, and he'd donned grief every time a loved one breathed the last. Yet for Blossom, death was an error. She risked being taken out of turn.

She'd been pushed to the front of a line she hadn't known existed. Stand up, walk over, take a number. She was a child only beginning to understand life, to get a firm grasp on everything the world had to offer.

Yet she'd been yanked to the front of the line, which left her emotions in a constant state of flux.

Now, glimpsing her surrounded by her doting family and one special friend, the state of a dying child's emotions were all the more remarkable. For there *was* an emotion he hadn't seen her display since entering St. Barnabas Hospital.

Blossom was laughing.

Chapter 27

At the podium, the auctioneer rustled papers and adjusted his bifocals.

As tall as Abe Lincoln and rail thin, Billy Bob leafed through a stack of papers while people from across the county filled the rows of chairs rented for the auction. Delia stood nearby to hold items aloft or gesture at larger items like a game show host. They were all feeling low, Delia included, but she was taking her duties seriously. Grim-faced and attentive, she wore what Mary supposed was her best outfit, a navy blue dress with red piping on the sleeves and white star-shaped buttons running down the bodice.

In the front row, Theodora sat with a man's bowler hat planted low on her forehead.

An elegant brunette in ivory silk and pearls swept into the dining room. An out-of-towner, the woman began nosing around the furniture crammed against the walls. Mary pulled her attention away.

All the antiques will be gone by sundown. She clamped her hands at her waist in a futile attempt to calm her roiling emotions. *Think of Blossom instead.* None of the antiques equaled the worth of a child's life. Given the size of the crowd, the bone marrow transplant appeared all but paid for.

Clinging to the thought she stepped back, allowing a young couple to find seats. Like dozens of others, they risked whiplash by craning their necks to take in her bald scalp, which Mary felt she'd accented nicely with silver hoop earrings and careful attention to her makeup. Twelve hours after the fact, everyone in Liberty knew the story of how most of the Perinis—and Mary—had willingly shorn their hair like a herd of sheep. But hearing the tale wasn't the same as seeing, and a woman as bald as a newborn lifted more than a few eyebrows.

As the young couple continued to gape, Mary slipped behind the counter. Crystal sparkled and brass gleamed on every inch of available space. She trudged past and into the kitchen.

Finney was tagging a familiar gold bowl with scalloped edges. "Why don't you keep this as a souvenir of your time in Liberty?" she asked Mary. "I've never seen anything so pretty."

"The porringer is solid gold."

"Good heavens! What do you think it's worth?"

"More than you or I have in our respective bank accounts." Mary ran her thumb across the scalloped edge. "Think of the money it'll bring for Blossom's care. Theodora is sure to bid."

Next the cook tagged a porcelain gravy boat. She nodded toward the hallway in back. "There's someone waiting to speak to you."

Anthony? Hope surged through Mary. The thought of moving away without healing their rift had haunted her for days.

"Not Anthony," Finney said. She tipped up Mary's chin. "Now, wipe off that frown. Meade asked to speak with you. I don't mind saying I've left her stewing for a good ten minutes. Least I can do."

"Why is she here?" Given all the trouble she'd caused, putting in an appearance was in bad taste. "Throw her out. I'll have enough trouble keeping myself together while everything in the restaurant is sold off. I can't talk to her."

"Oh, you'll listen. I'm the last person in the world to defend Meade, but you need to hear her out." The cook reached for a silver platter, her polishing rag at the ready. "Go on, now."

Obeying, Mary went to investigate. She felt defensive and angry, in no mood to dredge up a civil tone.

By the back door, Meade paced with her poodle cradled in her arms. Beneath her heavily made-up face, her features were somber. Her platinum hair was mussed, as if she'd run her fingers through the locks countless times.

She lowered Melbourne to the ground. "Thanks for seeing me. I didn't think you would."

Entreaty burnished the comment. Unimpressed, Mary said, "Why don't you call tonight? The auction is about to start."

"Yes, the auction—that's why I'm here." She withdrew a check from her purse. "Will you take a donation for Blossom's care? I'd like to contribute."

Despite her reservations, Mary took the check. Reading the amount, she murmured, "This is five thousand dollars. *Five thousand.*"

"The least I can do."

'I don't know what to say."

"Then let me talk." Meade stepped closer. "I never should've been jealous of you. We weren't competing for Anthony—he belonged to you from the start. He still does even if he's too foolish to see the truth."

Her sincerity threatened to overrun Mary's heart. "He doesn't belong to me. He never will."

"He loves you. I heard he was against the auction—you know about men and their pride. Deep down, he's surely grateful you've given so much to save his daughter. Still, I suspect he feels he's broken some chivalrous code by allowing you to bail him out."

"I'm not bailing him out." Anger surged through her. "This is about Blossom. He should understand that."

"He does." Meade laughed suddenly. "You know, I didn't believe the news about how you'd shaved your head. You pull it off well."

Mary palmed the tender skin above her ears. "I'm getting sunburned. Can you believe it?" Despite herself, she grinned. "I need to buy a hat."

"Then do."

Without asking permission, Meade brought her into a tender hug. The affection was almost motherly. Drawing apart, they gazed at each other with newfound respect.

"I'm sorry to see you go." Meade scooped Melbourne into her arms. "You would've taken good care of Anthony and Blossom." She pulled Mary in for another quick hug. "I have no idea what a bone marrow transplant costs. If you don't raise enough money, call me. I'll do whatever I can."

With the grace of royalty, she pivoted on her heel and swept out.

Heat rippled off the pavement outside the Gas & Go. Needing shade, Anthony trudged toward the sadly abandoned service island. Not one soul had stopped at the gas station since opening this morning. In contrast, the other side of the Square gave off a carnival-like energy. People knocked elbows and jumbled together with shouts and laughter. Most of Liberty's inhabitants, and an increasing number of out-of-towners, were streaming into The Second Chance Grill.

Anthony's heart urged him forward. Yet his feet remained planted on the hot asphalt beneath the glittering sun.

How to patch things up with Mary? At the least, she deserved a sincere apology before she sold everything off and moved back to Cincinnati.

Kicking at gravel, he searched for words beyond the abilities of his fumbling heart. Fact was, he couldn't bear to think of losing her at all.

What right did a man have to put his needs before a woman's dreams? Mary was a healer, a woman with special gifts and a caseload of patients waiting for her services. His love for her didn't enter the equation. She was making the right decision, which left him with the sole task of begging her forgiveness before she was gone.

His father strolled out of the gas station, where he'd camped all morning in a touching display of parental support. "Son, go over to the auction." He rested his hand on Anthony's shoulder. "Your sisters are helping Mary hand out flyers. Liza is too."

"They think people will bid higher if they read about Blossom." *They're hoping the money will save her life.*

He wanted to believe, too. Lord, he wanted to believe. Dr. Lash's increasing reticence regarding Blossom's prognosis warned against optimism.

"I'd like to go over," he admitted. "I'm not sure I'm welcome at The Second Chance."

"You aren't sure how to apologize."

SECOND CHANCE GRILL

"Basically."

"You're a horse's ass," his father announced. "I'd knock some sense into you if I thought it would work. Everything Mary's done? You owe her a debt of gratitude."

"Give it your best shot, Dad." Hell, he deserved a lot worse after the way he'd treated her.

"I'd rather hand the job to your brother." Mario pointed to Nick, coming across the center green with his legs pumping like a train gaining steam. "He isn't stopping by for a social visit."

Anthony groaned. The jovial expression Nick usually wore was nowhere in evidence. His head was held high, his eyes mere slits. Sunlight glinted off his newly shorn head.

"Why are you standing here feeling sorry for yourself?" Nick demanded. "Mary is selling off everything she owns to save your daughter. Why aren't you lending her comfort? A jackass like you doesn't deserve a woman of her caliber."

"I *am* a jackass." Anthony's shoulders sagged.

"Damn right you are!"

"And a horse's ass," his father put in.

Anthony sighed heavily. "Don't you think I tried talking to her at the hospital?" he said to no one in particular. "I wanted to."

Nick cornered him, standing nose-to-nose. "I was at the hospital, ugly boy. If you tried apologizing, you sure didn't try hard enough."

"I couldn't get her alone, not with all of you chopping your hair off. Hell, Nick, you'd turned the place into a madhouse—" He stopped abruptly, and stared in wonder at the commotion in the center green. "What's going on now?"

In tandem the men took in the surprising sight of Mayor Ryan dragging Blossom's friends Tyler and Snoops toward the Gas & Go. Finney brought up the rear with her mouth running a mile a minute. It was anyone's guess which woman was more furious—both the cook and the mayor looked griddle-hot.

Skirting the mayor, Finney arrived first. "Anthony, tell the mayor to let the kids go. They were only trying to help."

Fleeing the mayor's clutches, Tyler added, "It's true, Mr. Perini. We only built the websites to help Blossom. We didn't know there'd be so much email."

"Email?" Anthony glanced questioningly at Mayor Ryan.

She muttered a few choice words then said, "These troublemakers posted the courthouse email address on five websites—*my email.* People from New York City to San Diego have sent so much mail our server went down. *Twice.*"

Nick scratched his armpit with the finesse of a Great Ape. "That's not good."

"You think?" The mayor landed her fiery regard on Anthony. "I've also been inundated with calls. The phone hasn't stopped ringing. Anthony, I understand that everyone wishes to help your daughter. I do too, but my office isn't equipped to handle donations. I have a town to run."

Snoops fiddled with her purple-framed glasses. "I didn't think there'd be so many calls to the courthouse. Honest, I didn't."

He gave her shoulder a squeeze. "Snoops, what exactly did you do?" Given her IQ, which hovered in the stratosphere, anything was possible.

Her black bean gaze found his. "I, uh, built the websites and did some blogging. After I set up the blogs and wrote a bunch of posts, I designed an algorithm."

"What's an algorithm?" Evidently Snoops thought the gizmo would raise money for Blossom's care.

"No offense, Mr. Perini. You wouldn't understand." She rubbed the side of her nose, deep in thought. After a moment, she added, "See, me and Tyler figured more people would show up for the auction if they saw the photograph of Blossom when she had cancer the last time. So I scanned a picture I took of her in fifth grade. I uploaded everything, wrote copy about the auction, built the websites then seeded other sites. Oh, I also transmitted to AP, CNN, CTV, BBC and Univision."

Anthony grabbed his brother, whispering, "Are you getting this?"

"Sort of," Nick replied. "Snoops transmitted info about Blossom across the Internet. Half the journalists on six continents are reading the story. Millions of average Joes like you and me are doing the same."

Mayor Ryan flapped her arms. "Would someone explain in English?"

Finney shoved the mayor, sending her stumbling sideways.

"Shut up already," the cook said. She'd picked up tech basics from her unruly son. "This is getting interesting."

Anthony regarded Snoops, nervously toeing the ground. "You made Blossom an international story? You did this to bring more people to the auction?"

She blinked rapidly. "I just wish there'd been more time. If I'd heard about the auction sooner, maybe I could've brought in more people."

"Like the entire population of China," Nick said.

Finney chuckled nervously. "That's fine, but I'm not making rice for a billion Chinese. I've already packed up most of the kitchen."

Mayor Ryan glared at her. "Go on back, Finney. At least you won't be answering the phone all day . . . as I will." After the cook stalked off, she added dryly, "Mary's auction has drawn a mostly local crowd. I'm sure I would've noticed the Chinese if they'd stopped by in the thousands."

Despite the mayor's incredulity, a marvelous expectancy danced Anthony. He looked off to the center green. The breeze rustled the treetops, and leaves fluttered like a thousand waving hands.

"Maybe they haven't arrived yet," he said.

Chapter 28

Naked bulbs threw ribbons of white across the dining room's empty walls. The lighting fixtures that had encased them were gone. Like everything else, they'd been sold.

The auction had gone well, even if they hadn't raised quite enough money to cover the bone marrow transplant and the accompanying expenses for hospital care. Still, thousands of dollars *had* been raised. If the shortfall seemed depressing, Mary assured herself other avenues for raising cash would appear in time. Perhaps she'd take out a loan for the rest or a buyer would come forward to purchase the building that no longer housed The Second Chance Grill.

Her fatigue was bone deep. She'd sent everyone home and planned to catch a few hours' sleep before driving to St. Barnabas. Rising from bed after so little rest didn't appeal, but twenty-four hours had passed since her last visit with Blossom.

She feathered her palm across her shorn head. The dining room seemed overlarge with the furniture gone, and her footsteps echoed with disturbing sound. Scraps of paper littered the floor. Finney had returned the folding chairs to the rental store after the last buyers hurried out with boxes and bags of the restaurant's historic treasures. The last moving van had fired up its engine and drove away. Afterward, she'd urged Finney to call it a day. The cook was so downcast, she hadn't argued. Mary's solitude was absolute.

"Mary?"

Swiveling around, she found Anthony hovering beside the counter. Evidently he'd entered from the back of the building, his footsteps muffled by her gloomy thoughts.

Regret sifted through her. He stood in the exact spot where he'd been on the day they met. The day Blossom began her quest to spark a romance between them.

"Why aren't you at the hospital?" she asked. The urge to wrap her arms around him was difficult to suppress. "One of us should be there."

"I just got back." His beautiful eyes, dusky with emotion, remained fixed on her. When she frowned with worry, he added, "She's fine. My parents are with her."

"How is she?"

"Weak, but holding on."

"I'm glad." On impulse, she motioned to the spot where he stood. "Do you remember the day we met?"

He rubbed his jean-clad thighs with nervous movements. "Of course I do. Blossom came into the Gas & Go in a fever about you. She made me come to the restaurant so we'd meet. She said your cooking was special."

"I'd spent weeks redecorating. It would've been smarter to learn the basics of cooking." A thread of amusement nudged past her heartache. "I wanted to bring something special to Liberty."

"You did." Anthony gentled his tone. "You do."

"I didn't know who you were," she rushed on, the heartache returning so quickly she feared she'd brim over. "You were simply a good looking man who came in with his daughter for ice cream. I was devastated over Sadie's death, losing her friendship and carrying on without her . . . but I felt something for you the moment we met."

"You did?" He rubbed his chin. "I thought I was the only one."

"When you shook my hand, you didn't let go." Not knowing the reason still bothered her. "I thought there was food on my face—I'd been helping Finney in the kitchen." She hesitated. "*Why* didn't you let go?"

Smiling, he pulled off the bar. "Keep the questions simple. Makes it easier for a guy who has a lot of groveling to do."

"Then tell me," she said with faint irritation. The heat in his voice sent a trill down her spine but she needed more, an explanation sure to speak directly to her heart.

Which he must have sensed because he caught her gaze and held fast. "I didn't let go because I fell in love with you the minute we met," he said in a slow, steady voice that began to heal the wound he'd placed on her heart. "I went down the first minute. And I was upset—not at you, not at falling in love—I was irritated with Blossom. She'd been nagging me to stop by and meet you. I didn't want to go. Later—"

He broke off, and the memories grew thick in his gaze.

Though the pain seemed more than he could handle, she prodded him on. "And later?"

"I didn't understand how my daughter saw my destiny, everything I yearned for and needed. Finally I understood."

Slowly she walked toward him. "*What* did you understand?"

"Blossom wasn't seeing my destiny as much as her own. You were meant to be her mother." He met her in the center of the dining room. Carefully, he took her hand in his. "If it means losing everything I've put into the Gas & Go, I'll do it. Blossom and I will move to Cincinnati. No matter how much time she has left, she *is* your daughter in every way that matters." He hesitated, his expression tender. "And I'm your husband, if you'll have me."

"I can't ask you to give up so much." The cost was too great. His life belonged in Liberty.

"You don't have to ask," he insisted. "I won't lose you. You're everything to me."

Common sense ate through the passion rising between them. "We're both exhausted," she said. "Let's not decide tonight."

"Whatever you say, doctor." A lopsided grin eased the tension on his face. "For the record, you aren't the only one with a stubborn streak. I know how to get my way too."

"So I've been told."

He pressed his palms to her cheeks, anchoring her. "Blossom understood I'd get another chance at love. She knew you deserved a second chance, too."

"So does she," Mary said. "Blossom *will* live."

The amusement vanished from his features, and her heart overturned. "We might not save her." When the comment weakened Mary's legs, he clasped her shoulders, adding, "You can't choose whether a child lives or dies. If this is her time, you'll have to accept it. We both will."

The tears ran hot down her cheeks. "It's *not* her time."

"God knows I hope you're right. But there will be other children," he said firmly. "They deserve a chance, too. We owe it to them to go on. Blossom would want us to go on."

"Other . . ?" Her vision blurring, she canvassed his face.

"The children we'll bring into the world together." He rubbed his nose across hers, the gesture so comforting she pressed her forehead to his on a sigh. "They want to feel the grass beneath their feet and hear the sound of rain falling. They'll be beautiful, and we'll love them."

As he spoke, she imagined the softness of a baby's skin. In her mind's eye she heard the voice of a three year old, smelled summer's first hot dog, and tasted the glory she'd experience at Anthony's side. She owed much to the future they'd build. Even if he must give up Liberty, give up the world he loved to become part of hers, wasn't the sacrifice worth the richness of a life together? Yet imagining such an outcome was difficult. How much easier to envision their children growing up in Liberty—all of their children, including Blossom.

She let out a gurgling laugh. "You're a convincing man."

"I can never repay you for all you've done," he said, pressing her face to his chest. "I *can* promise I'll spend the rest of my life trying. Let me try, Mary. Will you?"

Closing her eyes, she nestled close. "Yes," she said. "Yes, of course."

He led her upstairs with a sense of completeness he'd never before experienced. Overcome by exhaustion, they slept twined around each other.

When Anthony woke before dawn to find her fingers weaving through his chest hair and her mossy gaze lingering on his face, he made slow, thorough love to her. After long, pleasurable minutes, the haunting calls of the mourning doves and the upbeat music urged him from the bed.

Music?

He followed the thumping sounds of drums and guitars to the window. Dew sparkled on the center green's thick lawn. Daylight's blush seeped across the courthouse.

Locating the source of the music proved easy. On a picnic table at the east end of the green, a teenager sat next to a boom box straight out of the 1970s. The red, white and blue bandanna on his head was clearly inspired by the American flag. His three-day-old beard growth, torn jeans and neat penmanship gave the impression of a university student.

Penmanship?

"Mary, get over here," Anthony said, his voice hoarse with emotion. "A kid has planted a sign and a banner in the center green."

She grabbed a robe. "What does the sign say?" she asked.

Anthony swiped at his eyes. "It's shaped like a heart and reads, 'Save Blossom. We love her.'"

"What's on the banner?"

"Save America's Second Chance Grill."

She threw her hand over her mouth.

Grinning, he gave her a peck on the forehead. "Jump in the shower and put on some clothes," he suggested. "More people are coming into the Square, and a news van is pulling up."

By the time they showered and dressed, the music was increasing in volume. They hurried through the dining room humming the familiar notes to *The Star-Spangled Banner*.

At the picture window, they stared in wonder at the ragtag crew of teenagers converging on the picnic table with cups of coffee and donuts. Lined up in a row, the kids looked to the restaurant with clear anticipation. Spotting Mary, standing with her mouth hanging open, they lifted their fists and cheered.

She gave a jerky wave. "Is this from Snoops' websites?" she asked Anthony.

He chuckled. "Beats me."

Behind the rapidly growing crowd of teens and young adults, the passenger door of a CNN van swung open. A man got out. He carried a hand-held camera and began barking orders to the woman who'd leapt from the back of the van. The woman unloaded a tripod, sound equipment and a larger camera. Within minutes two other news vans joined them.

Soon, a whole fleet was lined up outside. Thunderstruck, Mary watched them fill the parking spaces surrounding Liberty Square.

Anthony knelt by the front door. "Mary, come look."

"What is it?"

"The kids slid something under the door."

He handed over a collection of notes and a handful of wrinkled cash—a twenty, a ten and a fistful of one-dollar bills. No doubt the meager donation represented all the pocket money the students possessed.

Thinking of Blossom, she stuffed the money into her jeans. "What do the notes say?" she asked.

He gave a delighted shrug.

Tearing open the first envelope, she read, *We're praying for Blossom*. The next missive said, *Blossom deserves a second chance. So do you. We'll fight to save her and The Second Chance Grill.*

"Oh, Anthony." Her heart brimmed over. "Where did they come from?"

"Kent State," he supplied confidently.

"You sound awfully certain."

"My sister Frannie joined them. She's chowing down on a chocolate éclair and making a sign." He gave Mary a quick squeeze. "I'll make coffee. Put on your show face, gorgeous. Those reporters are on their way over."

By the time the staff arrived, she'd given on-camera interviews to five broadcast journalists and spoken with nine print journalists representing newspapers in Ohio, Pennsylvania and New York.

She'd just sent the last reporter on his way when an elegant woman in a cobalt blue suit parked her Mercedes before the restaurant. Gliding past the crowd on the cobblestone walk, she waved affectionately to Mary like a long lost friend.

"I'm Angie Rosenbaum, a friend of Meade's," she said, rifling through her purse. "Ah. Here we are." She unfolded one of the flyers about Blossom. "Meade put this right in my hand. She knows how enthusiastic I am about bidding on valuables. Unfortunately, I didn't read the flyer until after I'd left your auction."

The woman's bubbly personality drew Mary close. "I recall seeing you," she murmured.

"I wouldn't have missed it. I own an antique shop in Shaker Heights and, frankly, I was so excited! Well, Meade handed me the flyer, and I slipped it into my purse without a second thought. If Jared hadn't rousted me from bed at dawn, I still wouldn't know about the girl with cancer or how you'd sold off the restaurant's valuables to save her." Angie patted the side of Mary's head. "Not to mention cut off your hair."

The woman's hazel eyes sparkled, and Mary decided she liked Angie Rosenbaum very much. "Who's Jared?" she asked.

"My son, the insomniac. Last night he was surfing the Internet. He found the sites about you and Blossom."

Anthony walked over. "A girl named Snoops built the websites," he interjected.

The antique dealer gave him a bright smile. "She may have created the first websites but there are dozens now. Some are raising money for Blossom. Others are working to save The Second Chance Grill."

Mary drew a startled breath. "People are donating money for Blossom *and* the restaurant?"

"One of the sites for Blossom is darling. The landing page has a cartoon of Uncle Sam holding a bag shaped like a heart. Every time someone makes a donation the heart expands. Another site, for your restaurant, is decorated in the Stars and Stripes." Angie beamed. "There's also a site about you."

"Me? Why on earth did someone build a site about *me?*"

"People find your story inspiring, dear. The site covers your medical career with clippings from medical school and the free clinic where you volunteered," Angie said. "You're fast becoming a national treasure—the young doctor willing to sell everything to help a girl in small-town America."

Breaking off, Angie swiveled toward the picture window and the rumble of an engine idling. "Oh, good. They're here."

Outside, three men got out of a large grey truck. The truck's back doors swung open with a grind of noise. The men began unloading items from the restaurant—tables and chairs, brass lamps and countless boxes. Angie waved them inside.

"Mind helping me arrange the tables?" she asked Mary. "I have no idea how everything was set up."

Mary dodged the men carrying in the first table. "You bought most of the furniture yesterday?"

"My staff helped with the bidding. They were planted in the audience."

Worry shot past the exhilaration that had accompanied her since she'd risen this morning. Every last piece of furniture, every gorgeous antique from the storage room was sold to raise money for Blossom.

"I can't take everything back." She took Angie by the wrist. "Blossom needs the money we've raised. I hope you understand."

The cheer on Angie's face deepened to sympathy. "I'm not here for Blossom alone. My son, the insomniac? Jared was a preemie, barely two pounds at birth. We nearly lost him. A doctor—a doctor like you—refused to give up." She clasped Mary's hands. "Yesteray I spent forty thousand at your auction. Keep every penny. This is my way of paying back on good karma."

Too choked up for words, Mary leaned against Anthony's sturdy bulk. She was still trying to compose words suitable to convey her gratitude when Finney rushed in from the street.

"You'll never guess what Theodora's doing!" The cook dragged Mary back to the picture window. "She's live on half the television stations in Ohio. Look at her out there!"

Past the crowd growing larger by the minute, Theodora stood in the center green with a group of reporters thrusting microphones in her face. With expressive gestures, the fast-talking Theodora held the reporters transfixed.

Mary leapt out of the way as the men carried in another table and began putting the dining room back together. Grinning from ear to ear, she peered back out the window.

What *was* Theodora doing?

Chapter 29

Finney's comment proved accurate. Theodora *was* live on all the local television channels.

Within minutes, she was also the lead story on CNN, FOX and MSNBC.

The sheer eccentricity of a small-town matriarch railing against the world propelled Theodora before an attentive public. Her fierce intelligence, combined with her feistiness, wooed the nation. When she hiked up her dress to show the reporters how well Mary had patched up her knee, the whole country listened. Dressed smartly in blue silk and pearls, with a Winchester rifle propped at her side, she spoke of a nation gone wrong when a town like Liberty couldn't keep its one and only doctor.

As far as Theodora was concerned, what right *did* a big city like Cincinnati have to steal Mary away? Cinci had more doctors than all the stinking deer pellets in Theodora's back yard, she explained to the reporters.

Thanks to antique dealer Angie Rosenbaum, the dining room was set back up within minutes. As the last table was shoved into place, someone rushed in from the street with a portable television set. Finney commandeered the set for the kitchen. She pushed Mary down in a chair to watch in open-mouthed amazement as Theodora made the case for a national discussion on healthcare that wouldn't involve special interests or the self-serving lobbyists behind political parties. Her speech was a plea for the country's citizens to work together to ensure good-hearted doctors like Mary continued their work as healers wherever they were needed.

Snoops, still on the outs with Mayor Ryan for driving a thousand calls to the courthouse, merely whimpered when the mayor appeared in the restaurant's kitchen, confiscated her laptop, and sat down to surf websites. The mayor seemed giddy over the bonanza of free advertising for her beleaguered town.

"Look at the voting on this website," she said, drawing Mary's attention from the television and Theodora's impromptu press conference. "People want you to stay in Liberty and set up a practice here."

Anthony, pacing behind their chairs, concurred. "She's right, Mary. What you've done for Blossom has struck a chord with lots of folks. They think you belong here."

The idea of staying *was* tempting, if unrealistic. "What about Abe?" she said for the hundredth time. "I have to take over the free clinic. I can't let him down."

A familiar voice boomed, "Who do you think you're letting down, young lady?"

Eyes twinkling, Abe Goldstein walked through the swinging door.

"Abe!" He looked rather winded, and Mary quickly steered him into a chair. "What are you doing here?"

He stroked his goatee, grinning. "I hope you're joking, dear. I would've arrived an hour ago but every street in Liberty is clogged with traffic. Look at this." He thrust a sheaf of email printouts into her hand. "Your publicity has blindsided my clinic—in a good way."

She skimmed the pages. The bulk of the email contained resumes and notes from doctors across the United States. Most were medical professionals starting out in their careers as residents at hospitals. Several were physicians at teaching hospitals. Every last doctor who'd contacted Abe wished to take over management of the clinic.

Stunned, she handed the sheaf of papers to Anthony.

"CNN is doing a feature on how general practitioners are a dying breed," Abe said. "Seems Liberty's press coverage got some nice young specialists thinking about how important it *is* for general practice to survive. Mary, every one of these doctors is willing to take over my clinic immediately."

She caught Anthony's startled gaze. He looked like he'd just won the lottery, which was exactly how she felt.

"We're staying in Liberty," she told him. "We're staying here!"

Abe appraised Anthony will ill-concealed delight. "I presume you're Blossom's father?" When Anthony nodded, he added, "Take good care of your daughter—and Mary."

"I will," Anthony promised. Unable to suppress his delight a moment longer, he grabbed Mary and spun her in a joyous circle.

He'd just set her down when the door to the kitchen banged open. Delia stumbled inside. "Everyone, get out here," she said. "You've got to see this."

En masse, they returned to the dining room.

What they discovered took Mary's breath away. People from throughout Liberty, young and old, rich and poor, were returning lighting fixtures and pewter bowls, silver candlesticks and Persian rugs—all the antiques they'd purchased at the auction. Overwhelmed, she leaned against the counter blinking back tears.

Luckily her staff took over. Delia thanked a brunette for the vase she'd returned. Finney accepted a box of antiques from a portly man. Items were left by the cash register or on the counter.

Outside, light bulbs flashed. In the green, a man planted a sign at his feet—*Save Blossom and Mary's Historic Restaurant*. Two women were handing out balloons and a man was setting up a snow cone machine. More cars arrived, many with signs taped on passenger doors and bumpers—*Hello from Kentucky! The University of Virginia is With You! Pittsburgh loves Blossom and Mary!*

One sign read, *Ohio IS the Heart of it All.*

Anthony followed her outside. "It's not our state motto but should be," he said. His voice catching, he added, "Personally, I think you're the heart of it all."

"Thanks," she whispered.

He gave her a lingering kiss. When he'd finished, he said, "I'm going over to help the kids from Kent State collect money. I'll head down to the hospital afterward."

"Tell Blossom I'll be down later."

"Will do." He sprinted off.

On the cobblestone walk a wicker basket brimmed with cash, checks and notes. Cradling the basket at her waist, Mary lifted her attention to the sheer size of the crowd bringing the Square's traffic to a halt. People milled around as if on holiday. In front of the courthouse, a petite Asian woman and a man in a wheelchair unrolled a banner—*Help save Blossom and Liberty's only restaurant.*

Finney appeared at her side and Mary said, "Looks like we're having an impromptu party. Why don't we hand out the rest of the parade flags? The least we can do."

"Blossom would like that."

A horn blared, startling them both. People shot out of the way. In a plume of smoke, Theodora ground her sky-blue Cadillac to a halt.

She leapt from the car and Ethel Lynn scrambled from the passenger seat. Evidently Theodora had taken great pains for her television interviews—the thinning tufts of her hair were neatly combed and lightly gelled, and her fierce brown eyes were framed with mascara.

"Go on." Ethel Lynn said, prodding her forward. "You know it's the right thing to do."

Theodora swatted her away. "Get off my tail! I don't need morality lessons from an old bag who spent her youth chasing half the men in the county."

"They were chasing *me!*"

"So you say." Dismissing the squabble, Theodora planted her attention on Mary. "Well? If you're waiting for an apology, let hell freeze over. I had every right to feel the way I did."

What was she talking about? Unsure, Mary tipped her head to the side. "Theodora, nothing you say will spoil my good mood. Not today."

The old woman took in the crowd. "Our town square is beginning to resemble a madhouse."

"You're partly at fault. Everyone saw you on TV." Mary smiled. "You were amazing."

"I was, wasn't I?" Softening, Theodora added, "You're a fine woman, Mary. I don't mind saying I'm proud of you."

"And I don't mind accepting your praise."

Theodora lowered what was left of her brows. "Buy a wig. You look like a fool with your hair gone."

"It'll grow back."

Theodora thrust out her hands. "Everything you've done for Blossom . . . why, if anyone should keep a love token from my family, you've earned the right."

Mary took the gift pressed into her palms, a shimmering sparkle of gold.

It was the porringer.

Chapter 30

For the remainder of the week, people arrived from across the country. The Second Chance Grill reopened, becoming something of a tourist attraction. Finney had the good sense to place a large mason jar by the register and whenever a patron started for the door, an extra tip plunked into the jar. Everyone, it seemed, had made the commitment to save Blossom.

When Mary wasn't racing between the hospital and the restaurant, she engaged in the delightful task of ferrying money to First Bank & Trust. Within days, five safety deposit boxes were stuffed full with cash and checks. There wasn't time yet for a complete tally of the donations, but clearly there was more than enough money to pay for Blossom's medical care.

Her bone marrow transplant took place on a Wednesday. She survived the procedure but hovered in grave condition. Frantic, Mary left The Second Chance to Finney's care and held a vigil at Blossom's bedside.

With each passing day, the healer's instinct warned Mary that Blossom might never leave St. Barnabas. The donations and cards, Mary's attentions and Anthony's devotion—nothing could guarantee a dying child would survive.

The non-stop worry left Mary's emotions barren. As her confidence in medicine wavered and the grey, paralyzing fear threatened to run her aground, the good doctor resorted to the only act she knew still offered hope.

Each night at Blossom's bedside, she got down on her knees

and prayed.

∾

In a fugue of exhaustion, she moved through days streaming one into the next. Anthony brought her changes of clothes, and his mother tried to get her to eat. Mary dozed with her chair pushed close to the bed, frequently rising from fitful dreams to whisper encouragement. Blossom remained unconscious with her lashes fluttering and her skin taking on a frightening bluish-white cast.

Day and night merged. A nurse checked Blossom's pulse. Dr. Lash read her chart. Monitors beeped and Blossom's graying lips tipped into a frown. One evening, when Anthony rested his hand on Mary's shoulder, she shrugged him off, irritated he'd try to disconnect her from her vigil or block her determination to bring their child back.

Their child.

Grief had stripped Mary of her reliance on her clinical training. Now she understood—she was a woman first, and not simply a doctor. She belonged to Blossom and Anthony. She'd knit them to her soul with a devotion meant to last a lifetime.

Now, as she climbed into the bed beside Blossom's slumbering form, she took refuge in memories as warm and comforting as the sun-lit surf washing over the beach. She recalled the day she met Blossom and Anthony, and how she'd needed to heal her heart after Sadie's death. She imagined Blossom with her cheeks covered in ice cream the day all hell broke loose at The Second Chance. And later, the heat in Anthony's lips when he'd first kissed her.

They were a family now. The events of the last months had changed their lives, sent them off in a new and startling direction. Which might have brought joy, if only Blossom would live.

Come back to me, baby.

Groggy from lack of sleep, she sat up and rolled the ache from her shoulders. After the pain subsided, she drew the covers up to Blossom's chin and regarded the dance of her lashes and the shallow breaths puffing from her mouth.

Moon-glow sent eerie patterns across the floor. On a yawn, Mary peered through the shadows; Anthony was gone from the hospital room. Was he napping on the couch in the parents' suite? Every member of his family had come tonight but they'd retreated to the parents' suite, leaving her alone with her inconsolable sorrow as the blip on the heart monitor slowed.

Lost in slumber, Blossom's head shifted. "Mom?"

She swung around. "What, baby?" she asked, finding Blossom's hand beneath the blankets and holding tight.

Blossom struggled to open her eyes. Giving up on the effort, she whispered, "I hurt so bad. Can I go back to sleep so it doesn't hurt anymore?"

"Don't go back to sleep!"

A doctor distances herself from her patients. She crushed the notion the moment it entered her brain.

"Are you listening, Blossom? Stay awake. Don't fall asleep, baby."

A mother fiercely protects her child.

She pressed her lips to Blossom's temple. "Can you feel that? Oh, sweetheart—can you?"

"Hmm . . . feels good."

"Wake up, precious child. Stay with me." She settled her hand on Blossom's forehead, willing the heat of life into the cold flesh. "Please, baby—don't go. You aren't supposed to sleep for a long, long time."

An ominous silence descended upon the room. Mary glanced at the heart monitor, slowing inexorably toward the unimaginable. Determination surged through her. She slipped her arms beneath Blossom's shoulders and lifted her lifeless body, nestling her close enough for their breaths to mingle. She refused to let it end like this, no—

"Mom?" Blossom's head lolled as she struggled from deep slumber.

"I'm here, baby."

"Why did you leave when I was small?"

Love held Mary's heart like a fist. "That wasn't me, sweetheart," she said, choking on a sob. "That was someone else. She was very young and confused. She didn't mean to hurt you."

"Did you leave because I was bad?"

"No, no—you were always good." Hugging tight, she sent fervent prayers to heaven. "I'm here now. I'll never leave."

The horrible silence lengthened. Greasy fear rolled though Mary with the prospect of losing her daughter, her precious daughter. Despair followed.

"Baby, come back. Please, sweetheart. Come back to me."

A shudder rippled across Blossom's chest. Then she said, "You have to say please."

"Like we do with Sweetcakes?" Humor was a good sign—a sign of life.

"Yeah."

"Please," she said, planting a kiss on Blossom's cheek. Gratitude spilled through her and she planted more kisses, a whole garden of love. "Oh, baby—please, please, please!"

On a sigh, Blossom steered out of the darkness.

She opened her eyes.

The first thing Anthony did upon returning to the hospital room was drop the two Styrofoam cups of coffee he carried. The second was cry out.

On the bed, Mary cradled Blossom loosely across her lap. The IV line from his daughter's arm snaked across the rumpled sheets. The heart monitor sang out a joyous *blip, blip, blip.*

"She's awake?" He slid through the sea of coffee he'd spilled. Arms splayed, he fought to regain his balance. "Mary, did she open her eyes?"

Mary laughed. "Give her a second, all right? Our chat wore her out."

"What happened?"

"I asked her to stay. She asked me to say please."

"Like we do with Sweetcakes?"

"You got it." She scooted over to make room for him on the bed, noticed his damp cheeks. "Stop crying, please."

He looked around. *Where the hell were the tissues?* "I can't."

"If you don't stop, I'll start all over again. It's contagious."

"Go right ahead." He nuzzled her ear. "Let me hold her," he added, jealous.

"No." She brushed her lips across Blossom's brow. "I can't share right now. Ask in a few minutes. Oh, Anthony—look at the monitor. Her heartbeat is stabilizing!"

He rubbed his wet nose. "A miracle." He bumped her, shoulder to shoulder. "Trade places. Let me hold my kid."

"*Our* kid," She landed a peck on his cheek. "Stop crying. I'm serious."

"No."

She wiggled her nose like a rabbit. "See what you've done?" she said, her eyes watering. "Now I'll start."

"What's the harm in a few tears?" he croaked, cupping Blossom's cheek. His heart soared as faint color rose in her skin. "I like your vulnerable side. Go on and sound the foghorns. Cry until the river runs dry. I'll hold you until you're done."

She brushed her damp cheeks. "I don't want to be vulnerable right now. I want to be happy."

"I wish you were naked right now. I'd thank you properly."

"You're bad," she said, but her eyes grew impish.

"Just honest." He left tears on Blossom's forehead before returning to his inspection of Mary. The suggestive tone of the conversation had widened her eyes in a way that was quite fetching.

Which was a lusty enough thought for Anthony to give himself a mental kick in the keister. This wasn't the time for thoughts of lovemaking. *Blossom was alive!* With glee, he lightly palmed her scalp and flicked the tip of her nose while Mary's attention wandered over his face like a loving caress.

"We *should* thank each other later," she said in a sultry voice, hitching his desire into high gear.

Blossom stirred. "I wish you'd both shut up," she said from behind her eyelids. A grin edged across her lips. "This hospital room is Rated PG. Take the R-rated stuff outside."

Mary nibbled on her ear. "No problemo, muchacha."

Anthony clamped down on his sobbing as Blossom opened her left eye then her right. "If you guys are getting frisky, go away," she said. "I want Grandma. She'll sing to me and I swear, she's got ice cream in her purse. How does she keep the stuff from melting?"

"You want ice cream?" Anthony snapped up his wrist.

How to sate his kids' dairy obsession at three A.M.? The solution came instantly. He'd break into the hospital cafeteria and haul out as many gallons as she wanted.

"What do you have a yen for, Blossom? Rocky Road, Cherry Chunk, Moose Tracks?" He was immensely grateful Ohio was a dairy state. "Double Chocolate? Strawberry Swirl?"

Mischief took a stroll through his daughter's sleepy brown eyes. "Yeah."

"Which kind?"

"Yeah."

He started for the door. "Five varieties on the way. I'll shoot for six but I'm not sure how stealthy I'll be lugging that much cargo."

Mary gave him a quizzical look. "You aren't planning to do something crazy, are you?"

He grinned like a pirate. What constituted 'crazy' on a night like this? "I'm not sure," he admitted. "I'm heading down to the parents' lounge to wake Nick. He does insanity better than I do."

"Don't forget the bananas," Blossom put in.

Of course! "And whipped cream," he said, excited now. "I'll find cherries, too. It's not a banana split without the cherries." He swung back around, approached. "Hey, Blossom."

"Yeah?"

"I love you."

"I love you too, Dad."

"Good." He rubbed his hands together, inordinately pleased with his daughter, the lucky invention of ice cream, and life in general.

Mary squeaked, "What about me?"

With effort Blossom lifted her head from Mary's shoulder. "Got a question," she said. "Do you mind if I call you Mom?"

A star-struck silence, then Mary's expression turned to quivering jelly.

Anthony, soaring above the moon, said, "I love you too, in case you need clarification." He shrugged. "Guess you're stuck with me and the goofball."

Cupid's arrow hit the mark, and Mary burst into tears.

Chapter 31

Outside the second floor's bank of windows, the treetops in Liberty Square trembled. The gust of wind shook loose the last of the autumn leaves. The firestorm of color whipped down to the cobblestone walk.

Drawing from the pretty sight, Mary finished rolling paint on the wall. In the months since Blossom's arrival home, so much had been accomplished. The waiting room for the practice of Dr. Mary Chance was nearly finished. Soon they'd hang a floral border paper. The carpeting wouldn't be installed until Monday, allowing Anthony time to finish the trim work over the weekend. Excited, she paused to imagine her new medical office bustling with patients.

The thump of footsteps rising up the stairwell caught her attention. With the sound came a tantalizing whiff of Finney's banana pudding, which she was whipping up in The Second Chance Grill.

"Mary?" Anthony called. "Still up here?"

She returned the roller to the pan. He met her midway across the spacious room, grabbed her around the waist, and swung her in a circle.

"You're in a good mood," she said when he put her back down. Mischief sparked in his gaze. "What is it?"

"Nothing. Just feeling good today."

"Good enough to help me paint the walls in the exam rooms? We should get started."

"Sure . . . if you'll talk to our daughter first."

Blossom, clearly hesitant to enter, stood in the doorway with her coat unzipped. "It's fifty degrees outside," she said before Mary could make a comment about bundling up. "We're having a November heat wave. Geez, don't you ever let up?"

"No," Mary said, folding her arms. "I don't."

Shrugging, Blossom scanned the waiting room. "How will old people get up here when they need a doctor?" she asked. "You don't have an elevator."

Anthony said, "We'll put one in as soon as our incomes allow." He hesitated before adding, "Listen, kiddo, Mary isn't up for your sales pitch. There's more painting to finish."

"What sales pitch?" Mary asked.

He sighed. "Don't ask."

Blossom picked at the coat's puffy sleeves. "Dr. Lash says I'm doing great. No more cancer." With a huff, she fumbled with something she'd lodged under her arm. A magazine? "Stop asking me to dress like a toddler. It's humiliating. I look like the Pillsbury Doughboy rolling down the street."

Mary lathered paint on the roller and headed for a wall. "You look adorable," she said, refusing to take the bait of another clothing argument. These days, the topic came up constantly. It arose nearly as often as the girl's other niggling complaint—why hadn't her dad and Mary set a date to marry?

Naturally Blossom didn't understand. There was much to celebrate, what with her health improving and the leukemia vanquished. Yes, they'd plan a wedding—eventually. But not until she and Anthony tired of spending every free moment taking Blossom on trips, buying her gifts, and helping redecorate her bedroom.

In a wide swath Mary drew the roller across the wall. "What do you think of the doctor's new office, kiddo?" With Finney now running the restaurant, Mary was free to set up her practice, slated to open in December. Many of the people in Liberty had expressed a desire to become her patients, a prospect that warmed her immensely. "Like the color I picked for the walls?"

"It's nice."

"The green color isn't too pale? I'm going for a relaxing look." She appraised her handiwork. "My offices *should* put people at ease, right? At least no one in town will have to worry about me cooking in the restaurant. I never thought I'd live that down."

"It's great you're going back to being a doctor." Blossom fumbled with the magazine beneath her arm. "Speaking of jobs . . ."

Mary stopped rolling. "Now wait a minute. If you think you're going back to work at The Second Chance, think again. I've had enough run-ins with the mayor. Besides, you need more time to heal."

"I'm fine!"

Anthony took the roller from her and began painting. "She's doing great, honey," he said. "Actually, she's here to badger you about something else. I'm staying out of it . . . even if I *am* on the kid's side."

"I hate it when you gang up on me." She grabbed her bottled water from the floor and swigged. "It's a real pain in the—" She caught herself.

Tenderly Anthony palmed her back. "You shouldn't swear."

"Yeah, yeah, yeah." She gave an elaborate sigh. "Let's review the drill," she announced, stepping back before the heat in his gaze made her brainless. "Number one: I have to get my medical practice up and running before I can think about a wedding. Number two: building my practice means you, Blossom, will have to wait a few years for a baby brother or sister."

"Three," Blossom mimicked, wrinkling her nose, "You're spacing kids apart because they're kids and not a litter of puppies . . ."

"And four," Anthony said, grabbing Mary around the waist and getting paint on both of them, "you refuse to promise you'll ever learn to cook, but you *will* stitch us up if we have an accident while playing Nerf basketball in the living room."

"Glad that's settled." A bad case of the giggles bubbled up her throat but she held them off. Blossom smacked the magazine against her thigh, and Mary decided she'd had enough. "*What* have you got, Blossom? Don't keep me in suspense."

She started forward but Anthony snagged her arm. "I lied," he said. He held Mary's gaze with longing, and the love she felt for him feathered heat across her skin. "Honey, this is a set-up.

I'm here to provide the kid with backup. We aren't leaving until you give in."

Demanding an explanation wasn't necessary. Blossom rustled the magazine in temptation then held it aloft for Mary to read the cover of—

Brides magazine.

Second Chance Grill
Book-Group Discussion Questions

1. Why does the reader meet Blossom before her father, Anthony? If Anthony's opening scene had appeared first, how would it have impacted the secret revealed by Ethel Lynn at the end of Chapter One?

2. The three characters of Mary, Blossom and Anthony carry the novel through point of view (POV). Each character delivers key aspects of the plot:

—Why does Mary receive the lion's share of POV?
—What does Blossom's POV add to the novel? How would *Second Chance Grill* change if her POV were excluded?
—Anthony's POV is the antithesis of the classical strong male. What does his vulnerability add to the story? Are his struggles as a single parent believable? Would a single mother harbor the same doubt while parenting a preteen daughter? Why or why not?

3. What do the secondary characters of Finney, Theodora and Ethel Lynn add to the story? How do they serve to augment the reader's understanding of Mary, Blossom and Anthony?

4. In many ways, Theodora and Ethel Lynn are opposites. They also provide backstory on the town of Liberty while providing comedic relief.

—Who is the stronger character?
—How does Ethel Lynn serve to characterize Mary's Aunt Meg, a character *in abstentia?*
—How does Theodora increase Mary's fascination and attachment to the town of Liberty?

5. The novel features several stories in parallel:
—How is Mary's childhood similar to the life she's destined to lead in Liberty?

—Both Dr. Abe Goldstein and Mary have suffered great loss. How do they handle grief differently? Are they both attempting to run away from the heartbreak of losing Sadie?

—How is Anthony similar to Blossom's boyfriend, Tyler?

6. Of the three main characters, who undergoes the most change during the novel? Or are all three characters equally altered by events?

Dear Reader: If you enjoyed Second Chance Grill and posted a review, please contact me at christinenolfi@gmail.com for a special gift. I truly appreciate the kindness. Please write "Review Posted" in the subject line of your email.

You'll also find me at www.christinenolfi.com or please visit my Facebook Author Page. On Twitter: @christinenolfi

About the Author

Award-winning author **Christine Nolfi** provides readers with heartwarming and inspiring fiction. Her debut *Treasure Me* is a Next Generation Indie Awards finalist. The Midwest Book Review lists many of her novels as "highly recommended" and her books have enjoyed bestseller status. Visit her at www.christinenolfi.com.

Also by Christine Nolfi

Treasure Me

The Impossible Wish

Four Wishes

The Tree of Everlasting Knowledge

The Dream You Make

The Heavenscribe series

Reviews Sell Books

Made in the USA
Monee, IL
25 February 2021

61328810R00154